THE FINAL FANDANGO

THE FINAL FANDANGO

BOOK THREE IN THE SPIDER TRILOGY

GUY BUTLER

POLKAJIG
PRESS

ISBN: 978-0-9848726-6-4

"In wartime, truth is so precious that she should always be attended by a bodyguard of lies."

Winston Spencer Churchill, 1943

ACKNOWLEDGEMENTS

This novel honors Chester Wojciechowski and Malcolm Butler, my inspiration for the main characters in this trilogy.

And Michael Johnston, a great Scotsman and friend, who passed away during the week this book was finished.

As always, I am most grateful to several wonderful friends and acquaintances for their diligent comments after reading countless earlier drafts: Krysia Blando, Janna Buckley, Alastair Collins, Don Collins, Mark Dillon, Bill Fagan, Tim Geary, JoBee O'Hara, Libby Jackson, Carlos Ontivero, Jeff Patterson, Bryan Thomas, David Urban and Amanda Velazquez. Especially my wife, Teri and our children, Jadzia and Remy.

In particular, very special thanks to Kristin Lindstrom and Victoria Colotta. If anyone dreams of writing a book without these two ladies on their team, they should wake up and apologize.

THE
FINAL
FANDANGO

PROLOGUE

Things Could Be a Helluvalot Worse

In August 1943, the Partizani in Yugoslavia conscripted a twenty-three year old Polish freedom fighter called Chez Orlowski to spirit a captured British football superstar from the clutches of Dr. Joseph Goebbels. Their subsequent adventures flirted with one disaster after another and served to build an indelible bond between the two men that lasted for the rest of their lives.

But for the war, they would never have met, one being an impoverished survivor of numerous Nazi labor camps, the other, Malcolm McClain, a wealthy, sophisticated professional athlete from Northern Ireland.

The ensuing Allied victory served to enhance the celebrity of both men. McClain, already a legend on the soccer field, was now a decorated war hero and Orlowski's exploits behind his nom de guerre, 'the Spider,' had exploded to mythic proportion. The oppressed children of an enslaved Europe memorized the folklore of his alter ego; the legend becoming a phenomenon because circumstances precluded solid documentation. In a time when youth craved a hero, the Spider received credit for defeating the Nazi Third Reich almost single-handedly. Even his best friend Malcolm McClain knew there were dark secrets beyond the astonishing bravery he personally witnessed—but he never pried. However, the simple fact that King George VI granted the Orlowski family British citizenship at the personal request of Sir Winston Churchill spoke volumes.

As improbable as the fable appeared, the Spider's secret past might indeed have turned the tide against the Third Reich, especially when you factor in his assassination of Adolf Hitler.

As Chez Orlowski attempted to adopt a normal life after the war, only four people in the world were privy to this astounding contradiction of conventional history. These unlikely bedfellows were Sir Winston Churchill, who passed away in 1965; retired SAS Colonel Paddy McBride, currently heading a global conglomerate called Black Widows Security; the Spider himself; and Reichsleiter Martin Bormann, 'the Brown Eminence of the Third Reich,' who mysteriously disappeared from the Führerbunker in Berlin at the beginning of May 1945.

As they plundered Europe, the massive wealth accumulated by the Third Reich became the vehicle to fund an emergency escape plan for the Nazi Party's entire upper echelon. Bormann, considered by MI6 to be the true genius behind Hitler's rise to power, began planning the preservation of German capital for escape contingencies immediately after the Soviets crushed the Nazi's ill-fated Barbarossa Campaign.

The GNP of Argentina spiked in return for President Juan Domingo Perón's assurance that 500,000 acres in Patagonia would provide safe haven for any jack-booted murderers and thieves who made it out alive. As he carefully orchestrated the emergence of a Fourth Reich, Martin Bormann planned to have Adolf Hitler reprise his role as Führer. The elaborate ruse was in full swing—until the Spider inconveniently slit the Austrian corporal's throat.

Now, almost quarter of a century after Hitler's death, the Reichsleiter was struggling to combat type two diabetes as he approached the twilight of his life. But, when an opportunity emerged to exact revenge on the man who had thwarted his grand plan, Bormann was fully prepared to martial his considerable resources, even if it meant risking the location of his secure base in the Andes Mountains.

His hatred for the Spider had fermented into an obsession; sacrificing his organization's anonymity would be a small price to pay.

PART ONE

CHAPTER ONE

1945, The Führerbunker, Berlin

Reichsleiter Martin Ludwig Bormann, absorbed in paperwork, scowled as he sat at the modest oak desk in Hitler's office. Its small surface was completely covered with neat piles of documents and he would have much preferred to be in his own spacious office at the New Chancellery. But in this last week of April 1945, the safety afforded by twenty-five feet of earth and concrete above the Führerbunker was fair trade. He was caused to lose his focus by the behavior of two people playing cards in Hitler's adjacent private living room. Hearing a snicker of laughter, he slammed down his pen and fumed towards the door, flinging it open.

"I am only going to say this once," he hissed at the culprits. "You have a simple contract with me; act out your adopted roles for just one week whilst the Führer recovers from his arm surgery, then go home to enjoy the million reichsmarks you will each receive. If you cannot perform that simple task and blow the subterfuge, you will both be shot." The two actors were stunned into silence, fear dancing behind their eyes from the confrontation. "It is of vital national importance that both the German people and the Russian invaders have no knowledge of the Führer's brief incapacitation. Do I make myself perfectly clear?"

"Jawol, Herr Reichsleiter," they both mumbled.

The woman, an unemployed actress from Hamburg, had covertly substituted for Adolph Hitler's mistress, Eva Braun, during the Führer's fifty-sixth birthday celebrations last Friday evening. Hitler's replacement had taken his place only this morning during an all hands meeting in the Führerbunker's conference room. Gustav Weler had performed the part of Hitler's stand-in several times over the past five years; in fact, most of the Third Reich's upper echelon used doppelgangers when the SS identified possible security issues. On this occasion, the million-reichsmark payday more than mollified Weler's reluctance to enter into the Russian artillery's bull's-eye.

Martin Bormann, a short, rotund Prussian with a prizefighter's face, grew up working on a farm in Mecklenburg. His hard work ethic and an intense, unwavering loyalty to Adolf Hitler rocketed him to his current position of unprecedented power within the Nazi Party. Even minimal research by the two actors would have revealed Bormann's prime character trait to be ruthlessness and that alone should have forewarned them that the next seven days would be their last.

On the following day, Monday, April 23, 1945, Martin Bormann began systematically taking complete control of the Third Reich's remaining power and finances. There were several tasks on his agenda and he intended to accomplish them all while Adolf Hitler, disguised as a bald businessman, was ensconced in a secret apartment at the Festsaal mit Wintergarten above the bunker. Heinrich Himmler, already ostracized for trying to cut a peace deal with the Swedish consul in Lubeck, was no longer a factor in the power struggle. Later this day, Bormann anticipated separating Hitler from Eva Braun by spiriting her away to Templhof Airport through the maze of underground tunnels Albert Speer had built into Berlin's infrastructure. However, in this quest for ultimate power, Bormann's most important task by far was to stymie Reichsmarschall Hermann Wilhelm Göring, the current Deputy Führer. If the Deputy Führer caught wind of Hitler's disappearing act, he could invoke a December 1934 decree that allowed him to assume complete control of Germany in the event of Hitler's incapacitation. By that afternoon,

Bormann had sent a message in Hitler's name to Göring giving him a choice between resigning all official offices and titles—or death. Within thirty minutes, Hermann Göring, the Reichsmarschall des Großdeutschen Reiches, made the only choice he could and was placed under armed house arrest.

Quite a Monday and a remarkable display of organizational skills from a former farmer, but not so surprising if you consider MI6's allegation that Martin Bormann had been responsible for the rise of the Deutsches Reich since the early days of its organization.

Adolph Hitler's magnetic personality and powerful oratorical skills made him the natural front man for the Party. Other major characters, including Himmler, Göring and Goebbels, became drunk with power, never hesitating to flaunt their riches in the belief that the Third Reich would rule the world for the next one thousand years. Through all these machinations, Bormann was a ghost in the background, a man in the shadows. His only honorific was 'Secretary to the Führer,' a position from which he controlled Hitler's appointments and manipulated all Nazi Party policies.

By Wednesday, April 25, Soviet forces had over two million troops surrounding Berlin. Eva Braun was on her way to Berchtesgarten and Bormann had neutered the power of all his main rivals. Now all that remained was to get Hitler and himself out of Berlin.

A salvo of Russian shells rained down on the Führerbunker, the final Nazi stronghold. The lights flickered and dust fell from the low ceiling onto the desk where Bormann worked.

I might be cutting this a little tight, he thought to himself. *I will soon be the richest man in the world but it won't do me much good if I'm dead. I will call Hannah Reitsch to set up Adolph's escape but quite honestly, at this point in the proceedings and with Gerda and our children safe in Austria, I am caring less and less about the rest of these fucking bloodsuckers.*

Early the next morning, Bormann picked up the phone and called Rochus Misch on the switchboard. "Obersturmbannführer, please put me in touch with Flugkapitan Hannah Reitsch. I believe you will find her at the Luftwaffe Test Center in Rechlin." Fifteen minutes later, Misch called back.

"Herr Reichsleiter, Flugkapitan Reitsch is on the telephone for you."

"Ah, good morning, Hannah, is Generaloberst

Robert Ritter von Greim ready to take over command of the Luftwaffe from that traitor, Göring? The Führer would like to have the ceremony this afternoon."

"Jawohl, Herr Reichsleiter. We are just waiting for a respite in the bombardment. How does it look to you from the New Chancellery right now?"

"Our intelligence indicates that there will be a window of opportunity in about two hours. Good luck, Hannah. I am looking forward to seeing you. Oh and remember, you are leaving von Greim here to assume his new position. On your return flight to Gatow, you will be accompanied by a very important Swiss banker, a man critical to the success of our war efforts."

Bormann hung up the phone, then left the study and walked to the telephone room. When he was certain no one could overhear him, he whispered conspiratorially to Misch.

"Rochus, I need to use our secure frequency. Stand guard outside the door and make sure nobody compromises me for the next ten minutes. This is a matter of immense national importance."

Obersturmbannführer Misch made the necessary adjustments to the radio, handed a headset to Bormann and checked his holstered Luger before leaving the room. Martin Bormann used the secret frequency to connect directly to a clandestine radio in Moscow, a private connection to the desk of Lavrentiy Beria, head of Stalin's NKVD.

"Lavrentiy, this is Sasha, greetings from beautiful Berlin on the Spree."

"Aha, Sasha, glad you have survived our target practice so far. When do you need me to get your sorry arse out of there?" laughed the secret police chief in his melodious baritone. Martin Bormann had been working covertly with Beria for over a decade and critical information shared between the two men on July 5, 1943, formed the basis for a secret grand bargain between Germany and the Soviet Union.

"Lavrentiy, I find it ironic that the 35,000 men and 550 tanks we lost at the battle of Kursk is being repaid by you saving my solitary, sorry arse."

"The circumstances under which we made our deal almost two years ago were quite different, Sasha. Germany and Russia were the two most powerful armies in the world and it made perfect sense that we should negotiate the future to our mutual advantage rather than fighting ourselves into oblivion. America and Britain are not to be trusted and the number of soldiers and tanks you sacrificed in return for Mother Russia being able to protect Kursk is paltry when compared to the twenty million Soviets who have died in your war."

Martin Bormann had recognized the impossibility of beating the Soviet Union when Operation Barbarossa failed in the streets of Stalingrad. The seeming unlimited reinforcements that Russia could call upon sparked his private call to Beria. By incubating this partnership with the Devil, Bormann agreed to contribute Germany's organizational skills and massive industrial wealth; Russia in turn provided an infinite labor force and the ability to stab the United States in the back after the war. In essence, the true genius was Josef Stalin. Russia had hedged her bets, winning massive control of the eastern bloc no matter who won the war. The cost to Stalin had been the lives of a mere twenty million citizens.

"Lavrentiy, I need to mop up some loose ends. The evidence you desire will be found buried in a shallow grave outside the bunker towards the end of this month. I am planning to be at your safe house by next Tuesday or Wednesday. After that, Berlin is all yours.

"Of immediate importance, I need you to pause the bombardment from noon until three this afternoon. I have to try and get someone out on a small plane."

"I'll do my best, Sasha, but my boys are drinking vodka like water and they are hunting for scalps. Good luck, my friend."

"Thanks, Lavrentiy; keep some of that vodka on ice for me."

Bormann disconnected and opened the door to let Misch resume his duties.

The Reichsleiter went back to the study, grabbed

his briefcase and locked any other sensitive material into the safe. Then he called the switchboard again. "Rochus, locate Obersturmbannführer Linge and have him come to the study as soon as possible."

Once Heinz Linge arrived, he and Martin Bormann immediately left the Führerbunker, proceeding through the outer Vorbunker in silence until they reached the long concrete tunnel connecting the old and new Chancellery buildings. Bormann turned north, heading towards the Foreign Ministry.

"Make sure the corridor is clear, Heinz," he commanded as they reached a deep recess in the wall.

"Not a problem, Reichsleiter. Both Chancellery buildings are in ruins. Not a lot of reasons for anyone to be down here."

Bormann pulled out a key and unlocked a heavy steel door within the recess; the two men disappeared inside. After ten minutes of negotiating the basement of the Festsaal mit Wintergarten, they climbed an internal staircase. Bormann then knocked on an innocuous brown door; four quick taps followed by two long ones. A clean-shaven, bald man peered at them through heavy-rimmed glasses as he cracked the door open.

"Mein Führer, how quickly can you be ready to fly to freedom?" The eyes of Obersturmbannführer Heinz Linge widened as he slowly put the pieces together. "Linge, stay here with the Führer," continued

Reichsleiter Bormann. "Hannah Reitsch will be landing in the gardens less than an hour from now. I am going to set up the promotion ceremony for Ritter von Greim on the rear steps of the New Chancellery and I need time to walk that idiot, Weler, through his role as your double. Hannah is going to stay with the plane and Linge will escort you to make sure there are no hitches. As we discussed, you are an important Swiss banker and will have no need to talk to her during the flight. You will be transferring to a bigger plane at Gatow so it looks like the next time we meet will be at Berchtesgarten. By the way, I received a coded telegram this morning; Eva is already there and sends her love."

"And what happens if our great flugkapitan does not make it through the bombardment, Martin?" Hitler demanded.

"In that event, Linge will bring you back here. I have contingency plans to get the two of us to Berchtesgarten by other means." Bormann pulled some papers out of his briefcase. "Here, sign this Last Will and Testament before I go. It allows me to act on your behalf during these last days." Without reading a word, Adolf scribbled his infamous signature wherever Bormann indicated.

"First chance I get, I will conscript some generals to witness this. Now, I have a lot to do today. Travel safely, Adolph, and good luck."

Reichsleiter Bormann left Linge in the apartment

with Hitler and returned to his study in the Führer-bunker. His first act was to summons Gustav Weler.

"Mein Führer," he said sarcastically. "Full dress uniform, please. You are going to appoint one of our great generals as the new Reichsmarschall of the Luft-waffe. Keep your mouth shut, I'll do all the talking. Remember, you have a severe tremor in your left arm so avoid touching people with it. Hurry up, you only have ten minutes."

As soon as Weler closed the door, Bormann opened the safe and extracted a large manila envelope containing several sheets of paper that modified key elements in Hitler's Last Will and Political Testament. The pages Hitler signed had been carefully crafted to contain no important information. But these replacement pages for the interior now expelled both Göring and Himmler from the Nazi Party and appointed Grossadmiral Karl Dönitz as the next president of the Reich.

Perhaps most important of all, these critical pages essentially transferred all administrative authority to Martin Ludwig Bormann. He dated the revised document for the following Sunday, April 29 and returned the envelope to the safe.

Artur Axmann, Edwald Lindloff and Otto Günsche joined Bormann and the doppelganger in the conference area. These three trusted officers were members of Bormann's sub rosa group and therefore well aware of the substitution. As they made their way south along the concrete passage from the bunker to the New Chancellery, they heard shots and shouting from the Chancellery gardens. Bormann halted the group with a raised hand.

"Otto, please find out what caused that commotion before we emerge from the relative safety of this tunnel."

Bormann fumed as he waited for Günsche's return.

Günsche was back with his report within a couple of minutes. "Reichsleiter, it is somewhat complicated. Generaloberst Robert Ritter von Greim made it to the New Chancellery Building but took a bullet during the flight. It is a nasty flesh wound in his leg; nevertheless, he is fully prepared to go through with the promotion ceremony. However, after he had been evacuated from the plane, an obersturmbannführer escorted an unknown businessman to the plane and it took off. Some guards taking a smoke break didn't like what they saw and took some shots at it... ."

Günsche was abruptly interrupted by Bormann.

"Goddamn fucking idiots," spat Bormann. "That businessman is someone immensely important to the fledgling Fourth Reich. Bring me those guards after the ceremony."

"Well, as I was about to say, when the ShutzStaffel went to check things out, they found Flugkapitan

Reitsch, Heinz Linge and some SS Gefreiters all unconscious on the floor of the greenhouse. Apparently Heinz Linge suffered a rather serious stab wound to his chest."

"WHAT?" shouted an incredulous Martin Bormann. "Then who the hell flew the plane?

"Otto, escort this Weler idiot back to the bunker. I'll handle the promotion ceremony myself. The rest of you line up those witnesses. If Heinz is able to talk, I'll see what I can get out of him."

CHAPTER TWO

The Death Throes of an Empire

An SS colonel informed Martin Bormann that Obersturmbannführer Linge remained heavily sedated after his emergency medical treatment. He had suffered a punctured lung but the knife had missed his heart and all major blood vessels.

The Reichsleiter had little choice but to return to the Führerbunker where he mulled over the turn of events for the rest of the day and into the night. Sleep would have been impossible anyway; the Soviet bombardment was now being hurled at them from less than one thousand yards away. Bormann recognized the irony of his perilous situation.

Twenty years of impeccable planning, seven hundred and fifty international corporations under my control, five hundred thousand acres waiting for me in Argentina.

Instead of trying to get Adolph out, I should have just disappeared last week while there was still time.

An explosion above the bunker interrupted electricity and paused his rambling descent into self-pity. Yellow emergency lights flickered on as the generators filled the musty air with diesel fumes.

If only I could buy an extra week. I might soon become the richest man in the world yet I cannot buy time. In fact, there is an increasing likelihood that I will die a pauper in this very chair. He reached for a bottle of brandy to help him wrestle his maudlin thoughts.

The night without sleep gave way to morning and Martin Bormann returned to the New Chancellery building to find Heinz Linge conscious but in considerable pain.

"Heinz, I apologize for having them hold back on your medications but it is critical you be lucid to relate what the hell happened yesterday."

"Herr Reichsleiter, I walked our Swiss banker friend to the gardens. Nobody seemed to be guarding the plane so we both became suspicious and retreated into the greenhouse. We walked in on four or five strange men who were squatting on the floor beside a pile of prone bodies. One was Flugkapitan Reitsch but she seemed unconscious rather than dead. I went for my Luger and then blacked out. I cannot remember another damn thing until I woke up in this cot. You are going to have to tell *me* what happened."

Linge coughed up some blood and winced as sharp pain surged through his chest. A doctor entered the room with a syringe and Bormann turned on him like a rabid animal.

"Get the hell out of this room until I am finished. You have absolutely no idea how important this interrogation is." The retreating captain closed the door as he left and Bormann returned his mouth to within three inches of Linge's ear.

"Heinz, you must try to describe these men. Were they Russian or American?"

"A couple were wearing SS uniforms; a couple were wearing hospital pajamas…. Wait a minute, as I was lying on the floor, I remember hearing someone talking in German. I opened my eyes for a moment and saw he was completely bald, just like the Führ…. I mean our Swiss banker. Come to think of it, he looked a lot like Koch, the bunker's janitor. I am very tired, Herr Reichsl……"

Bormann got up immediately and left the room, bumping into the doctor in the corridor.

"Reichsleiter, is it all right if…"

"Do whatever the hell you want, you stupid idiot!"

Martin Bormann then spent a considerable amount of time interviewing Hannah Reitsch, and any guards who had witnessed the debacle. After almost two hours, he retreated to the bunker, locked himself in Hitler's study and opened another bottle of brandy. Even inebriated, his superb analytical mind was able to plough through all the available evidence.

The pilot of the plane was wearing a Royal Air Force uniform. Apart from confirming the obvious, only the British would be stupid enough to dream up this hare-brained scheme. Little wonder we've had problems with the Brits; they are all fuckin' crazy and treat everything like it is just a public school prank.

Apparently, our janitor, Koch, could have been a spy. If he infiltrated the bunker, he must have overheard all the details and planned accordingly. Let me revise my thesis; maybe they are not so crazy. I'll give them the benefit of the doubt and surmise they could be Special Forces. Holy shit, if that's the case, the giant man that Hannah saw could be Colonel Paddy McBride, a certifiable nut case and uber-dangerous motherfucker.

Assuming it is the Brits who kidnapped Adolf, why do I care? At this juncture, I really don't. I must concentrate all my energy on getting my own arse out of this concrete coffin without getting shot.

The staged wedding of Adolph Hitler and Eva Braun began just before one o'clock in the morning on Sunday, April 29, 1945. Bormann pulled three of the privileged guests aside after the small ceremony and requested they help him formalize some particulars.

"Gentlemen, the Führer and his bride wish to consummate their wedding, so let us leave them in peace for the rest of the evening. I think it is obvious that our beloved leader is very aware that the end is near. He received word today that his friend, Benito Mussolini, was humiliated in death by the Italian populace and he is determined that a similar staged media event will not occur here. Unlike that Italian idiot, our Führer has backbone. I have here his last Will and Political Testament and request that you join me in witnessing his signature."

Dr. Joseph Goebbels, General Wilhelm Burgdorf, and General Hans Krebs solemnly joined Martin Bormann in witnessing the document, not realizing that they had unwittingly authorized Bormann to control more wealth and power than any human on earth—provided he could escape undetected.

CHAPTER THREE

The World Welcomes Peace

The next morning witnessed a comic opera. Russian shells were rocking the concrete bunker yet all the occupants tiptoed around lest they disturb the honeymooners. Lunch came and went but still no movement or sound came from behind the closed door of Hitler's private suite. Christa Schroeder, Johanna Wolf and Traudl Junge blushed and giggled only to receive a stern reprimand from Reichsleiter Bormann.

"If you ladies would be so kind, the Führer is not the only one needing a little respect for privacy. We are trying to have an important discussion over here. Please return in about five minutes with some tea and biscuits." He waited until the women had hurried to the kitchen then lowered his voice and turned to the fellow conspirators gathered with him around the large table in the conference room.

"Okay, gentlemen, we must maintain faith that the Führer made it out alive in that small plane. Hopefully, he will be able to escape but regardless, we still have to execute the final phase of our plan." Bormann's sub rosa group included Reichsjugendleiter Artur Axmann, SS-Hauptsturmführer Edwald Lindloff, SS-Sturmbannführer Otto Günsche, SS-Obersturmbannführers Peter Högl, and Rochus Misch. Heinz Linge was also a member but unable to attend for obvious reasons.

"I am encouraged by the way Heinz is responding to medical treatment. Unfortunately, his punctured lung will take several weeks to heal so we must proceed without him. Otto, Linge's role falls upon your capable shoulders." Otto Günsche did not flinch under the gaze of the other men but all noted the emotionless determination in his facial expression.

"You must quietly make your way into the study by way of the private bathroom. I need you to serve both those clowns a cyanide capsule. Before I left them alone last night, I slipped each enough sleeping powder to knock out a horse. Dr. Stumpfegger believes that the dose will render them unconscious for perhaps twelve hours, so you should have no problem.

"Kill the woman first; clamp her jaws down to break the glass phial." Bormann dramatically placed his own left hand on the top of his head and his right under his chin. "Once you see the foam come out of her mouth it will be over but keep her muffled until you are sure; I don't want any noise."

Günsche and the other five loyal confidants showed no reaction as Bormann continued.

"As for Weler, he should be even easier. Give him the capsule first if you can, then shoot him in the side of the temple from close range. Drop the gun beside his body, then retreat through the bathroom. I will wait no more than five seconds after I hear the shot and it is essential you be long gone.

"It is critical that I am first to witness the scene and that you men control anyone who follows me in."

Hitler and Bormann had hatched the plot several weeks before the two unwitting doppelgangers were lured into the bunker. The intent was that the staged suicides might bring closure to the war, thereby allowing the Nazi upper echelon to vanish without the scrutiny of a manhunt. That the Thousand Year Reich was on the brink of collapse looked certain, but core Nazi fanatics believed a Fourth Reich would rise like a phoenix within the next decade. Bormann's sub rosa group was key to the plan.

Each man around the table was fully prepared to surrender himself to the Russians, knowing that every detail of the next twenty-four hours would be scrutinized under brutal interrogation. All were committed to giving up their lives for the Fourth Reich, but if they survived, Reichsleiter Bormann personally guaranteed promotions, power and riches in reward.

"Otto, it is time. Find a towel in the bathroom. Use it as protection from Weler's brains when you blow his head off. I don't want to see any blood on your uniform when you rejoin us. Did you check out the Walther?"

"Jawohl, Reichsleiter, I recognize it as the Führer's personal PPK 7.65. To be honest, I never liked Weler, so it will be my pleasure," he said coldly as he rose from the table and headed for the bathrooms.

Christa, Johanna and Traudl returned to a smiling Martin Bormann. Each woman carried a tray of pastries and tea service. Axmann, Högl and Lindloff stood up to offer their chairs with a friendly demeanor that surprised the women. Less than five minutes later, at approximately 3:30 in the afternoon of April 30, 1945, a gunshot shattered the frivolity. Bormann jumped to his feet, a look of terror on his face.

"Everyone stay calm." He strode towards the door and knocked loudly. "Mein Führer, is everything all right?" He knocked again as the phalanx of Axmann, Lindloff, Misch and Högl closed ranks behind him.

Bormann crashed his shoulder against the door and burst in to see a lifeless Hitler slumped over a side table, Eva Hitler dead on the sofa beside him.

"Oh mein Gott, I should have never have left him alone." As the room filled with horrified witnesses, Bormann waited for them to take in the scene and then launched into a passionate speech.

"I could not be more proud of serving this great man. The bravest German and greatest leader the world has ever known. He has sacrificed everything for the glory of the Reich. Now it is up to us, his loyal friends, to make sure their bodies are never defiled by the heathen hordes at our doorstep." Noticing Otto Günsche at the back of the crowd he gestured, "Sturmbannführer, you and Misch must prepare to carry them out of the bunker. But first, in accordance with our Führer's wishes, the new chancellor of Germany is now Dr. Joseph Goebbels. He must be located immediately and informed of this tragic event."

It was another twenty minutes before a haggard Goebbels and his wife, Magda, burst in to witness the scene. Loyal to a fault, the gathered witnesses watched as the new chancellor of Germany physically deteriorated before their eyes. The devious and cruel Bormann laid a meaty hand on the shaking Goebbels' shoulder.

"Herr Chancellor, we await your order to create a funeral pyre outside the bunker for the Führer and his wife. The order has to come directly from you."

"The heart of Germany has ceased to beat; our Führer is dead," was the new chancellor's disjointed reply. Goebbels was never privy to the plot and with those sincere words, he added a great emotional credence to the farce.

The next day, Tuesday, May 1, Bormann handed an inconsolable Chancellor Goebbels a letter to sign. It contained a carefully crafted account of the suicides and would be presented by courier to Soviet General Vasily Chuikov, along with a plea for mercy on behalf of the German people. Chuikov's reply was a predictable rejection. Goebbels retreated into even deeper depression. The remaining personnel in the bunker seemed determined on drinking every ounce of alcohol they could find in an effort to fortify their resolve. Some steeled themselves to run the Russian gauntlet in an effort to escape, others resigned themselves to follow Hitler to Valhalla.

In Hitler's study, Bormann stuffed his briefcase with the contents of the safe as he gave final instructions to his sub rosa group.

"Gentlemen, good luck in your escape plans for

tonight. I have funded individual secret bank accounts for you in Switzerland. Your passwords are personalized and must not be shared. Should any of you be captured, you must disclose your rehearsed eyewitness account of my demise. The reason that each of you will report seeing me die in a different location is because no corpse will ever be found, unless of course, my escape is compromised. If you repeat the lie often enough, the Allies will believe I have perished, they just won't know where. With any luck, it will help loosen security enough for me to disappear...."

Dr. Ludwig Stumpfegger knocked frantically on the door as he begged excitedly for admittance. "Reichsleiter, Magda Goebbels poisoned all six of her children then walked hand-in-hand with Joseph up to the Chancellery Gardens. The new chancellor blew her brains out and then turned the pistol on himself. Who's in charge now?"

Martin Bormann, wearing civilian clothes, pounded his fist on the table. "Nobody is in charge, Ludwig, because there is fuck all to be in charge of. Let's get out of here, gentlemen. We will meet on the other side of Hell."

.

PART TWO

CHAPTER FOUR

1953, One Career Ends, Another Begins

"Good Lord, I think I'm having a heart attack!" wheezed Sir Arthur Singleton. Along with the other Blackpool Board of Directors and their guests, he was completely consumed by the events taking place within this cauldron of excitement. The uncharacteristic jumping up and down caused the wealthy Victorian's rose-gold pocket watch to flip out of his waistcoat and dangle like a fish on its way to the gaff. His pseudo-medical pronouncement raised no concern because nobody could hear him; he could hardly hear his own voice above the deafening roar of one hundred thousand spectators in Wembley Stadium. On May 2, 1953, everyone in and beyond the exclusive private box was witnessing a remarkable Cup Final. Blackpool had just clawed their way back to level the score with less than two minutes remaining in the game.

The Seasiders had been the dominant team in English soccer for over a decade, reaching the prestigious Football Association Cup Final in 1948 and 1951 only to receive runner-up medals after both Manchester United and Newcastle United bested them. This year had to be the charm, even though they were now playing without one of their legendary heroes, Malcolm McClain. However, the curse descended early in the match when the Bolton Wanderers scored during the very first minute of play. Everything continued to go Bolton's way and the Wanderers had a comfortable three to one lead with only twenty minutes remaining in the game.

Malcolm and Margery McClain were sitting in the directors' box with Chez and Jadwiga Orlowski. Disappointment loomed and Sir Arthur sucked his pipe with petulance, occasionally mumbling pathetic excuses to himself.

"Malcolm, this team is on a slippery slope without you. Use my name and go down to the dressing room. Joe Smith must put you in for the last ten minutes…."

"Sir Arthur, Tommy Garrett, the left defender, is playing great. I want to be on that field with my mates as much as anyone but these lads have played the entire season together, win, lose or draw. Let's cheer them on to the final whistle…"

His mother-in-law, Beatrice Singleton interrupted with a gentle laugh, "You're a wise man, Malky, unlike some people I could mention. You are almost forty years old and playing out your career with another club. Our lads must learn to play without you."

But Malcolm McClain's two best friends on the team were far from giving up on the game. Stanley Matthews, regarded as the greatest player in the world, systematically carved away the left side of Bolton's defense by flighting ball after ball into their penalty area. On the receiving end of these crosses was another Stanley, Stan Mortensen, the current English international striker. This relentless tandem tied the game at three to three with only two minutes left, all three Blackpool goals scored by Mortensen.

Every spectator was now standing and contributing to the deafening noise as the game entered its last sixty seconds and once again, the ball flowed through Blackpool's captain, Harry Johnston, to find the wizard on the right wing.

"Come on, Stanley, come on, Stanley, for Chrissakes swerve around him and GET THE DAMN BALL ACROSS," shrieked Margery McClain to the astonished amusement of the Orlowskis.

Matthews left a trail of defenders in his wake but held onto the ball when he noticed Mortensen being triple-teamed.

Good lad, Stan, now find Bill, whispered Malcolm to

himself. The Blackpool fans groaned as the Matthews cross seemed to curve hopelessly behind a diving Mortensen but McClain had seen and practiced this move a million times with the two Stanleys. All the defenders went with the center forward, leaving an unmarked Bill Perry to slam home the winning goal just before Referee Griffiths glanced at his watch.

He blew the final whistle and the Blackpool Directors' box shook as its occupants jumped up and down. The gold watch clattered onto the floor and was crushed underfoot—but Blackpool had finally won the Cup!

Two days later, the city of Blackpool closed its streets to welcome home their conquering champions. The team paraded the Cup from the open top of a double-decker, 'white lady' Ribble bus. As they passed by the Fleece Hotel on Market Street, Manager Joe Smith commanded the driver to stop. The players began to clap and on cue, the crowd chanted, "Malcolm, Malcolm, Malcolm." A second floor window opened and McClain waved down with a big grin.

"Get your sorry Ulster arse onto this bus, McClain. That's a direct order from your former manager."

The crowd went wild as two or three minutes later, Malcolm McClain appeared on the top deck of the bus, his teammates insisting he hold the trophy aloft as the parade continued into Talbot Square.

What a memory, and although his professional career would not officially end for another two years, this moment would always be remembered as its pinnacle, even though McClain did not kick a ball in the famous Cup Final.

CHAPTER FIVE

The Germination of a Plan

T he McClain and Orlowski families lived almost 150 miles apart but made a point of getting together several times a year. On one of these occasions, the venue was a pretty pub called the White Swan near the Roman ruins in Leicester. The four friends were in the middle of an enjoyable lunch when, much to Margery's evident concern, Malcolm suddenly doubled over and began to cough violently.

"Dammit, my age is catching up with me. I've never been able to shake off that wretched cough I picked up in the Bari field hospital during the war." He sat up, recovered and changed the subject. "How are things going with the restaurant?"

Chester, almost seven years his junior, shrugged. "The restaurant, I am happy to say, is doing very well. And I've finally completed my teaching degree. However, I'm getting bored, so if you think of another adventure we can go on together, count me in. Let's do something before we both get too old. I don't think a sedentary lifestyle was meant for either of us."

Both men were aware that they had a lifetime of knowledge and experience, along with an implicit obligation to pass everything down to future generations of gymnasts and soccer players. With that thought uppermost, there was little doubt in their minds that it was time to move on to the next chapter.

"Perhaps we should work together, start a business. Maybe a gymnastics and soccer academy..." Chez said.

Then Margery chimed in. "I think you guys would be a great team. If you get serious, I'll bend Dad's ear to see if he will finance your business venture. We should all sleep on it and then put some numbers together."

The lunch and the fire relaxed everyone and inevitably, the conversation wound its way back to Chez and Malcolm's adventures in Yugoslavia.

"Chez, when are you going to let me in on what happened after I left you in Semic?" Malcolm cajoled.

Chester demurred as usual and apologized that he was still bound by the Official Secrets Act and could not reveal anything that had happened during the final months of the war. He skillfully diverted the conversation by announcing that Her Majesty's Government was behind his mother-in-law, Bernice Brzozowska, and her five daughters owning and operating the first-ever Polish restaurant in the small Leicestershire town of Loughborough. The location had been driven by Chez enrolling in a fledgling degree course offered by Lufbra Training College, an institution created to focus on sports with an emphasis on gymnastics and athletic training.

However, Malcolm was like a dog with a bone. "Well, whatever special missions you went on, my friend, they must have been of colossal importance to merit the late King George giving you and your family British citizenship, let alone the government financing your education and a Polish restaurant!"

He knew his friend's word was his bond and he would likely take the secrets to his grave, but McClain's interest was understandably roused; after all, he knew the special talents of the Spider better than anybody.

Whatever the hell Chez pulled off, I bet it was a bloody doozy!

The next evening, all four friends dined together at *'Café Polska,'* the Brzozowski family's popular restaurant in the center of Leicester. The prior day's conversation was causing coy nervousness as they fiddled around with small talk, until Jadwiga uttered some harsh words to her husband in Polish. He responded to the table in English.

"Jadzie and I are very keen to know if you and Margery have thought any more about yesterday's lunchtime conversation."

"Oh, you've decided to tell me about your secret adventures, Chez?"

"No, I meant about…" Chez started, but then realized Malcolm was joking just before Margery interrupted.

"Stop playing the fool, Malky. Chez, we would be delighted if you and Jadwiga would consider being equal partners with us in a new business venture. I talked to my father on the telephone last night and our idea to train youth in mastering the disciplines inherent in sport is something near and dear to his heart. He offered to help us with any financing we might need.

"For the record, Dad seems to be in on the Spider's secrets, most likely through his friend Lord Acheson. He has apparently taken the same vow of silence as Chez but seemed very enthusiastic about backing almost any venture Malcolm and Chez decide to pursue. I remember times when the old skinflint wouldn't buy me an ice cream on the promenade. He definitely must know something we don't."

The prospects for the partnership fueled a flood of ideas as they enthusiastically devoured Bernice Brzozowska's famous Flaki soup and the specialty of the house, Bigos. The head chef finally made her appearance in the dining room to a ripple of applause. She raised her hand in sheepish acknowledgment as she made her way to her daughter's table.

"How was everything, my dear, dear friends?"

"Up until now, I thought the best Bigos I would ever eat was cooked in a barn in Blizna but this tops it easily; unbelievable, Ma," Chez offered as he raised his glass.

"Bernice, you certainly have a gift for cooking. Malcolm and I love tripe soup but we have never tasted anything quite this delicious," Margery said graciously.

"Good, save some room for dessert. I have just fried some fresh, assorted Paczki. Coffee for everyone?"

The consensus at the dinner table was to explore any prospects Malcolm's birthplace, Belfast, might hold for the new venture. If there was any place on earth that might open doors of opportunity for the famous McClain name, it would most likely be found in Northern Ireland.

"So, if Jadwiga and Margery are okay looking

after the kids for a week, Malcolm and I will take the Heysham boat over to Belfast. Once there, we should be able to determine if there is a market for an academy where we can use our combined lifetime experiences to train young kids. We might even unearth some gems that can go on to attain the highest levels in their chosen sports."

"We are going to contact my brother, Sam, and of course, our mutual friend, Paddy McBride," Malcolm said. "With their help, we hope to return home with a couple of possible locations and a construction budget. Chez surprised me by suggesting we name our project the Spider Academy. What do you girls think?"

Both wives voiced their complete support and clapped enthusiastically.

"Forget the coffee, let's drink some bubbly. Here's to the Spider Academy!"

During the next six months, their excitement escalated to a fever pitch. There were three trips to Belfast, and meetings with solicitors, accountants and the City Council. Armed with projected income and expenses, along with a tentative agreement on a location, the two men finally felt prepared to make a presentation to Sir Arthur Singleton, J.P., the man on whose bank account rested the entire future of the venture if it was to succeed.

Frankly, all four friends were quite nervous but none more so than Margery McClain as they waited in the plush living quarters of the Fleece Hotel in Blackpool. Her mother made tea and tried to calm everyone down with a little banter.

"You know, Arthur can sometimes appear a rather cold fish but deep down he has a heart of gold and loves his only daughter a lot more than his prudish upbringing allows him to show," Beatrice said. This theory took a jolt when the door behind her suddenly opened and a very stern Justice of the Peace marched into the room.

He sat down and lit his pipe without a trace of a smile before stating, "You children have exactly twenty minutes to make your case before I return to my club. What is this harebrained scheme you've been cooking up together?"

Two hours later, Sir Arthur was the one acting like a kid in a candy store. The site Chez and Malcolm had identified was in North Belfast, at the confluence of two major thoroughfares, North Queen Street and York Road. It had obvious potential because the Belfast City Council was prepared to designate it with special zoning, promising to invest in the infrastructure and build a major public swimming facility if McClain and Orlowski committed to building the Spider Academy there. Singleton picked over the numbers and then made a shocking announcement.

"I will fund your entire operation for a five percent annual return but I have three explicit demands you must all agree to." They all looked at each other nervously as they waited for him to elaborate.

"One, you are not asking for enough money so I am increasing both your construction and operating budgets by thirty percent. Two, Malcolm and Chez will take equal ownership and decent salaries; my daughter Margery and her best friend Jadwiga must be able to raise their families in a suitable lifestyle. Three, you have completely forgotten about your accommodations in that God-forsaken country. I will be buying you both houses so Mrs. Singleton and I have appropriate places to stay when we visit our grandchildren and godchildren.

"Oh, and a fourth condition: You must all join me in a glass of champagne to celebrate—assuming we are in agreement. Beatrice, have Tommy bring up a bottle of chilled Roederer from the cellars."

The four friends were completely speechless.

CHAPTER SIX

Buenos Aires, Argentina

F ollowing a military coup, Argentinian President Juan Peron had fled into exile. The event created a brief moment of concern amongst twenty thousand recent German exiles but they need not have worried. After all, their new Führer had proved himself to be a master criminal extortionist and the bullion that accompanied the fleeing Nazis across the Atlantic was but a fraction of the wealth concealed in the Party's Swiss bank accounts.

The new upstart military junta quickly realized that without the generous cash infusions that had flowed from their new German citizens into the Argentine economy for the past decade, their country would be on a path to bankruptcy.

Newly sworn in President Arturo Ferreyra and his

covert backer, millionaire businessman Rogelio Rodriguez, summoned de facto Nazi Ambassador Ludwig Freude to an emergency meeting at the Presidential Palace in Buenos Aires to clarify the situation.

"So glad you could make it on such short notice, Señor Ambassador. May I introduce my Minister of Finance Rogelio Rodriguez?"

"Pleased to meet you, Señor President and you too, Ministro Rodriguez. In anticipation of the agenda, I took the liberty of bringing with me a most respected member of our German/Argentinian community in Patagonia, Señor Juan Gomez. Both he and I are enthusiastic about offering substantial support to your new regime so that we might continue to enjoy security and prosperity within our wonderful adopted country during these turbulent times." A short rotund man in his mid-fifties stepped from behind his ambassador and shook hands with both Argentinians, honoring each with a polite bow. They all proceeded into a reception room to sit facing each other from high-backed velvet upholstered chairs.

For the next thirty minutes, President Ferreyra assaulted Ambassador Freude with questions about the whereabouts, past and present, of the Nazi treasure that had supported the Argentine economy since the mid-1940s. Throughout the escalation from an uneasy politeness to fierce bullying threats, Señor Juan Gomez sat silently in the background with a thin smile creasing his lips. He felt certain he was watching a marionette show and the puppeteer was Minister Rodriguez. The decisive moment revealed itself when the charade imploded with the minister of Finance rudely cutting off his president with a raised hand to take over the conversation.

"Listen Freude, you will grant the Argentine government immediate access to all Nazi assets in this country. We estimate the gold alone must have a value in excess of five trillion pesos, not to mention the diamonds, artwork and other treasure you thieves have pilfered. The entire Nazi inventory must be deposited in our national treasury by the end of this week or everyone in this country who eats sauerkraut will be shipped back to Europe to face the war crimes tribunal…"

Finally, Señor Gomez had heard enough. He spoke, not in the polite porteños of Ambassador Freude, but in textbook Spanish marred only by his distinctive German accent. His voice spat unmistakable menace as he interrupted Rodriguez.

"Basta," Gomez slammed his hand onto the table and glared at Rodriguez. "I do not appreciate being threatened, Rodriguez. As of this morning, your entire personal net worth was 18,261,052 pesos that equates to less than zero point two five percent of what I can write a personal check for as I sit here. In addition, I can co-sign for a thousand times more from accounts

I control outside this country. I also serve or have controlling proxy on the board of directors of over 800 Argentinian corporations. In my world, you are an insignificant, pathetic turd and I will remove your figurine president by noon tomorrow if you persist with this bullshit."

President Arturo Ferreyra, the titular head of the fledgling government opened his mouth as if trying to speak but Rodriguez immediately grabbed his arm. Señor Juan Gomez continued without any regard for their military uniforms, uniforms so overly embellished with gold braid they looked as if plates of fried eggs had been tipped over them.

"Now, before I get any angrier than necessary, I would be willing to persuade my associates to continue the same financial arrangements we afforded Juan Domingo Peron in return for the same security terms and accommodations; nothing more, nothing less.

"You must contact Ambassador Freude with your decision by three o'clock this afternoon. Whatever you decide, you will find me a man of my word."

Gomez never once looked at the president. He had determined correctly from whence the power emanated, so continued his unblinking stare into the shifty eyes of Rodriguez, eyes that now flickered from the rivulets of sweat pouring down from his hairline. It was, simply put, no contest.

"Yu...yu...you underestimate the p...power of

the p…presidency, Señor. I will have you arrested and th…th…thrown in jail immediately," stammered President Ferreyra.

"And you think we are not prepared for that? Let's get a few simple things straight. Should anything happen to the ambassador or myself, my associates will immediately transfer every single peso from our Argentinian accounts into our banks in Uruguay, Paraguay and Brazil. In short, if either of us sneeze, one of you comedians had better be there with a handkerchief. Do I make myself clear?

"You have until three to give me your decision. Choose wisely, Rogelio. You will both find yourself sleeping on a park bench if you persist with this crap and the parks provide little protection from the unsavory characters that roam after dark through Buenos Aires.

"Mr. President, Minister, it has been a pleasure meeting you both."

Señor Juan Gomez clicked his heels in a sharp bow and turned curtly towards the door. Ambassador Freude was not far behind but paused to shrug his shoulders at the military men, his upturned palms and pursed lips leaving no doubt that the die had been cast.

CHAPTER SEVEN

Belfast, Northern Ireland

T he McClains, the Orlowskis and all their possessions boarded the Heysham boat without fanfare to sail west for their new life in Belfast. The academy was still several months away from completion but they wanted to absorb the culture of Northern Ireland, enroll their eldest children in local schools and personally supervise the finishing touches to their embryonic venture.

It just seemed natural that the families would settle down in adjoining houses that shared a large back yard. The location they chose was Jordanstown, a small village between Belfast and the old Norman town of Carrickfergus.

Local newspapers, *The Belfast Telegraph* and *The Newsletter*, both speculated from time to time about what their favorite son might be up to and scrambled to uncover details about his Polish partner. Lacking facts, dogged reporters began to chase down snippets about the legend of the Spider. The result was a bonanza of half-truths that made the mysterious Chez Orlowski even more interesting than Malcolm McClain. Seldom a week passed without a project progress report from Belfast being featured somewhere in the European mass media.

Finally, construction was completed and all the equipment installed. The Lord Mayor of Belfast cut the red ribbon that ceremonially sealed the front doors, and the Spider Gymnastic Academy opened to tremendous fanfare.

Sir Arthur Singleton only knew one way to do things, and that was first class all the way. The large front-page headlines of the two local newspapers were eclipsed by a lead story on the BBC's Six o'clock Evening News from London and similar coverage followed in every major European capital. Northern Ireland was now acknowledged as having one of the finest fitness-training establishments in Europe, so the media elevated Chez to Malcolm's celebrity status.

The English language edition of Pravda broached the same inevitable question. "Mr. Orlowski, did you and Mr. McClain name your gymnastics academy after the Polish war fable, the Spider?"

"I am familiar with the legend, of course, but I have never known anyone who has met him," he lied smoothly to the Russian reporter. "Quite remarkable adventures for a man reputed to be over seven feet tall!" There were chuckles from behind the microphones. "Quite honestly, when I was about thirteen, I had a pet spider called Sebastian and was impressed at how he could defy gravity. We anticipate that the young graduates of the Spider Gymnastics Academy will impress the world with their own gravity-defying feats."

"You are so bloody smooth, Chez," whispered Malcolm to his friend.

There is an upside and a downside to this, thought Chez. *The Spider legend is a marketing godsend but I can think of several pissed off Russians and Nazis who might get curious.*

It seemed like every child in the province wanted to enroll under Chez and Malcolm's tutelage, so the two men made a sincere attempt at fairness by resorting to tryouts with Orlowski and McClain being the final arbiters on admission. As future events unfolded, this proved unintentionally shrewd judgment as nobody could ever accuse the two men of even a hint of racial or religious bias in their decision-making. Sir Arthur's strong financial commitment allowed them to offer scholarships to outstanding talent from economically deprived neighborhoods around the country of Northern Ireland so from the outset, all children at the academy trained in an egalitarian atmosphere that had simply never existed in Belfast before that time.

"Malky, it always amazes me to hear some of these young kids talking about the trouble in their neighborhoods. I can tell if they are Protestants or Catholics just by how they refer to each other. But you don't have to have a degree in social science to notice the powerful bonding that develops after a few short weeks on the same team," Chez commented.

McClain got a chuckle out of that. "If I am a Protestant player on a soccer team that wants to win and my teammate, a Catholic, scores three goals every game, he might become my best friend very quickly."

"The power of team spirit and friendship. But how long will it take for the young generations training at our academy to go home and break down the barriers in their own neighborhoods?"

"One can only hope. This social unrest has been going on quite a while, Chez; the Irish War of Independence was being fought when I was seven or eight years old. I didn't hear my parents talk much about it. I guess back then, Belfast was too busy building ships and weaving linen. I remember one day coming home from school to our house on Elswick Street to see my mother and father dancing a jig because Northern Ireland had voted to leave the Irish Free State and return to being part of the United Kingdom. That party came to a screamin' halt as hundreds of Protestants and Catholics killed each other over the next couple of years.

"I signed professional papers on my sixteenth birthday and lived in a fairly protected environment so in all honesty, Chez, I can't think of any incidents that would have made us wary about coming here from England. The province of Ulster has been peaceful for years but like you, I sense something bubbling under the surface."

"Well, I hope we're not making a giant mistake by using my *nom de guerre* over the front door. There is still a price on my head in most of Eastern Europe and the Spider attracts trouble like honey draws flies."

But, the flies would not come from behind the Iron Curtain.

CHAPTER EIGHT

1966, San Carlos de Bariloche, Argentina

Official history was content in the belief that Nazi Party Member 60508, Martin Ludwig Bormann, had died somewhere near the Lehrter Bahnhof bridge in Berlin as he made his desperate attempt to flee the Führerbunker in early May, 1945. Due to twenty years of time, considerable weight loss and some surreptitious plastic surgery, the aging man sitting on the porch with his collection of trout flies bore little resemblance to *'the Brown Eminence of the Third Reich,'* but they were, in fact, one and the same.

Bormann and his surviving family members perfected an elaborate escape from Germany, eventually arriving in South America by U-boat in mid-1948. Today, as Señor Juan Gomez, he assumed a tolerable lifestyle at the Hacienda San Ramon, a twenty-minute drive north on Route 40 from San Carlos de Bariloche in the Rio Negro province of Argentina. Located almost six hundred miles south, southwest of Buenos Aires, the Hacienda had allowed the former Reichsleiter and his six remaining adult children to live in secure anonymity insured by the plunder from Europe's finest homes and museums and its richest banks.

Over time, five of the six children suffered extreme shame and embarrassment when they learned that the man they called 'Padre' had been tried and convicted in absentia for killing millions of innocent victims. The fact that the malevolent face in the photographs beside their Uncle Adolph had been presumed dead by the victors' version of history provided little solace as they grew to realize that their father could not change his evil ways as easily as his name. One by one, they left as soon as opportunity presented itself, cutting family ties and all communication with their father. Now there was only one remaining; a young man named after Rudolph Hess, Martin Bormann's first hero in the Nazi Party.

This son was now in his mid-thirties; tall and good-looking, therefore nothing like his father. As a naturalized Argentinian, he had changed his name from Rudolph Gerhard Bormann to Rudy Gomez shortly after completing the chaotic escape from Germany at the age of fourteen. His formative years in the Fatherland had been dominated by the meteoric rise of National Socialism and his father favored him over his siblings by allowing him a front row seat at countless Nazi rallies. Rudy remembered his heart being filled with pride as he looked over the sea of red flags and heard the adulation from thousands of proud Germans as they strained for a glimpse of Uncle Adolf and his father at the rallies.

His pride in seeing his childhood heroes control the destiny of Germany was shattered by the catastrophic defeat of the Third Reich. To this day, he believed that the British contrived the Allied victory, justifying his theory with a conclusion that Winston Churchill was insanely jealous of the way Martin Bormann and Adolph Hitler had led Germany to replace the British Empire as the most powerful nation on earth. As each of his siblings fled, Rudy's loyalties remained unshakably with his father.

"You might find this very interesting, Padre. We received a telegram yesterday from one of our agents about an event that took place in Northern Ireland. It was the lead story on the BBC and even made *Clarin's* Buenos Aires edition." Rudy handed his father the telegram.

The faded but telltale horseshoe scar on Bormann's right forehead reddened slightly as he read the telegram. Then he tossed it onto the table and turned to his son.

"So, a Pole living in Belfast has been named gymnastics coach for the British Olympic team! Why would that be of any interest to me, Rudy?" he demanded irritably.

The once-powerful man who had ruled Europe now appeared much more focused on completing the final knot on a Zonker fishing fly than listening to his report. *How I miss the euphoria of Berlin,* Rudy sighed as he persisted.

"Father, please note that a significant number of men and women who qualified for the British team currently train at an establishment named the Spider Academy. Malcolm McClain, the famous footballer, owns the establishment along with a Polish gymnast called Chez Orlowski. When we lived in Berlin, I remember you being very excited that Uncle Josef Goebbels had persuaded McClain to defect to the Fatherland and coach our German national soccer team. Then, rather mysteriously, you never mentioned him again."

The old man continued to peer through a large magnifying glass at the intricate trout fly, but his son knew he was now feigning his disinterest so he continued. "Earlier this morning, I did some digging through the archives and found that Malcolm McClain caused the Party considerable embarrassment by escaping from Stalag XVIII-D in Maribor. It gets even more interesting when I learned McClain's escape was orchestrated by our arch nemesis, the Spider." Rudy looked thoughtfully at his father a moment before he continued pushing.

"That Maribor debacle is the first mention of the Spider in our files. After 1943, there is so much written about the bastard, you'd think he derailed our war efforts singlehandedly...."

The former Reichsleiter suddenly spun around and glared intently at his son before speaking in a low, menacing voice.

"You know very well how I feel about that miserable cretin and I never want to hear the words Spider, Spinne or Araña uttered in this house, do you understand me?"

Then Bormann dropped his head and took a deep breath. After several seconds, he ignored his own dictum and, with a pained look in his eyes, resumed talking.

"Rudy, for over a year, incidents involving the Spider flooded Dr. Goebbels' offices on Wihelmstrasse. Your Uncle Josef believed it was all part of a cleverly contrived propaganda campaign by the Polish Armia Krajowa. Despite intense efforts, we never caught him, or for that matter, even got a photograph of him. Worse, he created a legend that our illustrious Ministry of Propaganda could not seem to undermine."

"I never heard of him until after we arrived in

Argentina," Rudy said softly. "You called him the most evil person in the world and the mere mention of his name still throws you into a rage all these years later. Will you ever tell me what it is all about, Padre?"

Bormann drummed the fingers of his right hand on the table to create a long deliberate pause. Quite suddenly, the drumming stopped as he came to a decision and began to speak again.

"Maybe that time is now, Rudy. I just turned sixty-six and my diabetes is becoming increasingly problematic. The more I think of it, if there is anything I can do to crush the Spider before I leave this earth, I should do it. Telling my son about the bastard might be the best place to start. But, you must promise to continue this quest if anything happens to me."

"Of course, Padre, you have my oath," whispered his wide-eyed son as he felt an adrenaline rush course through his body. Martin Bormann turned his chair away from the table littered with his fishing paraphernalia and looked directly at Rudy.

"We recognized that most of the deeds credited to the Spider were either impossible or completely bogus; the youth of Poland believed he was well over two meters tall and could leap tall buildings. When you attended the University of Cordoba, did you ever read about an American cartoon character called Superman? There are many parallels with this Polish legend.

"However, three incidents happened between 1943

and 1945 that are categorically attributable to a man who used the nickname, 'Die Spinne.' The first was the embarrassing debacle in Maribor that you uncovered. Then, just a few weeks later, we had a major breach of security at our top-secret rocket lab in Blizna. Credit, as usual, went to the Spider but this time, enough evidence was pieced together that showed parallels with the same man who spirited McClain out of Stalag XVIII-D. We had a team from ODESSA track the mayhem from Maribor through Nowy Targ to Blizna and finally to Krakow. The report they presented to me in 1955 leaves little doubt that we vastly underrated this Polish freedom fighter."

"But why did you have to know, Padre, especially ten years after the war?"

"Because of the third incident. Dammit, I need a drink. Get us both some schnapps, Rudy."

When Rudy returned to the porch, it was obvious that Bormann was emotionally charged; his eyes were red and his nose sniffled from behind a large white handkerchief. He sensed it was not a good time to push his father so he reverted to the telegram.

"McClain's partner in Belfast is called Chez Orlowski. Our files tell us that the Spider was Polish and apparently an extraordinary athlete. Couldn't this

Orlowski person perhaps be the Spider? You have to be pretty damn good to beat a Brit out of the most prestigious job on the British Olympic gymnastics team."

"I see where you are going but the real Spider would not let his guard down by advertising who he was. Remember, we never laid a glove on him because most who encountered him ended up dead. In an immediate response to the Maribor escape, Goebbels personally assigned Sturmbahnführer Abelard Hans von Keller to clean up the mess. I knew this man; he was a very capable, you might even say, ruthless officer who made his SS contemporaries look like kindergarten teachers. We gave him unlimited resources yet in less than a week, he ended up with his throat slit and the Spider's calling card pinned to his dead body. No, Rudy, if this Orlowski person was the Spider, I doubt he would let his nom de guerre be used as a billboard."

"No, sir, but maybe he believes all his enemies are dead! There are just too many coincidences. Something tells me…"

"No, no, no, let me tell you what I want you to do. I have just had an idea.

"You were educated at the University of Cordoba, speak English with a heavy Spanish accent and have inherited your mother's height and good looks. Dye your blond hair jet black, take a couple of caballeros with you for muscle; Romero and Ramos both speak fairly good English. Why not take a trip to Belfast in Northern Ireland? My staff will build a cover for your identity and tailor the purpose of your trip as an excuse to visit this academy. Convince Señor Orlowski that you are immensely wealthy and would like to open a Spider Academy in, let's say, Barcelona." Bormann paused, deep in thought. Rudy sensed that the analytical parts of his father's brain were testing the spontaneous plan. The old man finally nodded his head as if accepting his own endorsement and continued.

"We must plan this very carefully so there are no links back to Patagonia. My most reliable agent in Europe is Hans Dietmar; he runs our Portuguese operation. Barcelona reports to him so you will have substantial resources to back you up," Bormann was on a roll. "I will send Hans a coded telegram about our plan and then transfer the necessary funds from Zurich; he will train and outfit you. You will need to be cautious but it should not be too hard to uncover details about this shadowy Chez Orlowski without anyone connecting you with Argentina.

"I will rely upon your assessment; do your job and come back with your report. If this man turns out to be the Spider, I will do whatever it takes to destroy him. Better yet, I'll have him brought back here. I will personally inflict him with the most painful death a human can imagine."

The two men had talked themselves back into good

spirits so Rudy refilled both glasses before pushing the question,

"You mentioned a third incident, Padre?"

The younger man watched his father stare off towards the distant Andes before spitting his reply through clenched teeth.

"The Spider killed your Uncle Adolf. The ODESSA report concludes the bastard abducted our Führer from the Reichskanzlei gardens and flew him to England. There are first hand reports from Flug-kapitan Hanna Reitsch and a couple of SS guards that the leader of the kidnappers was a completely bald young man who dropped a couple of Polish swear words into his near perfect German. Ober-sturmbannführer Heinz Linge told me that he firmly believes this man to be a fake janitor who managed to access the inner sanctum of the Führerbunker with the purpose of spying upon us. In hindsight, I am convinced that this charlatan was the Spider. He must have overheard that I was going to smuggle the Führer out of Berlin by small plane and was waiting in the Reichskanzlei gardens with an ambush. We are also fairly certain they made it behind British front lines but then the trail went cold.

"ODESSA subsequently interviewed a storekeeper in the village of Uchtdorf. Two clean-shaven, bald men appeared there on a bicycle one morning. The two men had an animated conversation, leading the storekeeper to conclude that the older man was a high-ranking party member. I am one of the few people in the world that know that Adolph had shaved off his hair and moustache before he left the bunker."

"But where's the evidence that the older man was captured by the younger?"

"In Uchtdorf, I don't think he was yet being held by force. However, there was a British army camp a short distance away and our agents managed to elicit some information from a corporal that served there. Two bald men were captured after the crash landing of a small Luftwaffe plane. They escaped from the British but the next day, all hell broke loose when the SAS suddenly showed up looking for the men. The corporal was positive that a couple of days after that, the younger bald fugitive returned to the camp and was treated like a long lost friend."

The old Nazi's eyes froze as a sudden thought interrupted his story. "Sonofabitch, that SAS squad was led by Major Paddy McBride...who happens to come from Belfast, if I'm not mistaken. You're right, Rudy, there are just too many coincidences."

"Padre, this is all very amazing but I have so many questions. Can you trust this corporal's account? What happened to Uncle Adolf? Did he escape?" Rudy's questions came out in a rush of excitement.

"Rudy, the corporal gave our agents his testimony as Odessa agents were pulling the nails from his wife's fingers; moments before both their lives were terminated. If you connect the dots, it is clear that the Spider handed Adolf over to the custody of the SAS. They in turn flew both men to a secret location in England where they concluded Adolph must have been murdered. Before you ask the obvious, yes, that arrogant, fat bastard Churchill let our subterfuge with the bunker suicide go unedited into the history books. You must assume that it suited the British better to have Adolph murdered and his body dumped where it would never be found rather than granting him his rightful stature as a great martyr.

"I have no doubt that the Spider helped cause and create this mayhem. Get the bastard, Rudy. Just get the bastard," Bormann concluded.

With considerable input from his father, Rudy Gomez began to focus all his energy on coordinating the itinerary for himself and his two bodyguards. They must journey on Argentinian passports to Portugal and then rely upon Hans Dietmar to help them vanish. After a suitable period, they would be able to travel incognito to Barcelona where the Spanish cell was instructed to transform Gomez into a wealthy Spanish industrialist accompanied by his two assistants. Spanish clothes appropriate for their ruse must replace their entire wardrobe but bodyguards Lucas Romero and Franco Ramos insisted they be allowed to carry their traditional facón knives at all times. Gomez knew they could never be talked out of this condition but on the plus side, both gauchos could become lethal weapons should any dangerous situations arise.

In the early spring of 1967, Rudy bid his father goodbye and the three men caught the train from Patagonia to Buenos Aires en route to Lisbon.

CHAPTER NINE

Lisbon, Portugal

H ans Dietmar met Rudy and his bodyguards in the terminal of Lisbon's Portela Airport and whisked them by limousine to his residence in Alcântara. The three Argentinians spent the first two days there, recovering from their arduous 6,200-mile journey. They found themselves waking up at noon and unable to fall asleep until the early morning hours. But by the third day, their minds and bodies had adapted to Portuguese time and their stomachs began to appreciate the incredible cuisine of the oldest city in Western Europe.

Comfortable with the tight security surrounding Dietmar's compound, Rudy gave Lucas and Franco permission to relax and explore the barrio of Alcântara. The privacy allowed him and Hans Dietmar to begin formulating details for the proposed mission to Belfast and, in preparation, Dietmar invited one of his close friends to visit the house for breakfast.

Professor Helmut Weiss was the well-respected head of the Department of Germanic studies at the Queen's University Belfast. He had lived in Northern Ireland for almost a decade and similar to many of his fellow professors at Queen's, he maintained a summer home in the Algarve region of Portugal.

The amicable conversation between the three men took place over coffee and croissants.

"Professor Weiss…"

"…Please, call me Helmut. May I call you Rudy?"

"Of course. Helmut, I will be visiting Northern Ireland within a few weeks and Hans thought you might be able to advise me about what I must see while in Belfast."

"It will be my pleasure, Rudy," began the professor and proceeded to talk non-stop for the next twenty minutes about Georgian architecture as it related to the façade of the Royal Belfast Academical Institution. He finally changed his focus to compare a long list of pubs and restaurants he could personally recommend.

Rudy feigned interest as he struggled to stifle several yawns, then grabbed an opportunity to interrupt the professor by slapping himself on the knee and laughing aloud. "Helmut, you make me feel like I already know every inch of the city. I would just save my money and stay here if I didn't have an ulterior motive for the trip!" He then adopted a slightly more conspiratorial tone as he continued.

"You have a couple of famous personalities living in Belfast: Malcolm McClain and Czeslaw Orlowski. The whole world seems to be talking about the Spider Academy they operate. Our organization is extremely keen on finding out if they might be interested in duplicating their facility in the Fatherland."

"I have met both men; they are enormously popular in Belfast but are you aware of their history? The Third Reich incarcerated both McClain and Orlowski during the war, so I doubt either could be motivated to help Germany."

"Well, perhaps not knowingly, but my group will be offering them a considerable sum of money to train staff for a replication academy to be built in Barcelona; I'll convince them it is planned for the youth of Catalonia. Once we learn about the new techniques and equipment they are using at the Spider Academy in Belfast, the trainers will be redirected to our state-of-the-art facility in Köln. Our goal is to create a resurgence of Aryan athletes in time to dominate the Olympic Games scheduled to take place in 1972 in Munich."

"Well, Rudy, you know where my heart is. Although I despise subterfuge, placing the German flag where it belongs—back on top of the rostrum in Munich—is a lifelong goal of mine. How may I help?"

"We will be visiting Belfast as well-heeled representatives of the Spanish government. Where do you recommend we stay? Are there any areas of the country we should avoid due to political unrest?" Then, with a casual innocence, Rudy threw in, "And before I forget, how did the academy come up with the name, Spider?"

"Well, they have joked with the press that that it was named after Orlowski's boyhood pet spider but common knowledge prefers to link it with a Polish fairy tale. Let me explain.

"During the war, the Polish underground created a folk hero called the Spider. There is absolutely no way this character could have been real, but if it amuses simple minds... Anyway, I believe the men decided to use the name and the legend to give them some instant marketing. It certainly has worked its way into a nice logo."

Rudy Gomez chuckled. "Helmut, I had heard it said that Czeslaw Orlowski might actually be the Spider."

"I have heard that old chestnut many times myself but it is just wishful thinking by the media. Those rascals would love to have a shiny object to chase but the fact that the legend of the Spider has him two feet taller than Mr. Orlowski is pretty hard to reconcile.

Besides, in the cartoons portraying the Spider that I am familiar with, he has long black hair and wears a Viking helmet; Orlowski is completely bald."

Professor Weiss proved himself a mine of information about the many nuances of life in Belfast and during his visit seemed completely unaware that he was contributing to the covert operation. However, contribute he did when he nonchalantly dropped a nugget in Rudy Gomez's lap.

"Come to think of it, Rudy, one of Belfast's biggest social events occurs later this year. Back in 1911, all the big wigs in the city attended an extravagant dinner to celebrate the launching of the Titanic. Quite the to-do at the time. Of course, they had no idea that half the people who attended that dinner would be feeding fishes less than a year later."

The professor became quite pensive before jolting back to reality. "The Anniversary Dinner is celebrated every May 31 at its original venue, the Grand Central Hotel. This dinner has become the Belfast social calendar's biggest charity fundraiser, so all the local celebrities should be there, maybe even Orlowski and McClain, though both must be busy preparing for the nineteenth Olympiad in Mexico City. Even if they are not on 'the list' you will certainly meet many people who can introduce you at a later date."

"That might be a fun thing to do, Helmut. I'll see if I can get invited," Rudy concluded with a smile.

By breakfast the next morning, the Argentinians had mapped out an agenda on which to spend a week in the capital of Northern Ireland. They then left Hans Dietmar and caught the overnight train to Barcelona. The conductor of the train was on Dietmar's payroll so Spanish immigration officials were not made aware that the three men had entered their country.

After the intercontinental express pulled into Barcelona's Estació de França station, Gomez, Romero and Ramos were asked to remain in the rear coach until the platform cleared of other passengers. There was a soft knock on the door of the compartment. When Ramos answered it, the conductor stepped forward and presented a pudgy man in a brown striped three-piece suit, who politely introduced himself as Otto Zeilke.

"Gentlemen, I will be your host for the next few days. If you would be so kind as to follow me. Danke, Willie, auf Weidersehen."

"Weidersehen, Otto."

The 1929 railway station is on the east side of the city close to the docks and as soon as their limousine pulled onto Avenida Marques de L'Argentera, the passengers felt the power of the city's stunning architecture.

Señor Zeilke escorted his guests into the reception foyer of his magnificent home. Four opulent leather couches surrounded a massive carved coffee table in the middle of the tiled floor and a waiter offered sangria after they relaxed into the cushions.

"Gentlemen, straight down to business," Zeilke said briskly. "The Maldà family technically owns this estancia. The old baron was sympathetic to our cause and the family has been rewarded well over the years. The current owner is his grandson, Rafael de Maldà, baron de Cortada. He is about your age, Rudy, and has agreed to pay a low-key visit to his family estate in Cap d'Antibes for as long as necessary while you assume his identity for your trip to the United Kingdom. The title is entirely honorific and here in Catalonia it has come to mean nothing more than a rich man, but you would still expect your personal assistants, Lucas and Franco, to address you as 'Your Excellency.'

"To enhance your adopted persona, you will be carrying a significant amount of British currency. A title and cash combine to blind the average man but if anyone decides to nose around, the credentials you carry will stand up to the closest scrutiny. However, I stress again that you must never appear to be close friends with your gauchos; from this day, you must become Rafael de Maldà, baron de Cortada, a

Spanish nobleman. If Lucas or Franco should have a weak moment and call you 'Rudy,' it might raise suspicion you do not need."

"But Señor, we have called him Rudy since he first came to Argentina as a young boy. Old habits die hard," laughed Franco.

"And so will you, if I hear of you jeopardizing the mission." Otto scowled without a hint of humor. "It must always be 'Your Excellency' followed by a polite bow of the head, comprendez?" The stern German looked at each of the three without blinking until they nodded their compliance with his demands.

"I have prepared extensive details about each of your identities. Lucas and Franco have little to worry about but the minutiae must match each of your travel documents. Rafael, by necessity, your homework will be significantly more demanding."

Rudy, caught off-guard, looked around the room to see whom Otto was referring to as Rafael before blushing a deep red. "My apologies, Señor, I will try to be more diligent."

"Tomorrow, I will escort you to Passeig de Gracia, one of our most elegant shopping enclaves. You will be outfitted with all the clothes and accoutrements that befit your new identities. As of this moment, you are required to live in character and my associates and I will be watching you very closely. We will question you about the food, the customs, the history of Barcelona and you will not leave my tutelage until I deem each one of you perfect in your role."

Then Zeilke cracked a smile and chuckled, "Truth be known, all anybody in the outside world is likely to ask you about will be football, so learn everything you can about our famous team, the current and past Barcelona players and the Camp Nou.

"Regardless, for your own personal safety in this city, you had better be a rabid Barça fan with passionate hatred for Real Madrid."

CHAPTER TEN

Belfast, Northern Ireland

I t took almost three weeks before Otto Zeilke felt that his three students were ready to infiltrate Northern Ireland society. At that point, he wished them well and organized a circuitous journey for them to travel through France before catching the ferry from Calais to Dover.

Rafael de Maldà, accompanied by Romero and Ramos, eventually took off from London-Gatwick on BEA flight 14. The Vickers Viscount landed at Belfast Aldergrove Airport at 12:40 in the afternoon of Tuesday, May 30.

Aldergrove was transitioning from a military base into the country's main civil airport and the new terminal still had the smell of fresh paint as the 24 passengers and crew entered from the transit bus.

It is only a 334-mile flight from London, so the three men were well rested and eager to explore the infamous capital of Northern Ireland. They had adopted their roles of a wealthy Spanish entrepreneur accompanied by his two personal assistants, with an air of elegance accented by swarthy good looks and romantic accents; women of Celtic descent tend to find such a combination irresistible. The baron de Cortada, several inches taller than his assistants, began to question why he had not dyed his hair years before. With an elegant moustache reminiscent of Clark Gable and hair slicked back with Brylcreem, his film-star good looks garnered him an almost embarrassing amount of attention from the British European Airways cabin staff, one of whom made a point of sitting beside him on the bus.

"Where are you staying in Belfast, Baron?" purred the attractive blonde stewardess. "I do not have to return to London this afternoon and thought I might spend a couple of days in Belfast. If you and your friends would like a little company for dinner—and perhaps breakfast?" But, although Rafael de Maldà looked every inch the impetuous Latin lover, innate Germanic discipline reminded him that their stay in Belfast had a specific purpose, one that could not be jeopardized by sexual distraction. Nonetheless, he used the encounter to develop his mysterious persona.

"My goodness, that sounds tempting but we are staying with my cousin and then taking the Larne/Stranraer ferry to Scotland in the morning. Give me your phone number in London and I shall call you next week when I am alone." As the woman pouted her disappointment, Rafael noticed a recent indentation on her left ring finger and smiled to himself that he was doing the woman a favor but within seconds, she slipped a note into his shirt pocket as she squeezed his knee and winked.

From Aldergrove Airport, a taxi took them directly to the Grand Central Hotel on Royal Avenue in the heart of Belfast. Opened in 1893, it had become a favorite of celebrities staying in the capital. The Beatles and the Rolling Stones stayed there and other notables who had occupied the much-coveted Suite 217 included Sir Winston Churchill, Bob Hope and Gene Autry. This famous suite, overlooking the bustling thoroughfare, was not available during their stay; nevertheless, Zeilke's Barcelona cell had done a remarkable job in securing three smaller suites on the second floor.

At a little after 3:00 p.m., the baron emerged from the rear door of his taxi and studied his surroundings while Romero snapped his fingers to summon an army of red-jacketed bellboys. They in turn gathered multiple leather suitcases from the boot and brought up the rear of a parade that proceeded through the brass revolving doors and into the magnificent Victorian lobby. Every piece of luggage bore the Maldà family monogram. As Rafael de Maldà presented their Spanish passports at the marble reception desk, a man wearing an elegant morning suit and sporting a glorious full beard, strode officiously towards him, a beaming smile creasing his face.

"Welcome, Your Excellency, I am the manager, William O'Malley. I hope you and your companions had a pleasant flight from London? Your suites are adjoining as requested and the bellboys will accompany you and your luggage there."

"Perfecto, Mr. O'Malley. I would like about thirty minutes to freshen up and then would very much appreciate a few moments of your valuable time."

"Of course, Your Excellency, my office is right over there; please join me at your convenience."

Wearing a monogrammed white shirt and expensive Italian slacks, the baron de Cortada carried a large black briefcase as he strolled from the bank of ornate mechanical lifts. The lobby of the Grand Central Hotel was abuzz with excitement about tomorrow's Gala event and decorations seemed to festoon every square inch of the vaulted space. He knocked politely on the manager's opulent double mahogany doors and within seconds, the cheery countenance of William O'Malley invited him into his office.

"Perhaps a glass of Spanish sherry, Your Excellency?"

"That is most thoughtful, Mr. O'Malley but I will be able to relax a little more if you can answer my simple enquiry." O'Malley gestured towards the studded Chesterfield sofa with a motion for his guest to sit as he poured Amontillado into two hefty Waterford snifters.

"What can I do to assist you, Excellency?

"This briefcase contains a significant amount of currency. I presume you have a vault on the premises?" O'Malley nodded in the affirmative. "Please count it and give me a receipt before taking it into your safekeeping. I use this money for day to day expenses so I will be drawing the amount down periodically during my stay."

"Absolutely no problem. It is a service the Grand Central Hotel provides to almost all our celebrity guests, whether it be in the form of currency or jewelry." Rafael handed over the briefcase and William O'Malley began to count the contents with practiced hands.

"Excellency, there are two hundred thousand and forty pounds sterling in front of me. Does that agree with your accounting?"

"Indeed it does, Mr. O'Malley. Please secure two hundred thousand in your vault and keep the forty pounds for your trouble."

"Oh my goodness, that is most generous, sir. If there is anything I can do to improve your stay, you have only to ask." The baron de Cortada waved a gesture of dismissal but then smiled with an apparent afterthought.

"Since you ask, Mr. O'Malley, it seems that there is some kind of party being arranged at the hotel. It might be an amusing distraction if you could arrange for me to attend. Can you tell me about it?"

"Please consider yourself my guest. Fifty-six years ago tomorrow, the Grand Central Hotel hosted a Gala Dinner to celebrate the launching of the RMS Titanic from the Harland and Wolff shipyards, right here in Belfast. Lord Pirrie was in attendance, as were the Board of Directors and several of the ill-fated first class passengers. The ship still had almost nine months of fitting out to complete before she headed to Southampton but we threw as grand a party as this town has ever seen that night.

"Tomorrow will be our annual celebration of the Gala Dinner and we always duplicate the original menu. The guest list is full but I have discretion to add an important personage such as yourself."

"Well, Mr. O'Malley, that sounds like fun, and much appreciated. Give me some idea about the makeup of the other guests and what dress is expected."

"The guest list is made up of mostly local celebrities and philanthropists. White tie formal dinner attire is requested, as the BBC will be filming a documentary throughout the evening with all proceeds donated to the RNLI."

"I have full formal attire in my luggage but I will need the hotel's assistance in getting everything pressed. After I am dressed, I will give Romero and Ramos the night off. Forgive me but what is the RNLI?"

"The Royal National Lifeboat Institution. It is a charity dedicated to saving lives at sea."

"Perfecto. Hold a thousand pounds from my deposit and donate it on my behalf to the RNLI to help pay for my dinner. Anyone whose name I might recognize on the guest list?" he smiled charmingly.

"I will give you the entire list but the most famous by far is Malcolm McClain, our local football star. He will be bringing his wife, Margery, but his partner, Chez Orlowski had to decline at last moment; his wife is about to deliver their ninth child. Seems like the Orlowskis are enjoying their life in Northern Ireland."

"That is very exciting for them and fortunate for me. As you know, football is very, very popular in Spain. McClain has been a hero of mine since I was a child. Is there a chance I might sit beside him?"

"Count on it, Your Excellency. You will have Mr. Orlowski's seat."

CHAPTER ELEVEN

The Grand Central Hotel, Belfast

Rafael de Maldà returned to his suite and asked Romero and Ramos to join him.

"So far, so good. I will be sitting next to Malcolm McClain at the Gala Dinner tomorrow night but unfortunately, Chez Orlowski will not be attending. I told the manager that I would give you the night off and he suggested you might enjoy visiting the Orpheus Ballroom. Apparently, there is not much to do on a Wednesday night in Belfast, but this ballroom is just north of here and within easy walking distance. Enjoy yourselves but, for heaven's sake, stay in character and keep your dicks in your pants. Remind me tomorrow to give you some folding money."

The next morning found the hotel hosting a frenzy of excitement. Enormous BBC television cameras were set up to cover the guests as they arrived at the main entrance on Royal Avenue. A champagne reception greeted the celebrities in the lobby before they proceeded to a large ballroom that was elaborately decorated to reproduce the atmosphere and style of May 31, 1911.

Rafael was the epitome of elegance in his white tie and full eveningwear, but remained in his room for at least thirty minutes after noticing the first limousine pulling up on Royal Avenue. He had decided not make a grand entrance into the festivities, preferring to blend into the crowd as he emerged from the elevator bank. His attempt at discretion failed, as most women in the room noticed the dashing baron almost immediately. He could feel their eyes focusing upon him so he picked a Waterford flute off one of the many silver-serving trays carried by waiters, flashed a dazzling smile and enjoyed the champagne. In no time at all, he began to feel like a hunted animal as packs of titillated femmes fatales closed in to introduce themselves.

"Seamus, who is that gorgeous man?"

Seamus Dunfey, headwaiter at the Grand Central

for as long as anyone could remember, answered the same question half a dozen times in as many minutes.

"His Excellency Rafael de Maldà, baron de Cortada, and yes ma'am, he is single and staying with us at the hotel."

I have to get into conversation with someone pretty damn quick or I will be eaten alive, thought the baron. *Wait a minute, that man has to be Malcolm McClain; dammit, he still looks fit enough to play.*

If there was any man in the lobby attracting as much attention as the baron de Cortada, it had to be McClain. Now in his early fifties, he portrayed every inch the athlete. His impeccably tailored white tie ensemble was highlighted by the Distinguished Flying Cross on his left breast and insignia around his neck indicating he had been honored by Her Majesty Queen Elizabeth II as a Member of the Most Excellent Order of the British Empire. Rafael maneuvered his way into the circle of sycophants surrounding the legend and waited for his moment.

"Mr. McClain, I am Rafael de Malda. I am most privileged to be seated at your table this evening." McClain gave him a warm smile and accepted the offered handshake.

"Aha, Billy O'Malley tells me you are a Spanish baron from Barcelona? Please, allow me to introduce my wife, Margery." The attractive brunette standing to McClain's left excused herself politely from conversation with the Lord Mayor of Belfast and turned to Rafael.

"Well, Your Excellency, my intuition tells me that every woman in this room would give her eye teeth to swap places with me right now." She laughed and held out her right hand, which Rafael kissed while making a polite bow. "And that, sir, will only acerbate the situation. I am certain that a hundred imaginary daggers are being thrown at me but, I must admit that I am rather enjoying the attention."

Seamus Dunfey took position beside a large bronze gong suspended in a mahogany frame. With practiced theatrical aplomb, he backhanded it with a leather-covered mallet to produce a low reverberating tone that silenced the babbling crowd.

"My lords, ladies and gentlemen, dinner is served in the Grand Ballroom." A phalanx of the bellboys dressed in smart red jackets majestically opened three pairs of tall wooden doors. The chatter resumed as the river of penguins and tiaras began to flow towards the rear of the lobby.

Romero and Ramos could not wait to get away from the Grand Central. They were both humble gauchos from the Pampas and although they spoke reasonable English, the hard edge of the Belfast accent confused their ears. After only one day in the city, the stress of acting out their rehearsed roles became incongruous with the simple outdoor life they were used to. They needed this break to relax.

The two men made their way from the south side of the hotel and found themselves on Rosemary Street.

"Let's have an early dinner and a couple of drinks, Franco. I don't much feel like going to that stupid ball-room Rudy was blabbering about. What was the name of that restaurant the professor we met in Lisbon raved about?"

"I remember he said it was close to the City Hall and think it has the word 'kitchen' in its name. Let's get as far away as we can from that damn hotel before Lord fuckin' Rudy thinks of something else for us to do."

The two men recollected seeing the green dome of the City Hall from their taxi so they hustled south along Royal Avenue until it transitioned into Donegal Place. The white Portland stone of the Baroque Revival building soon loomed large in front of them, so they stopped a pedestrian with a kindly face.

"Pardon me, sir, if that is the Belfast City Hall? Do you happen know a good restaurant close by? We think it might be called 'the something kitchen.'"

The man laughed and answered them with almost unintelligible gibberish. "Youse are likely lookin' fer the Cottars Kitchen 'cos they does a brilliant pork chop." Fortunately, he began to gesture wildly as he added directions. "T'other side o' City Hall; yous'll see the stairs going down to the dining room. All the best, now."

"Thank you, sir." Franco waved and hurried away from the man.

"What the fuck did he say? Was he speaking English, Franco?"

"Apparently the place is called *'Cottars Kitchen'* and it is located in a basement on the other side of City Hall. We can ask someone else when we get closer." In the end, they didn't need to, because right where the friendly local had directed them was a sign in front of a green, wrought iron railing. The Cottars Kitchen insignia had an arrow directing patrons down a flight of stone steps.

Their meal was hearty Irish cooking at its best and the two gauchos drained an entire bottle of Bushmills Black Label whiskey before they were finished. It was past ten o'clock when they finally emerged back onto the stairs. The liquid gold libation caused them trouble in climbing up to Donegal Square South and both were chuckling as they sat on the top step. Romero and Ramos now decided that perhaps they might be in the mood for dancing, so they retraced their steps towards Royal Avenue.

The Orpheus Ballroom was only a few hundred yards further north of the Grand Central Hotel and easily identified by the long line of people waiting to get in. But the queue moved quickly so Lucas and Franco found a couple of empty seats at the bar less than twenty minutes later and felt the need to reinforce their buzz. They waited patiently for the busy bartender to grant them an audience.

"Guys, what would you like to drink?" The middle-aged man behind the bar asked them in Spanish. The Spanish in itself would not have caused alarm but his idiomatic slang was unmistakably Porteños, the dialect of Buenos Aires. Ramos and Romero looked at each other in shocked silence before Franco made a clumsy attempt to recover.

"Señor, we are from Barcelona and speak Spanish of course but I am not quite sure I understood what you just said."

"Boludez!" said the smiling mixologist. "Bullshit! I was born and bred in La Boca and came to Belfast on a freighter a couple of years ago. I've been listening to the two of you since you sat down at the bar and, if I had to guess from your accents, I'd say you were both from Patagonia."

"You have a good ear," admitted Lucas Romero. "My friend and I moved to Spain five years ago but we now work as personal assistants to a wealthy Spanish industrialist. If you could pour us a couple of glasses of Black Bush, we'll get out of your way and find a table closer to the band. What kind of music do they play?" he asked in an attempt to change the subject. But the bartender clearly craved the companionship of compatriots from home and stalled the pouring as he continued to engage his two mysterious customers in their mutual version of Spanish.

"The band is '*Brian Rossi & The Wheels.*' Last night, their saxophone player walked out on them to form his own band called '*Them.*' I was worried that tonight would be a farce but they seem to have adjusted.

"Your friend, the industrialist, is he also from Patagonia? I can't believe a true Spaniard would be travelling with a couple of gauchos," he joked. "I'd like to meet him; maybe he could use another Argentinian assistant. I'll grab at anything that might rescue me from this lousy job!"

The bartender's pleas were not lost on Ramos and Romero. They tossed some shillings on the bar, grabbed their glasses and retreated.

"Lucas, I have bad feelings about this guy; he could be a massive pain in the ass. If he reads the newspaper tomorrow, the Spanish industrialist seated beside Malcolm McClain at tonight's dinner might intrigue him," he whispered. "Unless he believes in coincidences, he will tie us all together and jump on the opportunity to advance his career beyond bartending."

"Oh shit," Lucas concluded. "What if he goes directly to our hotel to meet Rudy and pegs his Cordobes accent. We both know Rudy is not going to hire him, but that big-mouthed bartender could create a scene and blow our entire cover. Lord Rudy will blame us for talking to him and there will be all hell to pay if we have blown our very expensive masquerade.

"We have to nip this in the bud; otherwise, Rudy's father will be pissed beyond belief."

During the dinner, Margery McClain switched places with Malcolm so she could chat with the mayor's wife, Maureen. This suited Rafael very well and he waited patiently for the waiters to serve the first courses before he opened the conversation. He chose the Sardines á l'Imperiale over the Consommé Petite Marmite and when the appetizers were served, offered a polite, "Bon appetite, Mr. McClain."

"Please, call me Malcolm and if you don't mind, I'll call you Rafael.

"Tell me how you think Barça is going to do next year. I remember watching your manager, Roque Olsen, when he played for Real Madrid. He is about a dozen years younger than I am, so we never met on the field. Have the Barça fans accepted him?"

"Only when they win. This season, Roque has an exciting young midfielder in Rexach but Zaballa, the legendary Spanish striker, is getting a little over the hill and not really producing. However, all we really care about is beating Real Madrid. The other games just fill in La Liga's schedule." Rafael laughed and Malcolm did too, just as the Saumon Natural arrived in front of everyone.

All in all, the Gala Dinner offered nine courses before dessert and coffee. The two men seemed to be getting along famously.

"So, Rafael, word of our Spider Academy has reached as far as Barcelona? I am flattered. Would you have time to visit before you leave? I'll introduce you to my partner, Chez Orlowski."

"Well, as I stated, my main purpose is to visit Short Brothers to get a preview of the SC.5, a heavy-lift freighter they are developing for the R.A.F. It's not really available to the civilian market but my company, Maldà Industries, might be interested in buying a couple of their Skyvans if I can cut the right deal.

"I note you were awarded the D.F.C., so you must know quite a bit about aircraft."

"I was a navigator during the war and I've maintained a fascination with flying. The SC.7 Skyvan is going to be a nineteen-seat, twin turboprop. I don't blame you for being interested, it sounds like it will be one hell of an aircraft. The chairman of Shorts is sitting over there. Would you like me to introduce you?" This caused a momentary panic to flicker through the baron's eyes.

"Thank you, Malcolm, but not at this time. If I

show my hand too early in the game, I will not get the deal I want.

"It is interesting that you mentioned visiting the Spider Academy. My family contributes a significant annual amount to help provide the youth of Catalonia with athletic facilities. We have built many gymnasiums, swimming pools and of course, soccer fields. Do you think that you and your partner would be interested in replicating your academy in Spain? Money would be no object, we could pay you and your partner hefty consulting fees just to train the staff and supervise the equipment installation. What do you think?"

"Tell you what, Raphael, I'll discuss it with Chez. Call me tomorrow and I will try to work around your schedule to show you the academy before you leave. The telephone number is Belfast 746907; I'll write it on the back of your menu so you don't forget."

Their conversation was interrupted by a series of toasts that honored those who died on the RMS Titanic and as the event concluded, Rafael took time to bid farewell to his new friends.

"Margery, I am so sorry we did not have more opportunity to talk; Malcolm, I will try to reach you tomorrow. You both have an open invitation to be guests at my home should you ever decide to visit Barcelona. Buenos noches to you both."

The impostor returned to his suite brimming with satisfaction over the success of his evening's encounter. He rapped on the doors of both adjoining suites but got no reply from Ramos or Romero.

Son of a bitch, it is after midnight, he thought. *Surely, they cannot still be out carousing?*

He himself was too charged with adrenaline to think of sleep, so when he heard the two gauchos return to their rooms at 2:00 a.m., he threw on a dressing gown and summoned them into his suite. Ramos and Romero looked at each other sheepishly and Rudy Gomez knew instantly that something was terribly wrong.

"Spit it out, compadres, I have a bad feeling that what I am about to hear is not good."

CHAPTER TWELVE

The Aftermath of a Hangover

"We felt relaxed for the first time in months and the evening started off well. Franco and I had a great meal and a small taste of the local whiskey. It was still early, so we decided to go to that Orpheus Ballroom you told us about and perhaps listen to a little music before we turned in......"

"....But something happened, didn't it? Was it girls, a fight? I would like the short story, so cut to the chase."

The two gauchos, both consumed with guilt, reported their encounter with the man behind the bar.

"So who could have guessed the bartender would be from La Boca? We told him we were from Barcelona and here as servants to a rich Spaniard, but every time he refreshed our drinks, he insisted in talking to us in Porteños, even though we only talked to him in

English," Franco explained. "Once he learned of our connection with a wealthy Spanish industrialist, we were certain that he would try to meet you, one way or another. So, we told him we had to pick you up at a restaurant before midnight and teased that if he could take a break, we would introduce you."

"And?"

"We left the bar and waited downstairs on York Street. He joined us five minutes later and…"

"Let me guess, he is no longer in this world," the pseudo-baron surmised as his blood began to boil. "First of all, why the hell did you have to tease him with the fact that you were with a wealthy Spanish industrialist? That was bloody stupid.

"What the hell did you do with his body and more importantly, did anyone see you?"

"We met him outside the bar and the three of us walked down some alleys in the general direction of the hotel. He began to get very nervous, so as soon as we felt it was safe, Franco slit his throat and we left his body in a doorway. A young couple walked by just before we left but I'm certain they could never identify us. At this point, we had no friggin' idea where we were and certainly didn't want to ask anybody for directions. It took us about an hour to sneak back into the hotel. We entered by an exit door and came up the stairs. Nobody could possibly have seen us." The two men stared at Rudy with dismal submission in their eyes.

Although he kept his voice down, his fury was evident.

"You goddam idiots, this changes everything," Rudy Gomez hissed. "Other people must have noticed your conversation with the bartender. How many swarthy, Spanish men were in that fuckin' nightclub? From what I have seen since we arrived in this miserable northern European outpost for white people, I am guessing three; you two and the recently deceased bartender. I will be shocked if the police are not knocking on our doors within twenty-four hours. I have an alibi; you two had better get one—and damn fast."

After lighting up a cigarette and inhaling several lung fulls of nicotine, Rudy seemed to calm down. "You were both drunk and perhaps now you have learned to respect the power of Irish whiskey. Your judgment last night was severely clouded—but what is done is done. I will have to accelerate my meeting with Orlowski and get us out of this God-forsaken country by Friday at the latest.

"As soon as you go back to your rooms, I want each of you to put every single item of clothing you wore during the killing into a pillowcase, shoes included. Then scrub yourselves thoroughly. Franco, before you turn in, take both your knives and toss them into the River Lagan. Walk towards that big clock we saw from the top of this hotel and you'll be headed in the right direction. As soon as you get to a bridge, throw both knives into the middle of the river. On the way, dump both pillowcases into the first rubbish bin you come across." Rudy stared hard at Franco Ramos to make sure he understood before emphasizing, "I mean it, Franco. It is critical that no evidence is ever found and for Chrissakes don't let anybody see you leave or return to this hotel. Are you sober enough for this?"

"Yes, sir, I am completely sober at this time."

"If and when you are questioned by the police, neither of you must deny having spoken with the bartender at the Orpheus. Instead, maintain that you don't know his name and never saw him again after you left the bar to return to the hotel. You would not recognize him if you saw him again. For all intents and purposes, last night was nothing more than two friends having a drink. Why should you pay attention to a bartender? And don't forget, you were back in your suites shortly after midnight and we talked about my evening at the Grand Gala.

"Comprendez?"

Early the next morning, Rafael de Maldà ordered room service and summoned his henchmen to join him for breakfast.

"Franco, I trust everything went smoothly last night?"

"Well, you already know it did, don't you, Your

Excellency?" he mumbled sardonically. "Did you think I would not notice Lucas following me?"

"It was for your own protection, Franco and don't blame Lucas. I instructed him to avoid contact with you. He was only to step in if you ran into trouble."

The lack of sleep and the shenanigans of the prior night created hunger cravings, so the three of them tucked into plates of potato pancakes with fried eggs and bacon and still had room for fresh soda farls and blackberry jam.

"So, we are going to try and meet this Orlowski character and see if he has any connection to the Spider. Thanks to your ill-advised escapade, the meeting will have to take place either today or tomorrow because the longer we stay in Belfast, the more chance the local constabulary will connect the dots regarding last night's debacle."

"What do you want us to do?"

"I need you to come with me to meet Orlowski but stay as low key as possible; the three of us stick out like sore thumbs in this part of the world but my father will look to the two of you to corroborate my physical description of him."

After breakfast, the gauchos left together to return to their own suites.

"Don't know about you, Lucas, but I think Rudy is taking this baron shit a little too far. Who the fuck does he think he is? You and I taught him how to ride a horse and wiped his ass whenever he fell off. Now he is the baron de fuckin' Cortada and he is treating us like idiots."

"You are right, amigo, all we were trying to do last night was protect our mission. Okay, sometimes shit happens but I am very close to smacking him up the side the head myself."

Rafael made a casual visit down to the lobby to see if he could engage in conversation with the head waiter he had met during the banquet. From what Margery McClain had said, Seamus Dunfey had his ear to the ground when it came to gossip and any news of a murder near the hotel would be unlikely to escape his attention. Then he waited until a respectable half past ten before calling the Spider Academy.

"Ah, good morning, this is Rafael de Maldà. I had dinner last night with Mr. and Mrs. McClain and he wanted me to select a mutually convenient time to meet with Mr. Orlowski and himself while I am in Belfast. To whom do I have the pleasure of talking?"

"This is Bette Tarleton, Your Excellency, Malcolm's office manager. He told me to expect your call sometime this week but you are catching me a little off-guard. He and Chez are both conducting clinics today; however, they do have some open time on Friday. How about they meet you for lunch tomorrow at the

Copper Room in your hotel and then bring you back to the academy for a tour. Does that suit you?"

"Perfecto. Mrs. Tarleton, I am accompanied by two travelling companions and we will meet them for lunch at one o'clock tomorrow. I apologize for accelerating our meeting. I have been called back to Spain unexpectedly but my flight to London does not leave until Friday evening."

As soon as he hung up the phone, Rafael ordered Ramos and Romero to return to his suite.

"Tomorrow lunchtime seems to be the earliest we will be able to tour the Spider Academy, so I thought it prudent that we get away from this hotel for the rest of the day." The henchmen nodded agreement as their boss continued. "I have befriended the head waiter, Seamus Dunfey, and discovered that ten pounds sterling will cement a solid friendship in next to no time. Anyway, apart from his eagerness to pass along gossip of a murder in Smithfield Market, Seamus and I were able to spend a little quality time discussing the political situation here in Northern Ireland. As our research has shown, the Protestants and the Catholics hate each other's guts but from listening to Mr. Dunfey, trouble might be closer to erupting than we thought."

He paused to top up his tea, Lucas and Franco following suit.

"Are we talking about our flight being cancelled tomorrow?"

The pseudo-baron laughed. "No Franco, but the revolution might start in months rather than years.

"Should Chez Orlowski prove to be my father's mortal enemy, the Spider, it will be my duty to kill him. However, due to the predicament caused by your over-enthusiasm last night, acting now would be foolish to an extreme. Our best approach might be to send an assassination squad from Argentina or one of our cells, but if a local insurgence is imminent, we might be able to use one of the warring factions to our advantage."

"Naturally, we favor the Catholics, Your Excellency, but does the underdog have a chance in this fight?"

"They would if we funded them, Lucas. Seamus Dunfey tells me there is a hotbed of Irish Republican Army sympathizers located in a city called Derry. It's about sixty miles northwest of here, so we'll order a car, go there for a late lunch and do a little scouting around."

"And do you trust this Seamus character?" chimed in Franco.

"He has been head waiter here for a long time which means he hears and knows everything that's going on; look how quickly he learned about your dead bartender! In addition, I have a suspicion he is a closet revolutionary himself and would love to stick it to the man. With all that in mind, I have invested some additional pounds for him to be our driver."

CHAPTER THIRTEEN

Derry's Walls

T he second city of Northern Ireland has been called Doire since 546 AD, when St. Columba founded a small monastery in an oak grove on the east bank of the River Foyle. The English translation of the Gaelic name is Derry and over time the population, driven by necessity of survival, gravitated west onto an island in the river. In the early seventeenth century, Derry's citizens built strong walls around the island to protect themselves from marauders and despite many attempts, Derry's walls have never been breached. She remains one of the finest examples of a walled city in Europe.

King James I granted the city a Royal Charter in 1613 and changed the official name from Derry to Londonderry. On the surface, this might seem confusing but to this day, those who refer to the city as Londonderry are loyal to the Crown and those still calling her Derry are Republicans at heart.

Sean Dunfey talked the entire journey from Belfast to Derry. The route he chose could not have been more picturesque as the Grand Central Hotel's Jaguar 420 hummed along the A-6, winding around the north shore of Lough Neagh to get from Antrim to Magherafelt. His anger at the British invaders, coupled with a burning desire to see Ireland as one country again, left his passengers in no doubt about the problems festering under the fragile skin of this small country's society.

From the front passenger seat, Rafael patiently lent Dunfey a sympathetic ear for every minute of their two-hour journey.

They crossed the River Foyle on Bridge Street and entered Derry's walls through the Ferryquay gate. The pale green Jag made two ceremonial tours around the Diamond, the city's famous main square, before finding a parking spot directly in front of Austins Department Store.

"Ah well, there y'are now. Austins is the oldest department store in the world and we'll be meetin' a couple o' friends of mine upstairs in the Rooftop Restaurant fer lunch."

The four men piled out of the car and stretched their legs, noting that the Diamond is the junction for four major streets and is dominated by an ornate gathering of sculptures. The visitors entered the quaint old store and climbed the Edwardian stairs. Rafael called a halt at the second floor, his breath taken away, not by the most beautiful glassware he had ever seen but by the stunning young lady serving behind the counter. Her pale Irish face was framed by curly hair the color of dark, burnished copper and when her sixth sense picked up his brazen stare, she focused emerald green eyes back at him and smiled. Rafael's heart began to race uncontrollably and he reached for the support of the wooden baluster to steady himself.

"Sean, what on earth......"

"Have ye ne'er seen Waterford Crystal before, baron?"

"As a matter of fact, no, I must buy some of it for my father before we leave."

"Neah bother, we'll bring ye back to this department after lunch, big fellah," laughed their guide. He too had sensed the chemistry between the two young strangers, nor did the incident go unnoticed by Ramos and Romero.

A brief word with the elderly waitress in the Rooftop Restaurant secured a window table for eight and the travelers enjoyed a panorama of the Diamond War Memorial as they waited for Sean's friends. The memorial features a winged Victory statue whose eyes were now at a level with the men. She had seen a lot in her time on the Diamond and the lunchroom's vantage point emphasized how perilous things must have been at times for Derry's residents, as they wagered their lives on the protection afforded by a one-mile circumference of stone walls.

Sean read their minds. "You know, around here they call Derry 'the Maiden City' because her walls have never once been breached."

As they were sipping their tea, three rough-looking men strolled up to the table and nodded to Dunfey.

"God bless all here." Sean stood up and shook each man's hand. "Ah Brendan, is it yersel'? Yer lookin' like you haven't missed many meals lately!

"Yer Excellency, this here is Brendan Mulcahy, and a finer Irishman never walked God's earth. His associates are Michael Tobin and Colm O'Shaughnessy." The three men nodded to the strangers and sat down to join them. There was an overt air of suspicion from the outset as the seven men tried to weigh each other up over the lunch. Dunfey had primed Rafael with information that Mulcahy was a very important man in these parts and a former area commander in Irish Republican Army.

"Mr. Mulcahy, I can assure you that nothing discussed around this table will reach unwanted ears. I only made the acquaintance of Mr. Dunfey last night, but when I expressed my organization's willingness to support the Republican cause against British oppression, he took the initiative and set up this meeting."

"Well, Mr. Malda, if that is indeed your name, you must know that I have a price on my head and the Brits could come barging into this restaurant at any moment if they suspect I'm here. I took the precaution of positioning twenty of my men around the Diamond to watch for anything suspicious. Hope and pray to God nothing happens because you three and Dunfey will be the first to die if they come for me." The over-weight Mulcahy pulled back his jacket to show Rafael and the others an old service revolver tucked into his ample belt.

"I can assure you we are unarmed and have no hidden agenda, Señor. I myself have a secret and personal reason for hating the British. For me, this meeting is as simple as seeing a potential opportunity for us both to exact a modicum of revenge on the bastards. I am here to offer you significant financial support during these trying times, if you have a mind to tell me the current status of your organization."

"Go fuck yoursel'," growled Mulcahy and rose to leave.

"Okay, okay, I completely understand that might have sounded inappropriate. You have no reason at all to trust me at this point in our relationship. So let me try to fix that by revealing something about myself. I will need Sean to take a walk with Lucas and Franco. It will just be you, your two associates and me; I only need five minutes."

Brendan Mulcahy thought about this unusual proposition as he rubbed his chin.

"Tell you what, I'll give you two minutes, no more. Colm will stay here with us but Micky will go with your men. Anything happens to make me feel uneasy, you're all dead men."

Four men left the restaurant to walk around Austins; three remained at the table. Rafael waited patiently for privacy before leaning forward.

"Okay, my real name is Rudy Gomez. My organization is based in South America and there are extremely important and valid reasons why my men and I are in Belfast posing as Spanish businessmen. The part I told you about supporting your cause and having the resources to back up my commitment is completely true. Right here and now, I am prepared to give you twenty thousand pounds sterling in cash to buy whatever you might need to keep your dreams alive. In return, I am simply asking for an assurance that you will not go straight to the bookies and put it on a horse. If the money is spent prudently, there will be plenty more forthcoming. You have the gun, Brendan." Rudy stared into the older man's eyes in the hope he had established the beginnings of trust.

"I will tell you what everybody around here knows. We live outside Derry's walls in a Catholic ghetto called the Bogside. Catholics are second-class citizens in this part of the world, Rudy. My job, as a representative of the Irish Republican Army, was to fight for the rights of my neighbors. However, the IRA, of which I have been a member for almost thirty years—my Dad since its inception in 1922— has been decimated by the recent British tactic of internment without trial. It might only be a matter of months before the IRA abandons the Bogside altogether, leaving us to our own defenses.

"All I can tell you as we sit here is that myself, along with some other leaders from around the six counties, are going to band together as an alternative. We plan to call our group the Fenian Brotherhood, reprising a name that strikes fear into the hearts and minds of any British tyrants who know their history. I give you my solid pledge that every penny of your twenty thousand pounds will go towards setting up that organization."

The silent stare between the two men resumed, but ended when Rudy Gomez placed a brown paper bag on the table in front of Brendan Mulcahy.

"Put it to good use, Brendan and I'll bring you another twenty thousand on my next trip. You'll understand if I check up on you once in a while?" Brendan did not look inside the bag but slid it towards Michael Tobin.

"Go ask Colm to escort Sean and Rudy's friends back to their car. Tell them Mr. Malda will join them in five minutes. Then get that bag into my fridge as fast as you can."

Turning to his new best friend, he whispered, "Rudy, thank you, you might have saved a nation today. God bless you but let me give you a word of brotherly advice on another subject. It has been brought to my attention by Sean Dunfey, that more than the Waterford Crystal on the second floor attracted your eye. Listen well. Every man in Derry is in love with Mary O'Connell, including myself. Anything inappropriate in that regard will cause some very important people to scrutinize your behavior, understood?" The Argentinian nodded, even though his heart was already downstairs.

"Now, before you leave, can you at least tell me why you are here under the guise of Spanish businessmen?"

Rudy Gomez laughed his response in a credible Derry accent that mimicked Mulcahy.

"Go fuck yersel', Brendan."

As he got back to the Jaguar, Rudy paused after opening the front passenger door and leaned in to talk to the occupants. "Listen my friends, I'm going to pop back into the store to buy some Irish crystal for my father. Shouldn't be more than five minutes." Ramos and Romero rolled their eyes and Dunfey offered his advice,

"Your Excellency, be very careful, this is Ireland not Spain."

Rudy Gomez returned in ten, carrying a beautifully wrapped box. His head was swimming with images of Mary, his stomach in knots; he had taken Cupid's arrow front and center, his raison d'etre transformed forever. True to his word and in fear of offending every red-blooded male within fifty miles, the young man had been as cautious and polite as he could but Mary O'Connell's green eyes, freckled nose and smile disarmed him completely. He very much wanted to kiss her and sweep her away to Argentina but he ended up stammering some gibberish and leaving the store feeling he had made a complete fool of himself.

He had planned to tell her his real name but for the life of him, he could not remember whether he had or had not.

He stewed silently in his thoughts all the way back to Belfast.

CHAPTER FOURTEEN

Belfast

T he baron de Cortada felt slightly nervous as they waited in the Copper Room for his Friday lunch appointment. What he anticipated happening in the next few moments had occupied considerable speculation, nonetheless, he was not quite sure what to expect. *Where the hell are they?* he thought as he felt stomach acid welling up into his throat. Then he sensed the mood of the restaurant changing as his fellow patrons began turning their attention towards the door. William O'Malley, the manager, entered and behind him, two men in smart green tracksuits.

He recognized McClain immediately, so the other could only be Orlowski. He felt deflated. *Surely this could not be the man who brought down the Third Reich.* He was completely bald and perhaps five foot eight inches in height. His shoulders were broad, his waist trim and, as the baron watched him and McClain politely greet other diners as they entered, he began to notice an athletic, cat-like grace about the way Chez Orlowski moved. After almost five full minutes, Mr. O'Malley finally managed to shepherd the two celebrities to the table where Rafael and his two cohorts stood politely waiting.

"Your Excellency, may I introduce Mr. Chez Orlowski, I believe you already know Mr. Malcolm McClain."

"Thanks, Billy. You are most welcome to join us if you like," said McClain. Mr. O'Malley respectfully declined the offer and bowed slightly to the baron.

"Your Excellency, I am sorry your visit with us has been cut short; it has been an honor and a pleasure. I will have your briefcase waiting in my office before you and your assistants depart for Aldergrove Airport."

"Thank you so much, Mr. O'Malley. Our stay at the Grand Central has been exquisite." Then he turned his full attention to his lunch companions. "I am very pleased that both of you could join me for lunch. I hope you don't mind if my personal assistants, Ramos and Romero, join us. We have a full night of travel to look forward to, so please, let's sit down; perhaps the rest of the patrons will stop staring at us." The men laughed.

Chez and Malcolm both ordered tea and as the waiter served, Rafael asked for an assortment of sandwiches. He noticed that several of Chez's fingers appeared to have been broken once or twice and numerous small scars on his face indicated that his journey through life had not been a bowl of cherries. His voice was rich and heavily accented; his laughter infectious. He and McClain acted like brothers throughout the lunch so the baron risked a casual question.

"How on earth did you two meet and become such good friends?"

Malcolm smiled as he glanced across the table.

"I ran into a spot of bother in Yugoslavia during the war. Chez was the hired gun sent in to save my arse…"

"…And Malcolm ended up saving mine a couple of times too."

Well, that was easy. They must be referring to the Maribor escape. I'll push my luck a little more, Rafael thought.

"And which one of you came up with the unusual name 'Spider' for your academy?" As he began his stock answer, Chez Orlowski put a cucumber sandwich in his mouth, managing to chew and talk at the same time. Rafael found this quite distracting but again, it showed the mark of a man who had grown up in circumstances that were less than gentile.

"I spent my childhood in Weimar, Germany, and had a pet spider called 'Sebastian.' My mother and real father were both gymnasts, so I always tried to stay in good shape. I would try to copy some of the amazing things Sebastian could do. Spider became my childhood nickname and Malcolm thought it would be a good title to inspire our students."

Rafael noticed that the embroidered logo on the tracksuits worn by both men was a soccer ball with eight legs surrounding it. *Remarkably like the calling card of the Spider during the war,* he mused. *I have no doubts at this point; I am sitting three feet away from the number one most hated man in my world. My father would be so proud if I blew the bastard to Hell right here in the Copper Room.*

"Aha, I see you staring at our logo, Rafael. If we are finished here, let's go to the academy. After the tour, I will escort you to our gift shop and all three of you can select Spider Academy souvenirs to take back to Barcelona."

The refreshing thing about the tour was that it was not a slick, canned, marketing extravaganza. The Spider Academy did not need to market itself to anyone. Instead, what the baron de Cortada and his henchmen were able to observe first-hand was class after class of extremely happy, fit children of different ages being trained on state-of-the-art equipment by diligent, attentive staff. Even though he was playing a ruse, the baron was genuinely impressed. After the tour of the facilities was complete, the five men sat down in Malcolm's office where Rafael had no problem in expressing his admiration.

"So, as I explained to Malcolm last Wednesday night, de Malda Industries would like to pay you both a significant stipend to launch a duplicate Spider Academy in Barcelona, aimed at benefitting the youth of Catalonia. I understand that your energies are currently focused on the Mexico Olympics but I am looking towards giving our Spanish kids a better chance in München. Will you think about it and let me know?"

The baron de Cortada exchanged cards with Malcolm and Chez, tucking two elegant Spider Academy business cards into his jacket pocket as they stood in the forecourt on York Road. A driver brought the car around; the men shook hands and waved their goodbyes as the limousine pulled away.

"So what did you think of them, Chez and why did you embellish your standard fairy tale by telling them your nickname? It's not like you to let your guard down like that."

"Trust me, my friend, I have my reasons. Something's not quite right there, Malky. I think Rafael's full of shit and the two guys with him are nothing more than hired muscle. There is no bloody way that I'm going to waste my time going to Barcelona."

"Damn it, Chez, that's exactly the conclusion Margery came to on Wednesday night."

Rudy Gomez grinned all the way back to the Grand Central Hotel.

If I just can get them both to Spain, they will never see the light of day again. We'll kill McClain and fly the Spider back to Patagonia for a formal execution. Helluvalot easier than risking another trip to Belfast.

Now, I must get Ramos and Romero back to Argentina before they kill anyone else.

Mr. O'Malley intercepted the baron before he was halfway across the lobby.

"Your Excellency, I have R.U.C. Inspector Larkin in my office. He would like to have a quick word with you."

"But, of course, Mr. O'Malley," Rafael replied, his pulse racing as he followed the familiar morning suit towards the double doors. Once inside the manager's office, he saw a tall man standing in front of

O'Malley's desk, waiting to greet them. He wore the dark green uniform of the Royal Ulster Constabulary, the peaked hat and insignia indicating he was a District Inspector, 1st class.

"Inspector William Larkin, may I introduce the baron de Cortada." The two men shook hands and smiled.

"How may I be of assistance, Inspector?"

"Well, sir, sometime in the early hours of yesterday morning, we had a nasty incident in Smithfield Market; Gresham Street to be precise. A bartender at the Orpheus Ballroom, name of Manuel Sanchez, was found in the doorway of one of the pet shops. He had been brutally murdered, his throat slashed by a long sharp instrument. Mr. Sanchez was from Argentina and was heard conversing in a foreign language with two gentlemen in the ballroom earlier that evening. The gentlemen in question match the description of your two personal assistants. Can you vouch for their whereabouts on Wednesday evening?"

"Inspector, I can indeed confirm that my valets, Lucas Romero and Franco Ramos, had a drink or two at the Orpheus Ballroom on Wednesday evening and that those drinks were served by an Argentinian barman. The reason they told me about it was, although he spoke Spanish, his accent was so thick, neither could understand a word he said. I'm sure your witnesses reported that my assistants' side of the conversation was entirely in English? We had a good laugh about it the next day. It would be somewhat akin to you understanding an American; you both speak English, but the idioms are very different." Rafael and O'Malley smiled at the humor in this but the inspector just frowned before continuing.

"Understood, sir, but a young couple walking down Gresham Street at about the time the murder might have taken place, thought they saw two or three men in a shop doorway. I'd like to have a word with your men while I am here. Just to get them cleared for the record."

"Absolutely, Inspector, but did you not say that the murder happened in the early hours of Thursday morning? Both my men joined me in my suite after I returned from the Gala Dinner. I woke them up shortly after midnight so I could tell them I had just met the famous Malcolm McClain. I hope that helps your timeline but regardless, Mr. O'Malley, if you would you be so kind to connect me with their suites, I'll have them come down immediately to your office."

The baron asked both men to get on the telephone in Romero's suite and spoke to them in English so the Inspector could hear his side of the conversation.

"Ramos, Romero, I am in the hotel manager's office with a very important policeman. Apparently, the barman you met on Wednesday night was murdered later that night and the inspector would like to know if you might recall anything unusual."

Taking a reasonable risk that the inspector had not taken Spanish in high school, Rudy Gomez then concluded by adopting a thick, Cordobes accent to warn his men, "Stay cool, guys, they know nothing."

"Excuse me, Excellency; I didn't quite catch the last part," Inspector Larkin said sharply.

"Forgive me, Inspector, I was just reminding them to leave a gratuity for the maids in each of their suites. We are flying to London this evening but you have my address in Barcelona. Inspector, please do not hesitate to telephone me if you need further assistance."

"Oh, this is just a formality and will only take a few minutes. I would prefer you stay in case there are any translation issues. Mr. O'Malley, might we imbibe a small glass of Spanish sherry to make everyone feel more comfortable?"

"Certainly, Inspector, I have a very nice Amontillado I think you gentlemen would enjoy at this time of the day. It is very light and smooth."

All five men enjoyed the amber liquid as Lucas and Franco parroted their prepared speeches to Inspector Larkin.

"Thank you all and I apologize for this inconvenience. Here's wishing you a safe journey back to Barcelona," Larkin said.

"Salud!" responded the so-called Spanish contingent before they left the manager's office. Larkin stayed behind and whispered urgently as O'Malley stepped forward to retrieve the sherry glasses.

"Not so fast, Billy, I need to borrow some hotel property for a while." The inspector produced three plastic bags from his pocket and marked them each with a different name. "The latent prints on these glasses will be documented by our new Dermatoglyphics Department. If we ever find a murder weapon, they might prove very useful."

CHAPTER FIFTEEN

Clues to the Puzzle

The baron de Cortada, Ramos and Romero prepared themselves to check out of the Grand Central Hotel within the hour. The baron knocked politely on Mr. O'Malley's door to bid farewell.

"Your Excellency, I have retrieved your briefcase from my safe. If you would please verify the contents and sign this receipt, I will have a driver take you and your assistants to Aldergrove for your flight." Rafael signed with a flourish and smiled at the manager.

"Muchas gracias, Señor O'Malley. We look forward to staying with you again in the near future."

Retracing their journey from Argentina, they spent a couple of days with Otto Zeilke in Barcelona before handing back their credentials and boarding the train from El Estació de França. When their rail journey terminated in Lisbon, they emerged from the station in Portugal as three ordinary Argentinian tourists: Rudy Gomez, Franco Ramos and Lucas Romero.

Hans Dietmar took them to Chiado Square for dinner that night. He had made reservations at the famous Café A Brasileira on Rua Garrett as soon as the Barcelona cell informed him they were safely on board the train. Dietmar could scarcely contain himself as the maître d' escorted them ceremoniously down the richly decorated entrance hall and into the main dining room. The table he had insisted upon was towards the rear and to the right of the café's iconic clock. Only two tables were close by and Hans had paid dearly to reserve all three, thereby ensuring the evening's acoustical privacy. The maître d' bid them, "Bon appetite" before floating back to the front door.

"Okay, Rudy, what did you find out about this Orlowski character?" The Café A Brasileira has mirrors between the pilasters and Rudy, who was seated with his back to the dining room, was able to steal glances at anyone approaching their corner table.

"Oh, he is the Spider, Hans, of that I am absolutely certain. The bastard is living the life of luxury in Belfast. I wanted to slit his throat right there but my father must not be denied that pleasure. When we return to Argentina, all the resources of the Fourth Reich will be mobilized to avenge the death of Adolph Hitler." Movement caught his eye and he ceased conversation as a waiter approached their table with a large bowl of cod casserole.

The next day, well rested and well fed, they parted company with Dietmar at the Lisbon Portela Airport to catch an Aerolineas flight back to Buenos Aires.

In Belfast, Inspector William Larkin had not closed his files on the death of Manuel Sanchez. The inspector did not like unresolved open cases any more than he liked leaving the Belfast Telegraph with an unfinished crossword. Lack of finality tended to haunt his sleep, so every Sunday morning, his habit was to walk the half-mile from his bachelor flat on Dunluce Avenue to the Wellington Park Hotel for breakfast. He would arrive there promptly at half-past eight and sit at the same large corner table where he could spread out his homework.

"Good morning, Bill, the usual?"

"Yes please, Fred." The preparation of his ham, egg

and chips with a pot of tea got underway as soon as Fred gave the nod to Fiona in the kitchen and Larkin would stay there, his teapot replenished every twenty minutes, until exactly eleven o'clock every Sunday.

There were three unresolved cases in his current portfolio but on this particular day, he had only brought one—the Sanchez murder. It had been several days since the body had been discovered in Gresham Street but instinct told him he was close to a breakthrough. Larkin topped up his tea, dropped another sugar lump into the cup and went over his notes one more time. He found himself returning to a couple of facts he had marked with bullet points:

- Several of the Orpheus patrons remarked that two customers spoke with Sanchez in a foreign language. The language was not positively identifiable as Spanish by two female regulars who were final year language students at Queen's University, but both of them felt that the problem might be due to an unusually heavy dialect.

- Sanchez was found two hours later in Gresham Street with his throat cut from ear to ear. *(It must have been a long, very sharp knife.)* Yet, two bloodstained

shirts, a pair of trousers and some
shoes were discovered the next day in
a rubbish bin at Pottingers Entry off
High Street. The blood type matched
that of Sanchez, but Pottinger's Entry is
a ways from Gresham Street.

What am I missing? pondered Larkin. *In all my inter-
views, most everyone in the Orpheus that night was from
Belfast; there to find out if Van Morrison's abrupt departure
from The Wheels would have any adverse effect on the band.
Hell, most of the crowd knew each other. The only strangers
identified were the Spaniards from the Grand Central;
contrary to the statements of the language students, they
denied being able to communicate with Sanchez. So why did
Sanchez persist in talking to them in what I must assume
was Spanish with a heavy Argentinian accent?*

*Another thing. It is at least a quarter of a mile from
Gresham Street to Pottingers Entry. The murderers
could have got away with bloodstains on their clothes in
the early hours of the morning and I doubt they carried
clean clothes to change into. No, they must have changed
somewhere and dumped the clothes later that night or
early the next day, but why Pottingers Entry? For that
matter, if you continue down Pottingers Entry and go*

east on Ann Street, within another quarter mile you will end up on the Queen's Bridge at Donegal Quay. I am starting to think that I should start looking for the murder weapon in the River Lagan under the Queen's Bridge. For that very reason, I am led to believe that the bridge might have been the ultimate destination; it's less than a fifteen minute walk from Gresham Street—or the Grand Central Hotel!

Bill Larkin scribbled his notes into the file and rushed back home to Dunluce Avenue to make a couple of calls.

A fortnight later, Inspector Larkin invited Malcolm McClain and Chez Orlowski to the Royal Ulster Constabulary's brand new headquarters at Knock Road in Belfast.

The two men sat nervously in the reception area.

"Did Bette forget to pay our business license, Malky?"

"Damned if I know what this is about, Chez...."

However, the fears dissipated when the tall inspector opened his door and strode towards them with a broad smile on his face.

"Mr. McClain, Mr. Orlowski, so good of you both to take time to meet with me at H. Q. I have an interesting update on the Sanchez case that I would like to share with you both. In addition, I have some interesting back-up photographs and evidence that cannot leave these premises."

McClain and Orlowski looked extremely puzzled as Malcolm replied to the back of the inspector's dark green jacket as it retreated into the inner sanctums.

"Inspector, you must have the wrong men. We have never heard of the Sanchez case."

"You might be surprised but please, take a seat and I will explain. Tea?" When the three men were comfortable and the tea fixed to their individual liking, Bill Larkin began his tale with a beam of personal satisfaction written all over his face.

"Do you recall a Spanish nobleman calling himself Rafael de Malda? He stayed at the Grand Central Hotel, I now believe with the express purpose of meeting you both, managing to persuade our friend, Billy O'Malley, to seat him beside you at the Gala Dinner. Does this ring a bell with either of you?"

"Who could forget Clark Gable? Jadwiga was in the maternity ward that night so Chez couldn't make the dinner but the two of us had lunch with him later in the week; in fact, we brought him by the academy for a personal tour."

"As you might recall, de Malda travelled with a couple of rough looking fellows called Ramos and Romero. While you and Rafael were at the Gala, his bodyguards washed down their dinner at Cottar's Kitchen with an entire bottle of Bushmills Whiskey.

To complete their evening, they staggered all the way to the Orpheus to listen to a local rock band.

"For some reason, as yet unknown, it must have been critical that everyone in Belfast believed that these three con men were from Barcelona. I asked you both here in the hope that you might shed light on their possible motivation." He paused to take a sip of tea, allowing him to note a puzzled look on his guests' faces.

"While Ramos and Romero were at the Orpheus, a bartender, Manuel Sanchez, identified them as being Argentinian rather than Spanish. Sanchez was originally from Buenos Aires and probably identified their accents. Apparently the consequences of them blowing their Spanish cover must have been so disastrous, they murdered Mr. Sanchez later that evening."

"What? Wait a minute, I do remember something about that. It was all over the *Telegraph* and the *Newsletter*. But I thought it was an unsolved robbery murder outside the pet shop in Gresham Street."

"It was, until about a week ago." Chez and Malcolm had no idea where the inspector was going but his enthusiasm was impressive.

"The murderers slit Sanchez's throat with a long bladed knife. They knew that someone in the Orpheus might identify them, so they ditched the evidence as quickly as possible. Within half a mile of the murder scene, they dumped the clothes they had worn into rubbish bins, as they made a beeline for the Lagan to toss their knives into the river. Those rubbish bins were in Pottinger's Entry, where the cleanup staff at the Morning Star Bar reported finding the suspicious clothing within twenty-four hours. Sanchez's blood type was identified on the clothing and we lifted the clean fingerprint of a third party off a belt buckle. While my men were interviewing the staff at the Morning Star, they searched any other bins they came across and found two pillow cases, both with traces of Sanchez' blood and laundry marks linking them to the Grand Central Hotel."

"I am beginning to put the pieces of this puzzle together, Inspector."

"Following a hunch, I took the most direct route to the Lagan from Pottinger's Entry and found myself on Donegal Quay looking at the Queen's Bridge. So we sent the frogmen down and recovered these." Larkin pushed a couple of photographs towards the men that showed two large, evil-looking knives.

"I consider myself somewhat of a knife aficionado, and these are extremely fine blades," remarked the Spider with admiration.

"This type of knife is known as a facón and it is the personal weapon of choice for gauchos."

"Argentinian gauchos?" Chez expanded and the inspector nodded.

"At this point in the investigation, I have

significant reason to believe that Rafael de Malda and his henchmen were from Argentina, not Spain. Interpol interviewed the real Rafael de Malda at his villa in the South of France. He has never been to Belfast, looks nothing like Clark Gable and has a cast-iron alibi in that he has been living in Cap d'Antibes since March. So, whoever those three men were, they went to elaborate and very expensive lengths, including murder, to meet both of you without disclosing the fact that they were from Argentina.

"I can tell you now, that the fingerprint on the murderer's belt buckle positively matches the index finger of Franco Ramos, one of the henchmen. I am hoping that you gentlemen might be able to help me wrap up the loose ends, hence your presence here today."

Malcolm McClain shook his head in astonishment. "I'm sorry, Inspector, you've got me on this one. He told me he was in Belfast to meet with Shorts in the hope of negotiating a contract for a couple of Skyvans. I was the one who convinced him to visit the academy. De Malda said he would pay us a hefty consulting fee to duplicate our gymnastics facility in Barcelona, though if I recall, Margery and Chez both felt he was not what he seemed to be. What did you pick up that I missed, Chez?"

The legend wore a serious frown.

"I can smell them, Malky, and I suspect our Rafael

de Malda's first language is German not Spanish. When he referred to the Munich Olympics, he could not help calling the city München." When the Spider turned to look at Bill Larkin, the inspector was startled to notice that the friendly light blue eyes of Chez Orlowski had lost their color in favor of a steely grey.

"Inspector, I am restricted by the Official Secrets Act as to what I can reveal and have a letter in my possession from Sir Winston Churchill to that effect. Apart from Mr. Churchill, my wife and Colonel Paddy McBride, no living person, not even Malcolm McClain, my best friend in the world, knows the full extent of my wartime adventures. Can you respect my confidentiality?"

"Do you want me to wait outside, Chez?" Malcolm asked.

"No, Malky. It would be ridiculous for you not to know my story at this point in our relationship."

PART THREE

CHAPTER SIXTEEN

The Fourth Reich Mobilizes

R udy Gomez, Franco Ramos and Lucas Romero were in a jovial mood as they stepped down from the train in the San Carlos de Bariloche station. After a night in Buenos Aires, they had spent the afternoon in Viedma before changing trains to finish their final leg on the Tren Patagónico. Their bodies were cramping after the exhausting two-day rail journey and it felt good to stretch and get the kinks out.

"Do you smell the lake, Rudy? God, it is good to be home," Franco said.

San Carlos de Bariloche fronts the south shores of Lake Nahuel Huapi. This lake funnels northwesterly winds across the city to maintain a unique microclimate with moderate year-round temperatures. The town is also less than a hundred miles from neighboring Chile, a major reason Martin Bormann had chosen this place as the Nazis' final redoubt. Having a back door into the bordering country through the Cardenal Antonio Samoré Pass might prove extremely useful in the event Argentina chose to renege on their covert agreement of finances for security.

"Yes, Franco, I have spent over half my life in this valley and I know exactly what you mean. It is indeed good to be home." Then he coughed, spat out some red flem and laughed. "Can't say I missed the dust though."

A couple of familiar faces from the ranch appeared on the platform, greeted them with handshakes and hauled their luggage to a large black limousine.

"Your father is anxious to see you, Rudy," the driver said.

"Then we had better go straight to the Hacienda."

The limo led a plume of fine red particles as it cruised northeast on Route 40 towards the Hacienda San Ramon. At certain times of the year, the humidity and winds of Patagonia combine to create a fog from the underlying soils. Whenever this anomaly occurs, the sun becomes a deep orange orb. It can last for days, sometimes weeks, but no matter how hard you try, the red dust permeates everything you own.

"Never thought I would miss this, Guillermo. How

many more days of the red dust can we expect?" Rudy asked the driver.

"It's on the wane, Rudy. Tomorrow should be a lot better."

After they checked in with the armed guards at the gatehouse, it took a further ten minutes of steady driving before the car pulled to a halt in front of the main residence, a beautiful, three-story building with a steep roof and exposed timbers. The hacienda was framed by the Andes to the west and the picturesque scene it created could have been photographed as a postcard from Bavaria and fooled anyone.

The guards at the gatehouse had forewarned el jefe, Juan Gomez, and he stood waiting for them in the forecourt. Guillermo held open the door and Rudy stepped out to embrace his father.

"I missed you, mi Padre. How is your health?"

"Never mind that, I'm fine. Come inside, the schnapps is waiting." Turning to the others he ordered, "Lucas, Franco, freshen up from your long journey, there will be food for you in the kitchen."

After an excited household staff took the opportunity to welcome Rudy back, Juan Gomez steered his son into his private study and closed the door. He unlocked an ornate mahogany drinks cabinet and began uncorking an intricately etched bottle of perfectly clear liquid.

"Well, did you see the bastard?" The old man grunted with his back to Rudy.

"Wait, Padre, do not pour yet, I have brought you a special present from Northern Ireland." The old man turned to see his son sporting a wide grin as he unwrapped two beautiful Waterford Crystal champagne flutes. "Not the drink they were designed for but I'm sure the schnapps will taste even better out of these." Rudy tortured his father by washing the glasses and savoring the moment until they both were ready to toast before stating, "And yes, Padre, not only did I see the bastard, I had lunch with him. I have lots to tell you but first—prost!"

The retelling of the adventure started with a tuneful clink from the Lismore patterned glassware and the bottle of schnapps was half-empty before Reichsleiter Bormann uttered a single word in response.

"Franco and Lucas have certainly complicated things with their foolishness but I am optimistic that you might be successful in tempting the dumb Polak to Barcelona. If we can abduct him from Spain to Patagonia for a formal execution, vengeance will be mine."

"The gauchos did what they thought was right at the time, mi Padre, but it severely limits our options in Belfast. The cell of revolutionaries in Derry that I decided to fund might prove useful surrogates if we need a backup plan. If you decide to allow them to kill the Spider, it can never be traced back to the Fourth Reich...."

"....You miss the point, Rudy. I must pull the trigger myself and I don't want to just kill him, I want to destroy him; crush him like a bug; death by one thousand cuts. Fuck the anonymity; I want to show the entire world that the Fourth Reich does not suffer assassins lightly." Bormann was shouting loudly and gripping the arms of his chair so tightly that a small vein in his temple started to throb. Then, as quickly as his rage had surfaced, it subsided and he calmed down.

"Now, let's have dinner and an early night. I have summoned my secret executive committee to come to the Hacienda in a couple of weeks. We have to strategize on a couple of projects I am working on and I will add 'Spider Extermination' to the agenda, so be prepared to present a full report. Remember, the Jews abducted Adolph Eichmann back in 1960, right around the time Malcolm McClain was starting up his business with the arch-criminal Orlowski. I tried everything to get Eichmann's trial into a German court or even an international court but the world let the Jews convict him in Israel. It was a kangaroo court and a total farce, so we have to be very, very careful. Unfortunately, these radical yids are becoming bolder by the day, causing the members of my committee to travel here incognito and by different routes. It is damn inconvenient and Argentina needs to start providing the level of security I am paying for."

The recent experience of travelling in the new, modern Europe caused the son to see his father with fresh perspective for the first time. Rudy listened dutifully to the unrelated and irrational ranting, concerned more than ever that the aging man was driven by so much hatred.

The animosity has always been there; I just never really saw it, he thought to himself. *Maybe my brothers and sisters were right to flee this house.*

"No doubt you will recognize some familiar names and faces among our guests. They were the crème de la crème of the Third Reich and destiny has brought them here to join me in leading the Fourth Reich. My plan is to keep everyone at the hacienda until we formulate a strategy to disrupt the Munich Olympics. We will use that stage to show the world that the Fourth Reich has risen again. That will be our main course; for dessert, we will discuss delivering that Polish piece-of-shit to justice. All our financial resources will be brought to bear on this final mission."

Rudy shuddered inside. *The old man is positively*

glowing with fanaticism. Total destruction of his arch-enemy is now the most important thing in his life. I just brought him proof that the Spider is still alive so I have become a collusive pawn in his evil machinations.

My chances of convincing Mary O'Connell to love me have suddenly vanished.

Rudy Gomez had finally to come to the same realization as his siblings; his father was a malevolent lunatic.

He had always been afraid of his father; now he was terrified.

CHAPTER SEVENTEEN

Evil Lurks in the Shadow of the Andes

A t the Hacienda San Ramon, several guest cottages had been spruced up in anticipation of the visitors. The guests began arriving intermittently over the course of the next week and gradually, the forecourt of the barn filled with expensive Mercedes. All but one were black; the exception, an ostentatious businessman named Herbert Kuhlmann, drove a powder egg blue 230SL Pagoda convertible.

Reichsleiter Martin Bormann had summoned his secret executive committee from all corners of South America. It would have been extremely unwise to ignore an invitation from the *'Brown Eminence of the Third Reich,'* as the man now hiding behind the sobriquet Juan Gomez controlled the massive financial resources that ensured their security in South

America. The last guest to arrive was Walter Rauff, who currently worked for the BND, West Germany's secret intelligence service in Chile. Herr Rauff was conducting an assignment in Santiago when he received the summons but the inevitable paperwork delayed his journey to Patagonia by forty-eight hours beyond the arrival of the others.

A breathless orderly ran the half mile from the barn to the hacienda and was directed to the rear of the house. Bormann was taking coffee on the back porch with his son and two guests who, although they lived locally, had been requested to stay within the confines of Hacienda San Ramon for the duration of the clandestine meeting.

"Señores, Standartenführer Rauff has just arrived at the barn. All of your guests are now gathered together for your address."

"Mein Herren, it is time. Guillermo will drive us to the barn." With that, local doctor Aribert Heim, infamously known as Dr. Death while practicing medicine at the Mauthausen concentration camp, and former Gestapo Captain Erich Priebke, currently employed as a social sciences teacher at The German School in Bariloche, joined their hosts for the short ride to the barn.

As the growl of the automobile approached the Bavarian architecture of the barn, a group of ten ageing men began to assemble in the forecourt. Nazi

Ambassador Ludwig Freude stepped forward to open Bormann's car door and the reunion began with a recognition of their host. Heels clicked in unison, right arms extended forward at forty-five degrees and the guests barked, "Heil Bormann," in unison.

All the men knew each other by reputation, though few had ever met during the war. With the exception of Rudy Gomez, they had several things in common. All were die-hard members of the Nazi Party, they had a price on their heads and were war criminals convicted in absentia for the murder of millions of innocents.

Good God, thought the younger Gomez as he silently recounted the histories of these men. *If the Mossad knew who was gathered here, they could kill almost every Nazi war criminal on their list with one well-thrown grenade!*

Nikolaus Altmann lived in Bolivia and served as a lieutenant colonel in the Bolivian army as he fed intelligence to the BND. Back in the day, he was better known as SS-Hauptsturmführer Klaus Barbie, the butcher of Lyon. He chatted with his good friend and BND counterpart in Chile, Walter Rauff. The two men were laughing loudly over a shared joke.

"Shocking news about those Mossad bastards kidnapping and murdering Eichmann," murmured Dr. Josef Mengele to Franz Stangl, Eichmann's former adjutant. Mengele, the Angel of Death, was not the only one of the assembled Nazi luminaries to express his sadness over Adolph Eichmann's capture and subsequent hanging.

"Those Jewish bastards seem to think they can break any international laws they please," Stangl retorted.

This statement was ironic because Gestapo Captain Stangl had been personally responsible for the deaths of over 900,000 holocaust prisoners. Herbert Kuhlmann chatted with SS-Gruppenführer Ludolf von Alvensleben from Buenos Aires and SS-Obersturmbannführer Gustav Wagner from Brazil. The only man standing alone was the extremely anti-social Heinrich Müller, the Nazi accorded by Hitler himself with the responsibility for conducting the investigation after the 1944 assassination attempt at Wolfschanze.

I understand that Herr Müller has serious psycho-logical problems—as if the rest of these men do not! His investigation terrified the upper echelon of the Party and Müller even insisted upon personally joining the firing squad that executed Colonel Claus von Stauffenberg, Rudy thought, shivering internally. *I must admit, I secretly empathize with the bravery of those men. I can see now that they had the best interests of the Fatherland at heart. Had I been ten years older...*

"Welcome, my old friends and comrades, welcome," boomed the aging Reichsleiter. "I am glad to see you are all safe and prospering in our adopted homeland; I intend to keep it that way." Barely a few seconds into his speech, raucous cheers and applause interrupted him. He raised both arms to calm everyone down before continuing. "Let me assure you, a company of the 12th Mountain Infantry Regiment is guarding this hacienda and several kilometers beyond its perimeter. Coincidentally, other Argentine forces have been mobilized to conduct war games in the area and that essentially secures this entire region of Patagonia."

Ludolf von Alvensleben, former commander of the 46th SS Regiment in Dresden, gently interrupted with a question. "If I might ask, mein Führer, can we therefore assume you have persuaded President Ferreyra to follow in the footsteps of his predecessor, Juan Peron?" Living as he did in Buenos Aires, von Alvensleben had heard rumors about the attempted Nazi shakedown by Ferreyra and Rodriguez.

"Gruppenführer, I am pleased to report that the terms of our retirement in Argentina remain the same. The new regime has assured me that another Eichmann situation will never occur. However, in the off chance it does, the perpetrators will not escape Argentinian justice." The men clapped politely. "And if they do, Argentina will become a nation of paupers overnight!" This time, the men cheered loudly.

Inside the barn, a long trestle table had been cleared of lunch debris and covered with a crisp white tablecloth. Bormann sat at the head chair and the eleven guests, plus Rudy, searched for their names on the elaborately scripted place cards.

"Gentlemen, shall we get down to business?"

Martin Bormann spent almost an hour on what he termed 'general business.' It included the reading of recent telegraphed reports he had decoded from all the active and passive Nazi cells around the world and he finished with a blunt, "Any questions?"

"Just a comment if I may, Herr Reichsleiter," said Dr. Aribert Heim, a fairly recent arrival in San Carlos de Bariloche. "I spent seventeen years hiding out in Baden-Baden until the police traced me; I barely got out. Had I known about this massive Nazi underground, I would not have spent every day living in fear."

"Dr. Heim, we were protecting you as best we could. Did you not receive an anonymous telephone call warning you about the imminent police raid on your house?

"I can assure all of you that the network of the Fourth Reich is extremely robust, well-funded and ready to rise again when the occasion calls. Which is the perfect segue for the main item on our agenda, the Twentieth Olympiad in München."

The old warriors adjusted their seats in eager anticipation of this topic.

"Each and every one of us attended the 1936 Berlin Olympics, even Rudy, though he was only two years old at the time. What a magnificent event! It gave the world a foretaste of Aryan power. We are still the greatest nation on Earth despite having been betrayed by incompetent generals, aided and abetted by General Winter at Stalingrad, not to mention the British who manipulated the Americans into the war." There were various mumbles of assent from the men. Klaus Barbie stood up defiantly to pound his fist on the table.

"I did everything I could to rid the world of Jews, as did everyone in this room. If we could have had one more year to complete the task...."

Bormann held up his hand for calm as a rumble of approval from the aging Nazis began to grow. "So you will all agree that Israelis competing for medals at an Olympic Games held in the Fatherland is a massive insult to the German people? It is an insult that will not, must not be tolerated!"

The invited men worked themselves into a frenzy, banging clenched fists of both hands onto the wooden table. Water glasses tipped over but nobody cared. Rudy surveyed the faces, all reddened by blood pressure, as his father continued.

Why the hell am I here? These men are certifiably

insane. I cannot imagine the terror of being held in a concentration camp with one of these bastards in charge. What can I do to stop this madness?

"Well, gentlemen," the Reichsleiter continued after matters settled down, "the Fourth Reich is formulating a plan. We have identified a Palestinian called Luttif Afif. He leads a group within the Palestine Liberation Organization called Black September. This group is prepared to disrupt the Munich Olympics by holding some Israeli athletes hostage in return for the release of Palestinian prisoners currently incarcerated in Israeli prisons. Affif and his associates will be richer by five million untraceable U.S. dollars if they pull this off. Consequently, no country will ever invite Israel to another Olympics." Questions exploded from the men and Bormann held up his arms yet again to ask for silence.

"Okay, one at a time. If I miss any of your questions, ask them again. The money cannot be traced; trust me, I control almost every bank in Europe. Secondly, what happens if the Israelis release the prisoners and everybody goes home happy? Not going to happen. Odds are they will kill the athletes and German police will kill the Black September terrorists. Israel will keep their prisoners and we will keep our money."

The questions kept coming and the discussion went on until dinner was served and the group retreated for the night.

Rudy Bormann tossed restlessly in his bed, his conscience pounding the inside of his cranium. *I must be on the biggest guilt trip of all time. I remember as a child, seeing these men as giants. They were strong and my father was their leader. How could I have been so naïve to believe that crap? All I see now are withered, embittered murderers. The only common thread with my childhood is the role played by my father.*

Now, I am in possession of incriminating knowledge that will make me an accessory to mass murder if the Munich plan comes to fruition. What the fuck am I going to do?

But in the early hours of the morning, his rambling thoughts finally escaped to the comfort of Mary O'Connell's smile and he drifted off to sleep.

The next morning, his father thought it would be less contentious if he let Rudy recount his trip to Belfast rather than continue with the Munich plans. As the group of elderly criminals filled their stomachs with hot coffee and pastries, the elder Bormann instigated some casual table talk.

"I suppose all of you have heard versions of what happened to the Führer in those final days in the bunker? I was actually there, so allow me to share the truth.

"Adolph and Eva Braun did not get married or commit suicide. In fact, Eva and her sister Gretl Fegelein live on a hacienda about 500 kilometers north of here." Arched eyebrows indicated that several of the men were not aware of this.

The Reichsleiter continued. "What I am about to tell you is the result of my personal knowledge, supplemented by research and facts. I am going to give you the short version as it will prove important background information for this morning's presentation that my son, Rudy, has prepared.

"The two bodies discovered by the Russians outside the bunker were doppelgangers, personally hired by me. Our dear friend, Adolph, was to use the staged cremation to distract the Allies as he made his covert journey across the Atlantic to reunite with all of us in Argentina. Our plan was sabotaged by an unsavory character known as 'the Spider.'" There was an audible intake of breath at the mention of this name.

"Yes, mein herren, the same bastard that has been linked to several cowardly attacks on the Third Reich. The Spider kidnapped our Führer, flew him to London and, we have solid reason to believe, executed our brave leader as he steadfastly refused to capitulate to the fabricated public humiliation of our great cause."

"What a cruel bastard."

"I'd like to meet him and gouge his eyes out with my bare hands."

"I would not kill him but I'd remove his organs one by one, starting with his balls." These were just a few of the vivid comments expressed by the assembled group of war criminals.

"Well, you might get the chance, although I reserve the right to kill this man myself," spat Bormann. "As you all seem to know, this terrorist has led his life under a cloak of gutless anonymity—but he could not run from us forever. With my authorization, Rudy followed a lead and located the Spider in Belfast, Northern Ireland. He runs a gymnastics academy there and will be coaching the British team at the Mexico Olympics." After the incredulous gasps died down, Bormann answered the big unasked question.

"Make no mistake, we will bring this bastard to justice. My preference is to abduct him to Patagonia where we can all get our pound of flesh. Should that prove impracticable, it is still supremely important that we make sure he is annihilated no matter how, no matter where."

Bormann paused and looked at the weathered faces around him.

"Therefore, our primary plan is to dupe him into

traveling from Belfast to Barcelona. Once we have him alone and on our turf, it should be a simple matter to shanghai him to this hacienda. I am optimistic this plan is our best option but unforeseen circumstances might cause us to adopt an alternative approach, one that uses a similar strategy to the one I outlined yesterday for Munich. We are going to fund local terrorists to do our noble work for us." Discontent was evident at this remark and Dr. Mengele interrupted the Reichsleiter.

"Mein Führer, I think every man here would much prefer your primary approach. This Polish assassin needs to answer directly to the Fourth Reich for the sins he committed. I have some interesting medical procedures that will cause him to beg for death. Do not cede our rights to some Irish thugs." Roars of approval supported Mengele so Bormann raised his hand for silence.

"Josef, nobody wants this cretin's head more than I but we must plan for contingencies. Rudy has started to funnel untraceable cash into a Northern Irish organization known as the Fenian Brotherhood, a fledgling offshoot of the IRA in desperate need of financial support. If our efforts fail to entice the Spider away from Northern Ireland, we must carry out his death sentence by proxy. Our funding of the Fenian Brotherhood will be contingent upon them launching a guerrilla attack that blows up this gymnastics academy with the Spider inside. Once we confirm his death, we can revert to the Fourth Reich's main objective of monopolizing the world's economy, but I am sure you all agree that avenging the Führer must rise to our top priority at this time.

"To ensure success, I have formulated many backup strategies including offering extra money to the Black September PLO to take him out if he coaches at Munich. Make no mistake, this bastard is mine and cannot escape my wrath." The other Nazis thumped the table in enthusiastic approval.

The younger Gomez's face was pallid when his father turned to him. "Rudy, why don't you relate your recent experiences in Belfast."

The secret executive committee meeting of the Fourth Reich adjourned after breakfast on the fourth day. The night before, a final grand dinner had been hosted at the main hacienda. The alcohol was plentiful and several of the guests had to be assisted back to their cottages. Rudy also drank his share of schnapps but was the first to retire just after midnight, the never-ending Horst Wessel drinking song ringing in his ears.

"Die Fahne hoch! Die Reihen fest geschlossen! The flag on high! The ranks tightly closed!" Drunk old men, right arms extended in the Nazi salute, singing the Nazi anthem in western Argentina.

What a fucking nightmare, Rudy thought.

Rudy's bedroom faced the front of the house so the incessant clamor rattled his windows. He wearily climbed out of bed and removed a panel in his closet ceiling. After grabbing a pillow and blanket, he hauled himself into the attic. Rudy had used this space to escape from the family bedlam since he was fourteen. Not even his brothers and sisters were privy to his secret place and once up there, the noises faded away and he felt secure.

As he had done many times over the past twenty years, Rudy collapsed onto his bedding, his thoughts in turmoil. His brain tortured him by replaying the previous nights' scenarios in an endless loop. He began to sob uncontrollably until his exhausted body finally defeated his troubled mind with the onset of sleep.

The Nazi survivors departed in their Mercedes the next morning to retreat behind their faceless assumed identities. Calm and relaxation returned to everyone who remained at the hacienda—everyone except Rudy. The thirty-five-year old found himself still racked with confusion and guilt. What he had witnessed over the past few days bordered on a very dangerous lunacy and he was experiencing a bewildering transformation. Once a passive supporter of the indoctrination of his youth, now he had come to the realization that humanity had been completely justified in condemning Adolf Hitler and his cohorts for horrific war crimes. His father emerged as perhaps the biggest, most diabolical villain of all.

The committee had voted that he return to Belfast and attempt to perfect the original plan of enticing the Spider to Barcelona. His instincts were telling him to head west into Chile and disappear.

Yet if I do that, they will track me down and kill me. Those bastards will have no mercy. I have to contrive a plan to get away from here. His thoughts battled for a solution but could not find even a thread of hope.

CHAPTER EIGHTEEN

Baiting the Spider Trap

B ormann noticed his son's changed demeanor but attributed it to anxiety about returning to a country where he might be arrested for murder.

"Rudy, I don't appreciate your attitude since you returned from Europe. Whether you like it or not, you are going back to Belfast.

"I am having second thoughts about your chances of convincing the Spider to travel with you to Barcelona. He must be completely focused on the upcoming Mexico Olympics and it might be years before he would take on the distraction of developing another academy. The reality is, I don't have the luxury of waiting. I just want him dead. Go back to Northern Ireland and fund your pet terrorists to take him out, but tell them to make his death as painful as possible as a favor to me."

The younger man stared blankly at his father. He heard the words but his brain flashed a different message. *The terrorists are in Derry and so is Mary. I will not waste my next opportunity. Give me half a chance and I will beg her to disappear with me. There must be a quiet place in this world where there are no Goddamned Nazis.*

"Rudy, are you listening to me?" Bormann demanded sharply. "You have to lead this effort for obvious reasons. Because of the bollocks Ramos and Romero made of your last trip, you should return clean-shaven and with blond hair so you won't be recognized. Speak English with a German accent and odds are you will not be associated with the baron de Cortada. Besides, they will never be able to link you to the murder of that bartender because Rafael de Maldà had a perfect alibi. Was he not dining with the famous Malcolm McClain in front of BBC cameras?"

Rudy resigned himself to his father's rationale with a shrug. "Don't worry, mi Padre, I can handle this."

"Your primary role will be to convince those characters you met in Derry to provide a return on our investment. However, this time you will not be relying upon a couple of stupid gauchos to back you up. I have arranged for a 10-man staffeln of elite schutzstaffel to take care of your personal protection. Staffelführer Hans von Keller will lead them. He is the son of the late Sturmbahnführer Abelard

Hans von Keller, who you no doubt remember was murdered by the Spider in Maribor. If anything, the son is an even crueler bastard than his father. If the Fenian Brotherhood fucks up, unleash his chain and he will go after Orlowski like a rabid dog."

"Sounds like you have thought of everything, mi Padre, but we still have a lot of planning to do. Is this SS Staffeln based in Patagonia?"

"No, they live and train in the Fatherland. You will be leaving for Köln next week.

"The Fenian Brotherhood has the marked advantage of being untraceable back to the Fourth Reich but if for any reason they do not deliver, you must lead the elite staffeln into Belfast to finish the job. You and von Keller can strategize the finer points for as long as it takes but, assuming the Spider goes straight home after the Summer Olympics, I would prefer the bastard be dead by Oktoberfest. Knowing that Polish cretin is rotting in Hell will make my beer taste all the sweeter," Bormann concluded with a cruel laugh.

Bormann and Rudy encountered a completely unanticipated event that exploded a hole in the schedule. In his ongoing attempt to ward off the ravages of diabetes, the Reichsleiter had imported some expensive experimental medicine from Switzerland. Dr. Aribert Heim drove from San Carlos de Bariloche to administer the injection and the two veteran soldiers decided to spend a little time together watching the

Olympic Games that were being staged to the north in Mexico. The color television at the hacienda was the first in this part of Argentina and reception depended upon a series of relays from Buenos Aires. As this was to be the first Olympics broadcast in color, Bormann was eager to show off his expensive new toy.

Just as the tubes warmed up and the flickering steadied into a hazy picture, a Mexican announcer's voice crackled over the speaker.

"In breaking news, we are taking you over to the Mexican National Auditorium where a controversy has erupted at a women's gymnastics event. What is the latest, Santiago?"

"Czechoslovakian gymnast, Věra Čáslavská, had apparently won the gold medal for floor exercise when the judges unexpectedly upgraded the scores of the Soviet Union's Larisa Petrik to create a tie. Many believe this was in retaliation for Čáslavská's recent outspoken opposition to Communism. Several Czech and Soviet coaches squared off in the center of the mat and it looked as though a major brawl was about to break out, when the British head coach, Chez Orlowski, interjected himself between the factions and calmed the situation down. Let's go to the video." The two Germans in Argentina stared at the grainy screen as a small but powerful figure wearing a red, white and blue tracksuit forced himself between several larger angry men.

"An ugly situation averted. Not only did Señor

Orlowski show himself to be calm in a crisis, he apparently speaks fluent Russian and Czechoslovakian. Back to the studio, Ricardo."

Aribert Heim glanced over at his patient with concern. Bormann's anger was manifesting in white knuckles gripping the chair arms as his rising blood pressure turned his face a deep red trending towards purple.

"THAT IS HIM! That's the FUCKIN' SPIDER; in my house, on my television." Dr. Heim filled a glass with brandy and convinced Bormann to drink the alcohol in an attempt to calm him down. He threw the heavy glass at the screen, smashing it with a bang into smithereens. As he collapsed back into his chair, foam started to drool out of his mouth and the doctor concluded that an adverse reaction to the Swiss medicine had started. He yelled frantically for help.

"Emergency, emergency, Señor Gomez is very ill. I must take him immediately to the hospital in Bariloche."

Rudy called the hospital on a regular basis but it was two days before Martin Bormann was allowed visitors.

"Ah, Rudy, that bastard was on tele……"

"……Padre, please, no mention of the Spider. It does your blood pressure no good. Anyway, from what I understand from Dr. Heim, the picture was so bad you couldn't really make out who it was. Just calm down. I am going to take over the day-to-day operations at the hacienda until you have completely recovered. My trip to Köln will be postponed until I am satisfied that your health has returned to normal. The sooner you stop fixating on the bastard, the sooner I can kill him." Rudy smiled and raised his eyebrows, and after a few seconds, the aging Reichsleiter smiled back.

Being on the hacienda without his father for the first time in the young man's life felt very strange. Rudy acted as 'el jefe' and was able to roam and forage without interruption from the staff. He had a degree in agriculture from the University of Cordoba and for the past ten years had experimented with various crops and animal husbandry at the hacienda but the Gomez family was so extremely wealthy, they certainly did not have to depend upon the soil for income. The young man spent most of his time visiting the various investments the family held but had never been entrusted with access to the bank accounts of the Fourth Reich.

Now, because of his father's unexpected demise, his duties required him to conduct business from his father's massive oak desk in the library. He could not help himself from being inquisitive but found nothing of real interest as he poked around. One afternoon he came across a neat pile of light blue airmail paper and decided to write a letter to Mary O'Connell to tell her how much his father appreciated having Waterford crystal in their hacienda. It was a short letter but took him over an hour to get the words just right. He was down to the last piece before he was able to turn it over. With neat script, he addressed the outer fold, *'Miss Mary O'Connell, care of Austins Department Store, Derry, Northern Ireland.'*

As the days passed, he could not be sure if his correspondence even reached her. Then one day in late summer a light blue envelope, stamped *'par avion'* was waiting alongside his breakfast setting.

Rudy used a clean butter knife to slice through the three sealing folds. His heart was racing and he almost dropped the knife twice so he took a deep breath before unfolding the document.

Dear Rudy,

I am sorry it has taken me so long to respond to your beautiful letter and yes, I do remember when you came into Austins.

Derry is in turmoil right now and hardly a day goes by that the R.U.C., backed by the British Army, does not launch a raid into the Bogside to arrest a bunch of our brave young men. I have had several friends killed and there seems no end in sight.

I hope you can find time to write to me again because it transports me away from Derry and into the wonderful world you describe in the Andes. Someday, you must invite me to Bariloche and take me to dinner at the Salamander. If they serve lamb, they must have an Irish chef.

Let me know if you are coming back to Derry any time soon; I'll take the day off work.

Best wishes,

Mary

Rudy read the letter five times, and then read it again—and again. That evening at dinner, he decided that his father must have fully recovered from his medicinal setback and it was time to reschedule his trip to Europe.

CHAPTER NINETEEN

From Köln to Donegal

L ess than a week later, Rudy Gomez flew to Köln to
meet with Hans von Keller. The two men arranged
to rendezvous at the Brauhaus Früh am Dom, an old
brewery located half a mile south of the famous cathedral. Rudy arrived thirty minutes before their appointed
time and sat alone at one of the twenty or so umbrella
tables set out in the square. He nursed a glass of the
local Früh beer and pretended to read the *Kölner
Stadtanzeiger*, as he compared anyone who approached
the restaurant with his photograph of von Keller.

At precisely two o'clock, a tourist wearing expensive designer sunglasses approached Rudy's table and
asked casually, "Excuse me, sir, I heard there was an
excellent Argentinian steak house in this square but I
don't seem to be able to find it."

"You would be better off eating German food in Köln. Good afternoon, Hans." Hans von Keller shook Rudy's hand and sat down.

"You are absolutely correct, Rudy. Before you leave Köln you must try this Brauhaus's specialty, pig's knuckle with potatoes; it is absolutely delicious. Waiter, a glass of Früh, bitte, and another for my friend."

As the waiter headed for the bar, Hans whispered, "So, Rudy, you have actually met the bastard who murdered my father?"

"Jawohl, Hans, I had lunch with him in Belfast a couple of months ago. As you well know, the Spider is the number one target on our list of traitors. When I came across a possible lead, my father sent me to verify; I'm positive it was him."

"I am honored that you flew all the way across the Atlantic to join my staffeln and that your father chose us for this mission. Will you at least allow me the honor of vengeance? I will slit his throat and pin a note to his chest, just like he did to my father."

"I deeply respect that, Hans and perhaps if all else fails; it might prove a last resort. However, we have determined that our primary strategy must use a third party so that the Fourth Reich cannot be linked in any way to the assassination. For his entire time in exile, Reichsleiter Bormann has been building a financial network that is within a decade of restoring our control over the global economy. When that happens, we will be untouchable. As such, the elimination of the Spider cannot be allowed to jeopardize our end goal. Rest assured, regardless of how and when he dies, he most certainly will be dead. Our mission is to monitor from afar and then verify the death."

It was no more than a ten-minute walk from the Brauhaus to the Köln Nazi headquarters, located in a grim stone building on the corner of Appellhof-platz and Elisenstrasse. In post-war Köln, the Fourth Reich was hiding in plain sight, knowing the Gestapo used this same location, the EL-DE House, as a notorious prison throughout the Second World War. Rudy's celebrity entitled him to a top floor suite with a window that looked east towards the twin spires of the cathedral. With no effort at all, he slept for the next 12 hours.

Serving staff loaded the ground floor conference room table with sandwiches, pastries and coffee as soon as word filtered down that Herr Gomez was awake and showering. Ten men in casual street clothes jumped to their feet as soon as Rudy entered and snapped their right arms in salute.

"Heil Bormann."

"I appreciate your loyalty to my father and the

enthusiasm for our cause, mein herren, but until we return to this building after the successful conclusion of our mission, there must be no indication that you are members of an SS Staffeln. Do you understand?" The men relaxed reluctantly and sat down around the table.

Rudy smiled and continued.

"First, some good news, my father has authorized 10,000 DM to be deposited in each of your personal accounts." There were wide grins and appreciative mumbles at this announcement.

Staffelführer Hans von Keller had honed his men into an impressive unit. Their average age was twenty-eight and they had trained together for the past two years. Rudy was understandably fascinated and found an occasion to ask von Keller a nagging question.

"Hans, apart from your staffeln I have seen no others in the Braunsfeld Park, are there many similar groups of young Schutzstaffel around Western Germany? Most of the young Germans I see on the streets of Koln are wearing Manchester United jerseys and listening to the Rolling Stones."

"There are reportedly thousands of us but we never meet. By necessity, all are clandestine but tell your father, the youth of Germany will be ready to serve whenever the need arises."

"My father is meticulous about planning for contingencies. In the unlikely event that the local terrorists I hire completely screw up the assassination, our staffeln is ordered to swoop in and kill the Spider ourselves. You have my word that if it comes down to it, the honor of pulling the trigger will be yours. Any ideas?"

After two intense weeks of planning and training, Rudy Gomez informed Hans that transportation had been arranged to take them by train to Paris. Once there, they would break into two groups, one with a connection to Le Havre, a port city in western France, the other travelling further west to Cherbourg. From these channel ports, they would pose as wine salesmen and travel across the Celtic Sea on merchant ships to disembark at Rosslare Harbor on the southeast corner of Ireland. Clearance through customs and immigration at Rosslare was assured and rental of four VW Squarebacks would allow each of the two groups to transport their cases of German wine independently to their final destination, Gortlee Castle in Donegal.

Gortlee Castle occupies two hundred acres of heavily forested land outside Letterkenny, the industrial capital of County Donegal, and currently served as the home of prominent banker Hermann Schmidt and his wife Kathleen. Mr. Schmidt emigrated to Letterkenny in 1944 and owned several car dealerships throughout northwest Ireland in addition to his private bank.

The weary travelers arrived at Gortlee over a four-hour period and were shown to their rooms. The household staff had been told that the young men were mechanics from Germany, visiting Donegal to analyze and train the service departments of Herr Schmidt's dealerships. Rudy sought out Mr. Schmidt and met with him in private.

"It is good to meet you again, Uncle Hermann. My father sends his sincere regards, several cases of fine German wine, and this personal letter," Rudy said politely, handing him an envelope.

"Rudy, you were eight or nine when I last saw you. The world has changed but I am flattered you still refer to me as your uncle. Your father is a great visionary and I was one of perhaps a thousand young men whom he funded to start businesses around the world. Here are the details of how to access your private account at my bank. You will find the manager, Mr. Kelly, extremely helpful, and above all, discreet.

"Kathleen and I do not need to know what is really going on but if you can protect the integrity of Gortlee Castle and its staff, I will most definitely appreciate it."

The Schmidts hosted a dinner for the travelers and then left the next morning for an extended stay at their villa in Garmisch Partenkirchen, Bavaria. Amazingly, the Schmidt family had managed to retain continuous ownership of the villa since Gerhardt Schmidt originally built it in 1738.

CHAPTER TWENTY

1970, Everyday Life in a Violent Society

By the late 1960s and early '70s, a rumbling turmoil erupted that turned Northern Ireland into a war zone. Almost every week, terrorists identifying themselves as Catholics or Protestants committed acts of barbarity. Violent proclamations usually took place in the middle of the afternoon, giving sufficient advance notice for the television stations to capture footage and read the obligatory righteous justification for the violence on the evening news. High profile buildings became high profile targets and there was no bigger target in Belfast than the Spider Academy. But even in this extremely volatile political climate, opposing factions seemed to recognize that some targets were strictly off limits.

Since the academy's famous opening, a dispro-portionate number of Northern Ireland's young gymnasts made their mark on the Olympic stage. Chez, shamelessly exploiting his heavy Polish accent to great effect, became a legend, not only as the current National Olympic coach, but as a generous local philanthropist.

In another sport, football, Spider Academy co-founder Malcolm McClain was appointed special consultant to the Northern Ireland Football Asso-ciation. His keen eye for talent allowed the cream of Belfast's sixteen-year-old soccer players to have the same opportunities he had been given. A few even crossed the pond to make their mark in the English First Division. Malcolm's eldest son would not be one of those few.

"Yo, Malky, happy birthday, my friend. I read that your boy scored two last Saturday against Glentoran. Did you go watch?" Chez asked.

"Chez, it hurts me when I don't go to his games but I don't want to seem like I'm offering him any encouragement. He's not as good as he thinks and needs to stay in school. Tough love, but he really doesn't have what it takes to play at the next level in England."

The former professional player had his toes tucked under the wall bars of the gym and grunted out the words as he pushed to complete his morning regimen. The two men always supported each other through their exercises each morning; it was their time together. The Spider, seven years younger than McClain, was hanging from the upper bars and performing crunches in cadence with his friend. He noticed Malcolm's sensitivity and changed the subject.

"Sounds like the Brits might have a solution to the Troubles with this Sunningdale Conference they're proposing. How long have the Protestants and Catholics been going at it now?"

"No good answer to that, Chez. This latest outbreak of violence started to rear its ugly head in 1968 but four hundred years ago could also be a correct response. I'm afraid I won't see an end to it in my lifetime. Both sides have legitimate beefs and giant intransigent egos."

"I never understood what caused the two sides to get so pissed off at each other in the first place," the inverted Polish gymnast pondered. "Don't they all believe in the same god?"

"There's a joke in these parts, Chez. A thug wearing a balaclava sticks his gun in the face of a rabbi and demands to know what religion he is. 'Obviously, I'm a Jew,' protests the rabbi. Undaunted, the thug asks if he's a Protestant Jew or a Catholic Jew!"

Chez chuckled. "Let's take a break, Malky."

The two men toweled off and walked towards the

water cooler. The short journey took almost twenty minutes as each student they passed called for and received the undivided attention of both men.

"Siobhán, I want to see your toes pointed in all movements. The judges add points for length and form. Come on, young lady; let me see that handspring again."

Siobhán McKenna was twelve years old and in her eighth year at the academy but Malcolm and Chez were the only people in the building that knew what her father, Barry, really did for a living.

The men eventually made it back into their executive area, grabbed fresh towels and sat at the conference table with large glasses of water. Unbeknownst to Malcolm, the Spider was on a mission. He had been charged by Jadwiga and Margery to get his best friend out of the academy for an hour so the staff could organize the setup for Malcolm's surprise fifty-seventh birthday party later that afternoon. But Malcolm wanted to talk and the opportunity did not make itself immediately apparent to the Pole.

"This latest outbreak of violence must have been bubbling under the surface for almost fifty years. I am sorry my naiveté is exposing both of our families to the danger; I take full responsibility," Malcolm said.

"If you are still looking for an actual date, it was probably July 12, 1968, when everything began to spin out of control. The Orangemen did their usual thing, a confrontational, six-mile parade to celebrate King Billy's victory over the Catholic King James at the River Boyne. Up 'til then, the Catholics sucked it in and played nice but that year, their frustrations boiled over. The Nationalists started their own marches, which resulted in a whole bunch of heads being cracked in the Bogside area of Londonderry. It hasn't let up since then."

Malcolm sighed before continuing. "The British Army was deployed to Northern Ireland last year to keep the two sides apart but they only exacerbated the whole situation. We've been losing about five hundred lives a year and I'm not sure if it's ever going to end."

"How come we've been relatively untouched?"

"I can only think it is because we accept and love all our students. And perhaps because of our reputations. Your family is Catholic, mine Protestant but we've never discriminated against anyone joining the Spider Academy."

Chez Orlowski was street smart, with an uncanny ability to cut through a Gordian knot. He offered Malcolm his unsolicited take on the complicated problem.

"Nobody talks about it, but I wouldn't be surprised if there are bigger forces in play here. In every labor camp I was thrown into, a prison hierarchy had evolved. Inevitably, I would be asked by the bully-in-chief to contribute something; this could be cigarettes, clothing, or food, in return for his protection. It was always referred to as a little insurance to make sure I didn't get beaten up by the guys from another barrack. Total bullshit! He was the one handing out the beating if I didn't pay the freight.

"Malky, my gut tells me a lot of the violence we are seeing is making some local bullies very rich; it smacks of the same protection scams I've seen a hundred times in my life."

"I have always suspected that too, but it is impossible to prove. I must say, I have personally known many leaders of the UVF and UDA on the Protestant side and the Official and Provisional IRA on the Catholic side since we moved back to Belfast; what you are saying would not astonish me."

"We don't pay protection money for the academy, do we, Malky?"

"Absolutely not! Do you think crusty old Sir Arthur would give up a hard-earned sixpence to a bunch of thugs? No, Chez, paying protection money is not the reason we haven't been hit. Much more likely it's because many of the children of those men I mentioned spend several hours a week here."

At this pensive pause in their conversation, Chez finally seized his opportunity.

"Tell you what, Malky, let's get out of here for an hour. Remember that engineer we met several months ago, Danny Fitzpatrick? He has just installed a state-of-the-art machine that can cut intricate shapes into metal. It'll be perfect for the signage we're considering…"

"…Oh, I don't know, I have a training session with the U-14's this afternoon at Seaview Stadium. The Crusaders professional team is going to surprise the boys by joining in."

The Spider smiled contentedly. "I'll get you back in time for that, no problem."

CHAPTER TWENTY-ONE

Back to the Diamond

S ome cases of wine concealed a smorgasbord of small arms and explosives and one of the staffeln's first tasks was to check that everything had survived the circuitous trip from Germany to Gortlee Castle in working order.

"I am going to drive to Derry. I have to make contact with the Fenian Brotherhood and give them their orders. I am going to sweeten the deal with a little cash and the promise of more. Needless to say, if they manage to eliminate the Spider, we will have no further need of their organization and I'll take the rest of the money back to Argentina."

"My job is to protect you so I'll bring a couple of the lads to make sure you come to no harm…"

"…Hans, I don't want to risk crossing an international border with you and your men carrying weapons. I will meet Mulcahy in the same place I did before. I appreciate the concern but I'll be fine. I should be back by dinner.

"If the Fenian Brotherhood lives up to their side of the deal, you and I must make a trip to Belfast to assure ourselves that the bastard is dead. Then we'll meet the rest of the unit back in Köln. Tell the men to enjoy the fishing; this might turn into a fairly short, well paid vacation for them."

"If I might suggest an additional detail to your plan, Rudy?" Hans looked at Rudy and schemed, "If our backup strategy becomes unnecessary, perhaps an anonymous note to the local police might lead them to your friends, the Fenian Brotherhood."

"Hans, my father speaks with great respect about your father's intelligence. The apple has not fallen far from the tree." The two men laughed but Rudy added a serious afterthought. "Should your earlier caution not be misplaced and they double-cross me today, prioritize our mission rather than trying to rescue me. If I am not back in three days or you find out they failed to kill the Spider, implement the backup strategy we trained for in Cologne."

Rudy Gomez left the men at the castle to sort out the shipment and took one of the VW Squarebacks. His first destination was the Schmidt Bank on Upper Main Street in Letterkenny where he introduced himself to Mr. Kelly, the manager. After the formal niceties had been completed, Rudy proffered an unusual request.

"Mr. Kelly, I need some operating capital, in British pounds. How much can I withdraw?" John Kelly was unperturbed by this question.

"Mr. Schmidt anticipated that might be the case and Letterkenny does not let an artificial border with the six counties to our east get in the way of commerce. You have almost six million pounds sterling in your account. How much do you need?"

"Thank you, Mr. Kelly, I'll leave a million in the account and take the rest." Kelly flinched this time around, but responded with a suggestion.

"Would you consider a cashier's cheque? Five million pounds takes up a lot of space and the Brits are bound to want to poke around your car at the border. A cheque is easy to conceal and redeemable at any British bank in the United Kingdom."

"You make an excellent point. Give me twenty thousand sterling in used notes and the balance as a cashier's cheque. Please put the cash in a brown paper bag and stash it in a file storage box. I'll need four or five of these boxes and want each of them to be filled with old bank statements, the lids cellotaped closed and 'BANK RECORDS' stamped all over the outsides. Mr. Kelly, I'm sure my request will take a little time to accomplish so I will grab myself a cup of coffee and wander around Letterkenny. I'll be back in about ninety minutes."

Two hours later, Mr. Kelly requested that two security guards accompany Rudy to his car. The back seat of the Squareback was already folded flat so they were able to slide the boxes into the rear, leaving them uncovered so the 'Bank Statements' signage could be read easily. He pulled out of the parking lot and drove the car east on the N14 before turning left towards Manorcumming.

Gomez encountered the border-crossing half a mile east of a village called Bridge End. Six British troops blocked the road with their armored Saracen and a rosy-cheeked corporal waved him to stop. The young man in the center of the road cradled an Enfield L1A1 while the rest of his squad focused on Rudy's rental car from behind cover. He slowed to a halt and wound down the VW's window. He proactively held out his West German passport and flashed a friendly smile at the corporal.

"Guten morgan, Corporal. Am I on the correct road to visit the famous walled city of Londonderry?" The soldier diligently compared the photograph in the passport with the blond driver before returning the passport.

"I need you to step out of the car, sir, and let me look inside the rear."

"Certainly, Corporal," Rudy responded. "My Uncle Hermann owns the Schmidt Bank in Letterkenny. I volunteered for the assignment of transporting the banking collateral you can see in my car to the Ulster Bank in Northern Ireland. Having always been fascinated by walled cities, I am really looking forward to photographing Londonderry on this trip. I'm afraid everything is crammed in rather tightly, but pick any box you want and I'll be happy to open it for you." The soldier hesitated and Rudy thought his bluff had failed. *Mr. Kelly did me a favor with the cashier's cheque. Even at five to one odds, if the corporal picks the right box and discovers the cash, I can claim I hid it there for security purposes.*

"Don't fuss yourself, sir, you are good to go. Keep going straight, Mr. Gomez. This road dead-ends in two and a half miles. Once you get there, you'll turn right onto Strand Road and be in Londonderry within five minutes."

The Saracen burped some black diesel fumes before moving forward to let Rudy continue his journey.

He located a parking space for the white station wagon in the Diamond, locked all the doors and tried to walk casually towards Austins Department Store. There were two things working against him; he was carrying a large amount of cash in a brown paper bag and was closing in on seeing Mary O'Connell. His heart pumped rapidly as his impromptu plan unfolded. On the second floor, he saw the flaming red hair as soon as he reached the stair landing. Knowing she would not recognize his face, he planned to leave her a note at the cash register. All he had to do was negotiate a few hundred square feet of fragile Beleek pottery and Waterford crystal while walking on legs that shook nervously with every step.

Nevertheless, he made it, left his note and managed to retreat to the stairs without incident. In the third floor Roof Top Restaurant, he sought out the pay telephone, fished a piece of paper out of his pocket and dialed the number. He instantly recognized the voice that answered.

"This is your friend from Argentina," he said in a low voice. "Meet me at the usual place at four o'clock." He hung up immediately as instructed in case the phone was being tapped.

As expected, Michael Tobin and Colm O'Shaughnessy nodded to Rudy as they cased the restaurant. Ten minutes later, at exactly half past three, Brendan Mulcahy appeared, walked over and sat beside him, his back to the wall.

"Good to see you are still living the life, Brendan," Rudy greeted him.

"And good to see you got rid of that stupid moustache, Rudy; and did you run out of hair dye?" Mulcahy smirked.

Rudy shook his hand and then placed the brown paper bag containing the twenty thousand pounds on the table.

"I have a small favor I would like to discuss with you and this twenty thousand should make it worth your while."

"Talk to me, my friend; we'll see if we are able to accommodate you."

Rudy explained his conditions and added that a fifty thousand bonus would reward a verified successful conclusion. Mulcahy agreed. At a gesture from his boss, Colm O'Shaughnessy walked over to the table, picked up the bag and left the restaurant. Mulcahy rose to follow but not before whispering a veiled threat.

"Rudy, seeing as how you find yourself in Austins, I suspect you will try to see Mary O'Connell. So far, no harm, no foul but keep your dick in your pants or you will lose it."

"Have a nice day, Brendan."

Mary O'Connell noticed that the expensive envelope on her cash register had her name in script on the front. She was intrigued but waited until she had a private moment before opening it.

> *Mary,*
>
> *I am visiting Southern Ireland for a couple of weeks but could not resist coming to Derry to see if I could persuade you to have a drink with me, perhaps even dinner.*
>
> *If this is possible, please let me know a time and a place by leaving a reply on the register where I left this note.*
>
> *Your Argentinian friend,*
>
> *Rudy.*

Rudy Gomez was the man who bought the Lismore Waterford and then wrote to me from South America. He seems such a gentleman, what harm could there be? She thought a drink might be fun, so she turned the note over and wrote a reply. After re-sealing the envelope, Mary scratched out her name and wrote Mr. Gomez on the front.

Rudy finished his business with Mulcahy and after the Irishman left, returned to the crystal department. Mary was nowhere to be seen so he casually sauntered towards the cash register. His heart bounded when he saw the envelope with his name on it.

He waited until he was out of the building before he read the note and was ecstatic at her response. Mary would meet him at 6 p.m. in Peadar O'Donnell's pub on Waterloo Street but she said that she could only stay for one drink.

It was 5:30 already so he asked the first person he encountered in the Diamond for directions. After sorting out the nearly incomprehensible but friendly reply, he raced the butterflies in his stomach along Butcher Street. In half a mile, he passed through Butcher Gate and turned right onto Waterloo Street. This street was narrow and sloped downhill as it escaped the walled city but there was Peadar O'Donnell's on the left as promised.

Miss Mary is quite shrewd, Rudy thought. *An unknown man invites her for a drink so she picks a pub in the heart of the IRA fortress. I make one untoward move and I will not see tomorrow's light of day!*

Rudy found a table and sat on a green leather bench from where he could observe the front door. Thoughts of what he was going to say were flittering around his mind when a waitress stopped at his table and plunked down two pints of Guinness. He was about to tell her he hadn't ordered the drinks when he heard a melodious voice address him.

"Pleased to meet you, Rudy. The first round is on me."

And there she was.

"But how did you know who I was, Mary?"

She sat down and laughed.

My God, she is the most beautiful woman I have ever seen, Rudy reflected with awe.

"I asked one of the regulars if there were any strangers here and you were the only one. For some reason I remember you as having black hair and a moustache but I like this version better, so I bought you a Guinness. Sláinte!" Mary toasted him.

He sat mesmerized by her lilting voice, her dazzling smile and those green, green eyes. They talked rapidly, each trying to cover their entire lives in a couple of hours. He could not remember how it happened but their hands had found each other and were now clasped. Their faces were only inches apart.

In a calm, low voice, Mary said, "Rudy, I would like to continue our conversation but this is not the place. Can we have lunch tomorrow?"

"Of course, I would love to. I am not going to drive back to Donegal tonight. Can you recommend a place around here where I can stay for a couple of days?" As she was thinking, he risked adding, "You have made my head quite dizzy. Perhaps some sea air would do me good. And by the way, does Brendan Mulcahy know we are having a drink together?"

"No, he most certainly does not. That man is quite a nuisance and he caught me by surprise as I was reading your letter. Anyway, there is a wonderful little place about three miles from here called the Belfray County Inn. Take the bridge across the river and continue down the Glenshane Road, you can't miss it. I'll meet you in the restaurant at noon tomorrow. Now, you must leave first. I will be telling these local eejits that you are my cousin from Germany so you should be safe.

"Take care, Rudy."

Instead of pulling his hand away, he pulled hers towards him. She did not resist and he kissed them gently before leaving.

The three-storey Georgian hotel was exactly what Rudy needed to clear his head. By the time he checked in, it was almost ten in the evening, so he went directly to the dining room and used a ten pound note to persuade the manager to rustle up some food and open an expensive bottle of Cabernet. His thoughts were all about the evening with Mary. She was the woman of his dreams and all other reasons for being in Northern Ireland were suddenly irrelevant.

So, she is not married and apparently not seeing anyone special. I cannot get her smile out of my mind. What am I to do if she does not show up tomorrow?

"May I have a glass of that wine, Rudy?" A now familiar lilting Irish voice interrupted his thoughts. He stood up and turned to see Mary standing behind him. They embraced and kissed passionately.

"But I thought you said…" Rudy couldn't believe she was there.

"Oh, about lunch tomorrow? Yes, and I meant it. Got any ideas what we might do to fill the time?"

CHAPTER TWENTY TWO

The Birthday Party from Hell

T he old garage in the Bogside smelled of oil and tires. The weather could get hot in early August but the doors and windows remained closed. Brendan Mulcahy and his two sidekicks had been there for almost an hour and the modifications to their Bedford van had still not been completed. Mulcahy finished his coffee and kicked the soles of the shoes protruding from under the vehicle.

"Fer Chrissakes, Malachy, how much fuckin' longer? We have to drive down to Belfast and need to get there before noon."

The mechanic propelled his skid by grabbing the edge of the Bedford's bumper and emerged to confront the three members of the Fenian Brotherhood.

"I had to replace the shock absorbers. You stupid

gits are going to be carrying five thousand pounds of fertilizer and chemicals in the back of this rusty piece of garbage and you wouldn't have made it to the end of the street if I hadn't beefed up the suspension.

"Now, let me explain how this works. Who'll be doing the drivin'?"

"Micky is drivin' the van; Colm and I will be following him in the big Austin."

Malachy Kelly stood up and wiped his hands on the thighs of his dirty overalls before opening the driver's door with a rag.

"Yous'll be wise to keep your fingerprints off the Bedford. The police can find all sorts of evidence if yer not real careful." Tobin, O'Shaughnessy and Mulcahy crowded close to Kelly to hear the instructions.

"Micky, behind your seat is the timer from a parking meter. As soon as you park at the Spider Academy, set the timer for ten minutes. Oh, and try to find a spot in front of the paint store. You must lock the van and then get into the back seat of the Austin. Youse must all stay calm, ten minutes is plenty of time for you to get away but not enough for anyone to stop the bomb."

"You sure this is going to work, Malachy?"

"Please, I'm an artist; of course it's going to fuckin' work. When the timer winds down it triggers a detonator that causes all the chemicals in the rear of the Bedford to explode. I have personally designed this cocktail to destroy not only the academy, but the paint store as well. All that flammable liquid should set every building within a hundred yards alight. Don't worry, yous'll be well out of range in ten minutes."

The two vehicles were almost an hour behind schedule when Micky Tobin finally pulled to a halt outside the Spider Academy. He waited until he saw the blue Austin Cambridge park behind him and then turned the wheel of the timer as instructed.

Click, click, click, click. Tobin locked the van and strolled casually back to his cohorts. "Dammit Brendan, I parked illegally in a loading zone, think I'll get a ticket?" He joked before he climbed into the back seat of the Austin.

The three miscreants were still laughing as they accelerated east along York Road.

"I'm glad you talked me into going to Fitzpatrick's, Chez. That Belgium water-jet machine is quite entertaining to watch. I think we could use.........
What the hell is going on ahead?" Malcolm shouted in alarm as Chez drove toward the academy.

They were only a few hundred yards away but the road in front of them was completely blocked by emergency vehicles. A thick plume of smoke created a dirty column in the sky.

"That looks too close for comfort. I'll park and see if we can get closer on foot." Chez pulled left into a petrol station. They went inside to get an explanation from the owner, Jim Green, a man they had known for a decade. The instant they walked through the door, Jimmy quickly came around his counter.

"Malcolm, Chez, thank God you're both okay…"

"Talk to me, Jimmy, what the hell happened?"

"Sounded like a car bomb, Malcolm, 'bout twenty minutes ago. The police think it was parked at the Blundell paint store right across York Road from the academy. I've heard there's serious damage to almost every building in the area and a fierce fire is still being fed by the bursting paint cans. The police won't let you inside the lines; too dangerous…."

McClain spun around in time to see the Spider's back racing towards the parking lot and headed after him.

Both men cut through a side street and sprinted towards the flames. The east wall of the academy was badly damaged and billowing a thick acrid smoke. York Road was filled with ambulances all the way to the police barricades.

"Sorry, gentlemen, you cannot……"

"....We own the damn place. Tell me about the casualties."

"Oh, I certainly recognize you, Mr. McClain. God must have been watching 'cos about ten minutes before the bomb exploded, most of your staff and students left to decorate Seaview for some kind of party. They are all standing over there." The police officer gestured towards a large group of people beyond the barricades to the north and Malcolm could make out Jadwiga and Margery surrounded by their students. Chez was already sprinting in that direction, leaving Malcolm to look numbly at the wreck of his building. McClain turned back to the officer he yelled, "You said MOST of the staff and students. What the bloody hell does that mean?"

"The building is too dangerous to enter because of the roof collapse and we can smell ruptured gas lines but we have recovered the bodies of an adult and a couple of youngsters who were near the door."

By this time, Chez was back at Malcolm's side and caught the tail end of the heated conversation. "Malky, everyone in both our families is safe but Jadwiga has found out from Bette Tarleton that six kids stayed behind in the gym to practice with Billy Scott."

"That means four are still unaccounted for."

This time it was Malcolm in the lead as the two men hurtled through the police lines and into the rubble.

"Kids, anybody there? Give us a shout. We're here to get you out," Malcolm yelled.

The dust and smoke blinded and hurt their eyes; there were only small isolated pockets of visibility. The firemen, recognizing the new dynamic, began to lay down a curtain of water. Another section of wall collapsed and a hundred voices outside gasped. There was no sign of any noise or movement from within the building until a soft cry was heard. McClain appeared through the smoke carrying a coughing body covered by a wet towel. Orlowski was not far behind him. Chez was leading a young boy by the hand and guiding him over the treacherous piles of loose bricks.

Four medics burst forward to help them but as soon as their charges were handed over to medics, both friends looked at each other and without saying a word, sped back into the building. In less than five minutes, Chez appeared carrying another swathed body. An arm moved and a voice cried out as the ambulance's rear doors opened. Chez turned to look for Malcolm; he couldn't see anything but swirling dust. He lunged towards the building for a third time but two burly police officers grabbed him by the arms.

Jadwiga and a hysterical Margery evaded the barriers and ran to Chez's side; he refocused his energies on the two wives.

"Stay back, both of you. Malcolm knows what he is doing."

But as soon as the policemen relaxed their grip, the Spider turned around and was climbing back over the rubble towards the black void in the building.

"Malcolm," he shouted.

"Chez, over here." He heard the footsteps crunching over the rubble before Malcolm stumbled towards him through the smoke. His black, sooted face was smeared with tears; in his arms was the lifeless body of Siobhán McKenna.

PART FOUR

CHAPTER TWENTY-THREE

The Pot Boils

B elfast was in shock. Why had two of its favorite sons been targeted? The BBC program, *Scene Around Six*, scooped all media when presenter, Walter McCoubrey announced, "One of the three children who died has been identified as twelve-year-old Siobhán McKenna. Her father, Barry McKenna, is reputed to be commander of the Belfast Brigade of the Provisional IRA, the Irish republican paramilitary organization that emerged to prominence last year, just before Christmas. This unfortunate death would seem to indicate that any car bomb attack on the Spider Academy would not be the responsibility of that organization. Attention is being focused on the Ulster Volunteer Force, sworn rivals of the IRA. However, in a recent statement, received by the BBC just before we came on the air, the leader of the UVF, George McFadden, vehemently denies that his organization had any involvement in the bombing. McFadden stressed that his son also attends the Spider Academy."

The day after the disaster, Malcolm McClain walked over to his neighbor's kitchen for a cup of tea.

"Chez, that chat we had earlier in the week about the academy refusing to pay protection money, you don't suppose…"

"…Nothing's off the table, Malky, but I swear to you, I will get to the truth. The police are throwing all their resources at finding the culprits, but it still might not be enough. I am going to take some time off to do a little research of my own." The Polish war hero spoke the words with a menace that took Malcolm back to the days in Yugoslavia when he had first met the Spider a quarter century ago. In all that time, he had never witnessed any fear in his friend's demeanor, no matter how impossible the odds.

My God, he thought. *Whoever killed Billy Scott and those kids has gone up shit creek without a paddle. The Spider will stop at nothing until he finds the culprits—or dies trying.*

"Chez, I know better than to try and stop you.

Let's do this together, my friend. United, the two of us will have a better chance…"

"…No, Malky, I am asking you to look after and protect both our families. I will tell Jadwiga tonight, leave in the morning and be back after I have taken care of business."

An idea flashed though Malcolm's head. "Come over to my house tonight for a drink. I want to wish you luck and there might be a way I can help."

At ten o'clock that evening, Margery answered the familiar knock on her kitchen door. Chez and Jadwiga Orlowski were stoic as they entered but Margery could not help putting her hand over her eyes and weeping.

"I guess Malcolm has told you what I need to do. Jadwiga needs a drink so I thought you ladies could use each other's company. Is Malcolm in the study?"

The door to Malcolm's study was ajar so Chez walked in without knocking. Two men were standing in front of the fireplace. They were the oldest friends he had in the world; Malcolm, of course, and former Special Air Service Colonel Paddy McBride.

"I had a funny feeling that as soon as he and I parted this afternoon, Malcolm would jump on the phone with you, Paddy. I heard you just got back from Zimbabwe."

The highly decorated British soldier stood north of six foot five and, silhouetted against the McClain fireplace, looked every bit as fit as when he had first met and trained Chez in Semic, Yugoslavia.

"It is really good to see you both; it has been too long. I am spending the night here at Malcolm's, so I brought a special bottle of twenty-five year-old Bushmills with me. This fine whiskey went into the cask just about the time we were having our little tête-à-tête with Adolf and Sir Winston. The three of us are going to sip it for inspiration while we strategize what the hell is going on here. You are not going off without a plan, Chez and that's a direct order." The big man glowered at Chez as he uttered this ultimatum and the Spider, in return replied by smiling and shaking his hand.

The Spider was not afraid of anybody, not even McBride, a man awarded the Distinguished Service Order four times for meritorious service under fire during the war as he commanded the Special Air Service. After he retired ten years ago, McBride founded Black Widows Security, a very private organization consisting of former Special Forces operatives. B.W.S. now protected individuals, corporations and even small countries in every corner of the world. No, the Spider was not afraid of McBride but he was smart enough to realize that fate had just put a very potent arrow into his quiver.

The bottle was finished by midnight but the plan was formulated long before that.

"Clearly, the person with the most motivation to catch the bombers is Barry McKenna. He lost a daughter and will not sleep until justice is served. Have either of you talked with him?"

"I tried, Paddy, but he is grief stricken. Just a matter of time 'til that grief ramps up into fury," Chez said.

"I think you are right, Chez, and all the more reason why we should keep an eye on him. I am going to set up a meeting between Barry and the three of us. B.W.S. will secure a location and I'll request the Royal Ulster Constabulary and the British Army to leave us alone. In the meantime, I am going to call our friends at MI5 and MI6; my gut tells me this might be much bigger than a parochial Belfast affair. When Chez allowed his nom de guerre to be used to promote the academy, you both knew full and well that it might prove irresistible bait to some of the unsavory characters he might have pissed off in the past."

All four men agreed that the Crown Bar on Great Victoria Street was an acceptable venue for their meeting. As the most famous bar in Belfast, McKenna agreed that the more public the location, the safer McBride, Orlowski, McClain and himself would be. Colonel McBride gave personal assurances that the Royal Ulster Constabulary and the British Army had orders directly from Whitehall that Barry McKenna, the most wanted man in the Province, had total immunity for twenty-four hours.

The inside of the mightiest Victorian gin palace in Britain had ten private seating areas called 'snugs' that allowed total privacy to patrons who preferred to do their drinking in secret. Even the waiters could not see the occupants, as orders were placed on a circular tray with a central divider that revolved from the snug into the central service walkway.

For five hundred pounds cash, the owners of the bar agreed to evacuate the inside of the Crown for one hour. Black Widows Security performed a thorough sweep and the four men were ushered in and left to their own devices. On the table in the middle of Snug A was a bottle of Black Bush, courtesy of the management.

"Are you carrying, Barry?"

"Too fuckin right, Paddy, how's about yous'uns?"

"Of course…."

"….For the record, I am not," interrupted Malcolm, "And I feel bloody naked!"

"Barry, we appreciate you giving us this chance

to talk. Chez and Malcolm feel as though Siobhán was one of their own and, along with me, we will do everything in our power to find out who planned the bombing and bring them to justice."

"Fuck justice, Paddy. I find them, they're dead. You find them, you tell me and I'll kill them. Can we all agree on that?" The voice of the commander of the Belfast Brigade rose in volume, full of emotion. As soon as he had finished the tirade, McBride attempted to calm things down.

"Barry, how is your wife, Sinead, handling the situation?" McBride asked.

"Well, she was not the woman who gave birth to my daughter but since we adopted Siobhán at the age of three months, you would never know. Right now, she is inconsolable. God knows what Siobhán's natural mother is going through." Paddy, Chez and Malcolm all winced at the thought.

"What's the word on the street? Have you got any leads at all as to who these bastards are?"

"Well, I'm certain the bomb was not ours. We have a list of protected subjects and the Spider Academy is on that list. Besides, the Provos do not use fertilizer any more. I thinkin' it must have been George McFadden and his bloody UVF because they truly are that fuckin' stupid, but on my way to this meeting, I was given a tip that might hold the truth."

"AND?" the three friends asked as they leaned forward.

"That is for me to know and for youse to find out."

CHAPTER TWENTY-FOUR

The Back-up Strategy

Hans von Keller and his staffeln caught Walter McCoubrey's revelation on *Scene Around Six*, as they were playing cards in the main dining room of Gortlee Castle. Von Keller stared at the file photographs the BBC used when referring to Orlowski and McClain and then blew up in indignation. In addition, an early news crew was able to get brief footage of Orlowski as he talked in the background to an ambulance crew.

"Gott im Himmel, after all the money we have invested, those clowns did not even bother to check if Orlowski was in the building?"

"Where the hell is Rudy? He never did come back from the meeting with that Mulcahy character. How fucking ironic if the Fenian Brotherhood killed the man who funded them and then lets the target get away." Von Keller paused, fuming.

"Okay, gentlemen, time to turn in and get some rest," von Keller said finally. "Tomorrow at dawn, we are going to practice our back-up plan. I am declaring Rudy Gomez as MIA, so we will need to borrow three of Herr Schmidt's cars to get us in and out of Belfast. I don't want to use the rental VWs on this mission as they might draw unwanted attention."

When they trained for this mission in Köln, von Keller's staffeln had never liked the idea of the primary attempt on the Spider's life being conducted by an untested third party. Now that the Fenian Brotherhood had failed so miserably, they welcomed the opportunity to implement their back-up strategy.

Their background research indicated that the McClains had two children and the Orlowskis, nine. These children ranged from an infant to four young adults who attended the Queen's University of Belfast. Their plan would be to kidnap one of the three Orlowski daughters and transport her back to Letterkenny to serve as bait. Then they could threaten to kill her unless the Spider came to Gortlee Castle, unarmed and alone.

The most likely target was identified as Teréska

Orlowski, the eldest daughter of whom the Spider was known to be particularly fond. She was the same age as Janna McClain and the two girls were inseparable. Furthermore, the staffeln knew that both girls attended Belfast Royal Academy and went home together every day by taking a ten-minute walk to the Spider Academy. They decided to kidnap both girls rather than waste time trying to identify which one was the Spider's offspring.

The three vehicles crossed the international border at different locations and regrouped in the parking lot behind McAleer's Bar in Dungannon. This put them no more than an hour outside Belfast, so they decided to grab a quick lunch. As they were eating, one of the men asked, "Hans, those idiots from Derry destroyed the Spider Academy yesterday. Why would the two girls walk there anymore?" This simple revelation stunned the neo-Nazi.

"Mein Gott, you are right, how could we be so stupid? After what just happened, we don't know if they will even be attending school this week," replied von Keller. "However, we've come this far, so let's use today to practice in the field. There's always an outside chance that a grab and go opportunity might present itself if we compare any students we see with the girls' school photos. We'll stay overnight in Belfast and use today and tomorrow to reconnoiter." Lunch continued in silence, von Keller furious at himself.

Their careful rehearsals of the kidnapping would now require a certain amount of adlibbing, something he despised.

The next rendezvous was to be less than half a mile from the high school, in a large parking lot on the corner of North Queen's Street and Brougham Street. After the third car arrived and rolled to a halt, von Keller rallied his troops around a street map spread across the bonnet of his vehicle.

"We are going to split into four groups; one watching the school's front entrance on Cliftonville Road, the second covering the rear on the Antrim Road. I want a third group monitoring certain trains leaving from York Road Station; a train departs for Jordanstown every 30 minutes and it is now the most logical way for the girls to go home—if they are even attending today. Fritz and I will walk from the Spider Academy towards the school. You all have the photographs and only need concentrate on fifteen-year-old girls with long blonde hair who are wearing the school uniform of grey skirts and navy blue blazers. If any group identifies the girls, one follows, the others get word back to the rest so we can coordinate a point of convergence.

"The school day ends about thirty minutes from now, so let's plan on meeting back at the cars at around half past four if the girls cannot be identified. Good luck, we are going to need it."

And as luck would have it, the Antrim Road group positively identified Teréska and Janna from the photographs within minutes. In addition, both carried Spider Academy backpacks with their surnames embroidered on the top flap.

The two girls were giggling about boys and the Beatles as they turned east onto Duncairn Gardens, stopping to buy Lucozade and Maynards wine gums at a small newsagents.

"Pietr, find the men watching the front of the school tell them to get back to the cars. I believe these girls are on their way to the train station, which means they will be passing where we parked in perhaps ten minutes! Friedrick, I will follow them from behind but I think you should cross the street and see if you can intercept Hans. He and Fritz should be walking towards us."

The girls continued to giggle their way towards York Road station at a frustratingly slow pace. They stopped for the pedestrian crossing signal at North Queen Street and Franz Meyer stood right behind them as part of a small group of pedestrians gathered to wait for the traffic light to turn red. He could make out his staffeln's three vehicles parked in the southeast parking lot and saw four of his comrades loitering on the other side of the street. A low voice whispered in his ear; it was von Keller.

"Well done, Franz, we might be home for dinner after all."

Barry McKenna was getting up to leave the Crown Bar when he heard the side door of the bar open and the sound of feet hurrying in towards the snug. He reached under his jacket but McBride's massive left hand immobilized him.

"Hold it right there, Barry. You must trust me in this or you will never live to see your daughter's killers. What is it, Frank?"

"A group of men have kidnapped Janna McClain and Teréska Orlowski. There was a bunch of them and onlookers reported that they seemed highly organized, almost like a Special Forces team. Apparently, they must have known the girls' route because they were lying in wait just before they reached York Road station. They had the girls hooded, gagged and in their vehicles before anyone could react. It was over in seconds but not before one of the girls kicked an assailant in the shin. One witness said he yelled Chrysler or something and had to be assisted into the car."

There was a shocked silence in the Crown Bar as

those present tried to digest this terrifying news. But, the stillness was broken by a menacing conclusion with a Polish accent.

"When they bombed the academy, they were not trying to kill Siobhán and the other kids, they were coming after me. And I am betting the word the kidnapper yelled was not that of a car, it was scheiße; the German for shit.

"Barry, I am only going to ask you once. Tell me all about the tip you mentioned?" The Spider leveled his cold stare at the IRA leader.

McKenna, a man who had spent most of his adult life fighting fearlessly for a united Ireland, took one look at the Spider and decided to err on the side of prudence. He sucked in a deep breath and told everything he knew.

"Chez, the Provos are divided into several brigades. Each commander called me within twenty-four hours of Siobhán's murder to assure me that their men had no involvement with the bombing and to offer me their support. However, Padraig O'Hanlon, a good friend of mine who leads the South Derry Brigade, shared that he's been getting a bunch of shit from the Fenian Brotherhood recently and warned me that they could go rogue at any time."

"The Fenian Brotherhood," said Paddy. "I thought that group faded away before the turn of the century!"

"They surely did but when the official IRA left us

high and dry a couple of years ago, I helped form the provisional IRA to protect fellow Catholics living in the Bogside. The South Derry Brigade elected Padraig as their commander but a fat drunken eejit called Brendan Mulcahy got really pissed off when he was passed over. He and a couple of goons formed their own splinter group and decided to call themselves the Fenian Brotherhood."

"So what evidence do you have that Mulcahy might be responsible for the bombing?"

"Up until a few months ago, Mulcahy and his thugs, Micky Tobin and Colm O'Shaughnessy, were hitting everyone up for drinkin' money. Then, all of a sudden, they must have come into a ton of dosh because Mulcahy began sporting a solid gold Rolex. They were known to be buying all sorts of weapons and explosives and began lobbying Padraig to go on the offensive against the R.U.C. Nobody could figure out if they had robbed a bank or got real lucky at the horses but something or somebody changed their lifestyle for sure."

Having listened to Paddy and Barry talk for several minutes, Chez Orlowski did what he did best; he made a calm, calculated assessment of the situation.

"The bombing of the academy was sloppy and amateurish. Any professional would have made absolutely certain that I was inside the building. Even so, I might still have survived the blast by sheer bloody luck. Do you remember the assassination attempt on Hitler at Wolfsschanze? A sturdy table leg deflected the blast and saved his life.

"On the other hand, this recent kidnapping of our daughters is reported as being very professional—which leads me to believe that the two incidents were by entirely different groups."

McBride jumped in with his own thoughts. "Let's run with your thesis for now, Chez. I'll elaborate by speculating that a group of trained professionals is after your arse but they paid some locals to do their dirty work so they could watch from the sidelines and escape culpability. When the attempt failed due to abject stupidity, they stepped it up several notches. How does that sound?"

"It could sound a little paranoid, until you factor in all the people I have pissed off in my life. The most likely suspects would have to be Russians or Nazis, with the Nazis in strong command of pole position."

"Remember that fake Spanish count that Inspector Larkin unmasked? Why did you suspect he was a Nazi, Chez?" Malcolm asked.

"I spent a long time in labor camps run by those bastards. My antennae goes on full alert when they come near me, Malky."

Chez turned back to McKenna.

"Barry, would you be willing to go to Derry and find out if there is any truth to Mulcahy's involvement?"

"I will be there as soon as we attend Siobhán's funeral, assuming Paddy gets me out of this bar and back to the Markets without the R.U.C. claiming their bounty!"

"I know it is asking a lot, but could you hand him over to me for questioning if the lead proves to be good?" Paddy asked, though he fully anticipated McKenna's answer.

"If the lead proves good, Paddy, there'll be nothing to hand over."

CHAPTER TWENTY-FIVE

Love Is an Island

Rudy and Mary discovered they were hopelessly in love with each other. Their night of passion at the Belfray County Inn had not afforded either much sleep. They held each other close and talked until spontaneous lovemaking took over. The cycle repeated several times until Rudy laughed, "My sweet, sweet, Mary, why don't we have a shower and go downstairs for breakfast. How long can you stay here with me? I don't want you to leave, ever."

"Then book the room for a year. I don't want to leave either."

Although only three miles from Londonderry, the Inn was buffered by rolling fields, the grass kept as short as a golf fairway by sheep and the air cleansed by northerly breezes off the Atlantic Ocean as it joined the Irish Sea. After breakfast, the two escaped humanity by walking for miles through the beautiful countryside, their hands never separating.

"Tell me more about your family, Rudy, and what you did growing up."

"Well, sweetheart, before and during the last war, my father was a very powerful man in the Nazi Party who treated my mother, Gerda, as nothing more than a baby machine. I was one of ten children but the physical toll must have been enormous and she died of uterine cancer in Austria on March 23, 1946. She suffered for many months but still managed to evacuate me and my seven surviving brothers and sisters out of Berlin to Wolkenstein before the final defeat.

"I grew up in awe of my father's power but remember quite clearly that my siblings all blamed him for causing Mother's death. Luckily, we were adopted by a compassionate Catholic priest, Father Timothy…." Rudy paused to wipe a tear from his cheek so Mary picked up the conversation to allow him to regroup.

"I was named after my mother. She was very beautiful and worked the Dublin theatre scene as an actress. Men were her weakness and when I was about fifteen, she met a rich American and disappeared off to Boston with him. I have never heard from her since. My father, an engineer, was devastated. He brought up my younger brother and me on his own for a couple of years until the two of them were killed in a car crash on Christmas Eve, 1956. My whole world shattered and after the funeral, I fled Dublin and moved to Derry to live with my late Aunty Lucy; I was seventeen and very vulnerable. When's your birthday, my love?"

"I was born in Berlin on the last day of August, 1933. How about you?"

"You not going to believe it but I am EXACTLY six years younger than you. We share a birthday so we must be meant for each other. Sounds like both our families fell apart so I'm truly fascinated to hear more about yours." Then she paused and bit her lip. Rudy showed concern, asking if there was a problem.

"My darling, there is something in my past that I must tell you about." They stopped walking, Rudy held her close and whispered, "You can tell me anything; nothing can affect my love for you."

"Just after I moved to Derry, I fell in love with a married man twelve years older than me; I believe I must have been seeking a father figure in my life. I was careless, became pregnant and we had a little girl. His understanding wife asked me if they could adopt the child and I agreed. She is enjoying a much better life than I could ever have given her; all the best schools, holidays abroad and such. I do get to see her every year on my birthday and I could not receive a more precious present. She calls me Aunty Mary and her Mum and

Dad come up to Derry for the day and let me have lunch alone with her. We have spent several of those birthdays in the Roof Top Restaurant at Austins."

Mary wiped away her tears and sought comfort. "Rudy, you are the first man I have truly loved since then. Please don't break my heart."

"I would kill myself first. I am looking forward to meeting your daughter and perhaps we can celebrate our first birthdays together by both taking her to lunch.

"Now it is my turn to tell a dark family secret; one which you must never repeat to anyone. The world believes my father died as he tried to escape from Berlin in 1945. The devious bastard wrote the entire script and planted sufficient evidence to satisfy the Allied Press. As you now probably realize, the Waterford crystal I bought when I first met you was for him. Today he lives in secrecy on a ranch in Argentina that is the size of an Irish county. He might very well be the richest man in the world, but as he approaches his eighties, diabetes is slowly ravaging him.

"To this day he remains a fanatical anti-Semite, an extreme racist beyond anything you could possibly comprehend. I have grown to hate my own father and everything he stands for. With all the evil he has spawned, I pray for the day when God takes him from this earth."

"Do any of your brothers and sisters live with you and your father?"

"No, Mary, I am the only stupid one. My oldest brother, Martin, is an ordained Catholic priest; the rest either have died, or are living in hiding from my father. It has been exceedingly difficult for me to find the courage to break away from his tentacles but falling in love with you has strengthened my resolve to disappear and never return to Argentina."

"That is very sad, Rudy," Mary said. After a respectful pause she added, "Let's head back to the hotel and have a drink. I pretty sure I can make you forget about all your family problems before we have dinner."

Dinner at the hotel was excellent and a small Ceili band entertained the thirty or so guests. It was close to eleven o'clock when they returned to the bedroom.

Mary laughed as soon as they stepped into the room. "Oh my gosh, it looks like a hurricane hit this bed. You use the bathroom first and I'll try to tidy up this mess." Despite his objections, she started picking up the bedclothes from the floor in a futile attempt to return the room to some semblance of order. Rudy was in the bathroom loading his toothbrush when he heard the television announcing the late night news.

"A massive car bomb destroyed the Blundell paint store on York Road today. The explosion happened at quarter past one this afternoon and caused extensive damage to the Spider Academy directly across the street." Rudy came back into the bedroom, his ears alerted by the words 'Spider Academy.' Mary O'Connell sat on the edge of the bed, eyes transfixed on the screen with both hands pressed against her cheeks.

"The blast ignited hundreds of gallons of paint and the fire quickly spread to the academy. The owners of the Spider Academy, war heroes Malcolm McClain and Chez Orlowski, returned from a lunch meeting to find their establishment an inferno. Despite this, both men broke through police lines to search for survivors. They managed to rescue two of their students from the blaze but the death toll has currently risen to five: Billy Scott, a gymnastics instructor and four students.

"Earlier this evening, on *Scene Around Six's* Walter McCoubrey reported the identity of one of the children as twelve-year old Siobhán McKenna, only child of the infamous IRA commander, Barry McKenna...."

"....OH MY GOD, THEY HAVE KILLED MY DAUGHTER," screamed Mary as Rudy lunged forward and tried to wrap his arms around her.

Mary was in a state of shock and she sobbed for hours before finally falling asleep from exhaustion but Rudy Gomez was not as fortunate. His mind, riddled with guilt, ruminated on the incredible stupidity of his actions.

I should have never have returned to Argentina after I first came here. From the moment I laid eyes on Mary, I knew she was the one. How could I have been so irresponsible? To hell with my father and his evil games. When Mary finds out what I have done, she will never, ever forgive me. He tossed and turned, trying to think about anything but Mary's grief. As penance, his mind tortured him by replaying the tragedy over and over and over.

Mary stirred at dawn and noticed him staring at the ceiling. "Rudy, my love, I am going to get dressed and drive back to Derry. I need to contact the McKennas and attend the funeral; I have to pay my respects and see Siobhán's body. I do love you very much but I need some time by myself right now. Will you please, please contact me before you leave Ireland?"

Rudy got out of the bed and knelt in front Mary. He held both her hands in his and started to cry as he poured out the confession of his involvement in the bombing. Her mouth fell open in shock at what she heard.

"I have decided to drive down to Belfast as soon as you leave here. I will surrender myself to the R.U.C. as an accomplice and offer my full assistance in bringing the Fenian Brotherhood to justice. I will not seek any mercy, so this might be the last time I ever see your beautiful face.

"I desperately need you to believe two things: Yes, I ordered a man's death on behalf of my father but not for a second did I think those bastards would kill innocent children. I will go to hell for that. Lastly, I sincerely love you with all my heart and soul and beg your forgiveness, if that is even possible."

Mary turned her back on him and walked to the window where she stared silently over the fields for what seemed like an eternity. When she finally turned back to Rudy her countenance had changed to one of determination, her emerald eyes flashing as if they were shards of flint.

"You are not going to Belfast without me. Now that you've told me who the true villains are, we'll avenge Siobhán together; you do it your way, I'll do it mine."

With an apology to the management sweetened by five, twenty-pound notes, Rudy left the VW Square-back and contents in the parking lot of the Belfray County Inn, saying he would return for it in a couple of weeks. He took the keys of Mary's much smaller 1966 Hillman Imp and the two emotionally damaged lovers drove down to Belfast.

The drive, which would take them about two hours, had started in awkward silence until Mary patted him on the arm, and gave him a weak smile.

"I spoke to the manager at Austins. He had heard about Siobhán and wasn't expecting me in this week anyway......"

"Mary, I feel terrible right now. I was planning on asking you to marry me and the two of us running away to a place my father could never find us...."

"...Then why don't you ask me?"

"Because I am going to jail for a very long time and I could not do that to you..."

"...If you don't go to jail, will you ask me?"

Rudy pulled over to the left shoulder of the road, switched the engine off and gathered Mary into his arms. He kissed her and cried at the same time. There was no sexual tension or anticipation; both realized the kiss symbolized their pure love for each other.

"Here, hold onto this cheque, it is endorsed payable to Mary O'Connell. I want you to use the money to build a new life for yourself. If I ever get through this, I want to be part of that life—if you still want me."

When they entered Belfast from the north, Rudy fished in his pocket for a business card he had kept since his last visit. Handing it over to Mary, he kept his eyes on the road and asked, "Any idea where Knock is, Mary?"

"Easy to tell you're not from these parts," she commented dryly. "The Parliament buildings are at Stormont and you have to go through Knock to get there. It is on the other side of the Lagan so we'd best to go to the city center and look for signs."

After a further forty minutes negotiating Belfast heavy traffic, the Hillman Imp pulled into a parking lot in front of the Royal Constabulary Headquarters in Knock. Rudy and Mary got out and they walked together towards the security checkpoint.

"Give me just a minute, Mary, I'd like to fill my lungs with fresh air before they shackle me in chains."

She grabbed his hand. "Try to keep faith, Rudy and remember, I love you."

Hand in hand, they went into the station and stood at the receptionist's desk.

"Inspector William Larkin, please," Rudy said.

"And who may I say is here to see him?" Rudy hesitated and raised his eyebrows at Mary.

"Please tell him it is Rafael de Maldà, baron de Cortada."

Five minutes later, Bill Larkin walked into the reception area and, ignoring the young couple seated there, began to look around for his appointment. Rudy stood up.

"Inspector Larkin, I am the person you met in the manager's office of the Grand Central Hotel just over three years ago. However, I am not, nor ever was, the Spanish count I pretended to be. My legal name is Rudy Gomez and I live in Argentina. May I introduce my dear friend, Mary O'Connell."

"Please follow me to the conference room, Mr. Gomez. We have a lot to talk about. I will be asking a stenographer to join us. Do you wish to retain counsel?"

Foremost on the Inspector's mind was his open file on the death of Manuel Sanchez. Not only did a stenographer and her stenotype join them in the conference room, Larkin waited until two burly officers were in place before he began the proceedings. He read Rudy his rights and opened with,

"Mr. Gomez, I have in my possession, conclusive evidence that you and your two associates, Franco Ramos and Lucas Romero, were responsible for the death of Manuel Sanchez, a bartender in this city, during the early morning hours of May 12, 1967. I have forensic evidence, including a positive match between the murderer's blood-soaked clothes, specifically his belt buckle, and the three glasses you were kind enough to leave me in Mr. O'Malley's office. Interpol exposed your false identity and an International Warrant for your arrest is outstanding. What sayeth thou?"

Rudy had confessed all to Mary as they drove from County Londonderry but she was nonetheless shaken by the gravity and extent of her lover's criminal past.

"Inspector, my trip to Belfast in 1967 was an elaborate ruse financed by my father to confirm that Mr. Chez Orlowski and the person known to him as 'the Spider' were one and the same. The Spider and my father are archenemies despite never having met, but that is a completely separate story.

"I had absolutely nothing to do with the murder of Mr. Sanchez. As you are no doubt aware, I attended a charity event on the evening in question and sat beside Mr. Malcolm McClain, Mr. Orlowski's business partner in the academy. When Mr. McClain invited me to meet Mr. Orlowski, I saw it as a perfect way to accomplish my mission and report my findings back to my father in Argentina. It was not until the next morning that my servants, Franco Ramos and Lucas Romero, confessed they had murdered a bartender. I accept responsibility for lying to you in the cover-up and consequently understand that I am an accessory to the murder. I will provide international authorities with their current whereabouts in the hope that the courts might take my cooperation into consideration."

"Can you tell me their motive in killing Mr. Sanchez?"

"Sir, they are rogue gauchos but essentially simple-minded men who understood that my father, their boss, had gone to considerable trouble to disguise the fact that we were from Argentina. Mr. Sanchez apparently identified their Patagonian accents while they were having drinks in the Orpheus Ballroom that evening. They panicked and made a very, very bad judgment call."

"But that is not the reason you are here, is it?" asked the shrewd inspector. "And if I may, Miss O'Connell, what is your role in all this?"

"Inspector Lar..." Rudy started.

"Please, I would prefer to hear directly from the young lady."

Mary took a deep breath to control her emotions.

"Rudy and I met in 1967 when he first visited Derry. We have corresponded and he contrived this current visit to meet up with me. We have since fallen in love and still hope to marry despite recent circumstances."

"And what might those be, Miss O'Connell?"

"Yesterday's bombing of the Spider Academy. We drove here from Derry after we saw it on the tele last night...... Oh my God, I can't do this, Rudy." Mary covered her face with her hands.

"I am not fully understanding you, Miss O'Connell." Mary started to shake, then looked up and bravely continued.

"Inspector, I am the natural birth mother of Siobhán McKenna, one of the children killed in the collapse of the building." She started to sob and Rudy put his arm around her. With all the resolve he could muster, Rudy Gomez looked the inspector squarely in the eye.

"And I am an indirect cause of those deaths, Inspector. I will give you a full confession of my involvement but need your assurance that Mary will be treated courteously. She had absolutely no knowledge of my involvement until last night."

"My dear sir, you cannot come into my office, admit to your involvement in multiple murders and then ask me for assurances about anything.

"Rudy Gomez, you are hereby remanded in custody. Mary O'Connell, you are free to go but do not leave Belfast without asking my permission. I highly recommend The Wellington Park Hotel on the Malone Road. My sincere condolences for your loss."

As Rudy left Larkin's office in handcuffs the inspector offered the distraught Mary O'Connell a cup of tea and thought to himself, *I must say I did not see this coming, but a whole bunch of my loose ends just disappeared at one fell swoop!*

CHAPTER TWENTY-SIX

Payback Is a Bitch

At eleven o'clock closing time, Brendan Mulcahy, Michael Tobin and Colm O'Shaughnessy were wrapping up a typical evening of heavy drinking at their local pub in the Bogside. The three men eventually staggered out into the cold night air and headed towards their homes. A dirty, dark blue Ford Transit van was parked with two wheels on the pavement, leaving them barely three feet to shuffle by in single file. The side sliding door was open and a voice from within called out as Mulcahy drew level.

"I'd like a word, Brendan. Please, get in the van." As drunk as he was, the leader of the Fenian Brotherhood noticed that two rather large men had blocked his alternative exits along the pedestrian route.

Brendan thought he recognized the voice of the South Derry Brigade commander and casually moved his right hand towards his belt.

"Is it yerself, Padraig?"

"Indeed it is, Brendan, but please keep your hands where I can see them. Better still, if you, Michael and Colm would please clasp your fingers behind your heads, my men will look after your weapons so any accidents don't happen to interrupt our little chat." The big men flattened all three Fenian Brothers stomach-first against the side of the van and tied loops of fishing line around their thumbs, looping the free end of the line around the back of each man's belt. After they were frisked, the three were helped into the rear of the van, the door secured and the two muscle men got into the front seats.

"Well, it seems like you lads have been trying to make your own political statement down in Belfast…"

"Don't know what the fuck you are talking about. Where the hell are you taking us?"

"That's for me to know and you to find out."

The three captives could not see much through the front window of the van but could certainly tell when they crossed over the Craigavon Bridge, as it is famous for its unusual double-decker design. They continued in silence for another twenty minutes, finally coming to a halt in front of the abandoned

Ballykelly railway station on the south shore of Lough Foyle. Everyone exited the van and the three men all begged to be able to relieve themselves.

"I am not releasing any hands and definitely not going to hold any cocks, so you must own that Guinness for a while longer," said O'Hanlon before adding, "We have a special guest who would like to ask you some questions." A dark car, already parked at the side of the disused brick building, suddenly turned on its headlights to illuminate the group. The prisoners were looking straight into the lights as the newcomer got out and slammed his driver's door closed. His black silhouette moved towards them and they could tell the man had something in his hand that looked like a soup can on a stick. He stopped about five feet in front of Colm O'Shaughnessy and shot him in the right kneecap. PHUTT. O'Shaughnessy went down to the ground squealing in pain so O'Hanlon and his men rushed over to shut him up.

The drama was repeated with Micky Tobin. PHUTT. The sound from the silenced automatic resembled an angry release of compressed air and served to terrify Brendan Mulcahy. Every ounce of Guinness he had drunk that night poured through his trousers and onto the ground.

"Who the hell are you?" whimpered Mulcahy, frantic fear causing his voice to crack. The man turned so that his victim could see his face.

"I am Barry McKenna and you murdered my only child."

"That's a fuckin' lie, I recognize who you are but I've never even met your kid."

"I didn't say you met her but you sure as bloody hell killed her. On your knees, you lying bastard." Mulcahy was now crying as his alcohol-addled brain tried to search for who might have betrayed him.

"Three years ago, you accepted a load of dosh from a South American cunt called Rudy Gomez, money that could have helped a whole bunch of republican sympathizers through these rough times. By rights, that money should have been handed over to the South Derry Brigade to help defend the Bogside, yet you chose to spend it on drink and jewelry for yourself. This mysterious moneyman returned a couple of days ago and gave you even more money. This time, he asked you to assassinate a good Catholic man in Belfast. Yet again, you did it half-assed. As a result, children died, including my daughter, Siobhán.

"The person you tried to kill is Chez Orlowski and he happens to be a personal friend of mine; has been for several years. His daughter and her friend were kidnapped yesterday. On his behalf and against my better judgment, tell me where you are hiding these girls and you can live."

"All bloody lies, I never met any South American and never got any money. I don't know anything about a kidnapping and never went to Belfast," he spewed defiantly. "Who fed you this pile of shite?"

"Mary O'Connell, who happens to be my daughter Siobhán's mother. She knows this Gomez character and drove down to Belfast with him this afternoon. She came by the house to see my wife and myself, pay her respects and fill me in on your involvement. I drove straight here to ask you a simple question but if I don't get some fuckin' cooperation, I am going to waste your sorry arse. Last chance, where are the two girls?"

The resigned look on Brendan Mulcahy's face said it all and he hung his head and said nothing more.

"As for not getting any money! Padraig, rip that gold fuckin' Rolex off his wrist and shove it in his mouth. I hope he fuckin' chokes on it." O'Hanlon complied and then gagged Mulcahy to make sure he could not spit it out.

"I am not letting the three of youse die easy. Siobhán died a horrible death; that sweet innocent darlin' child asphyxiated on smoke and then burned. You fuckin' eejits are going for a short boat trip on the Lough. Unfortunately, the boat's drain plug is missing so I doubt yous'll even make it halfway across. When you go under, the longer you hold your breath, the longer you will have to beg forgiveness to my angel, Siobhán's sweet, innocent face."

McKenna nodded at one of his men, who dragged Mulcahy to his feet by his collar.

PHUTT. McKenna blew off Mulcahy's left kneecap before all three Fenian Brothers were unceremoniously dumped into the small skiff, Mulcahy screaming the entire time. The trolling motor spluttered into life after three tugs on the starting rope, and O'Hanlon assisted the boat into waist deep water before giving it a final push. When it was just a dark shadow in Lough Foyle, the men on the shore heard sounds of distant, frantic splashing. Then all went still.

"It must be very hard to swim when you cannot use your arms or your legs," mused O'Hanlon.

"Ah well, there y'are now," agreed McKenna as he got into his car and returned to Belfast.

Colm O'Shaughnessy tried to use his good foot to staunch the cold water as it gushed unhindered through the drain hole in the rear of the boat. The skiff had close to a foot of water slurping around in it by the time he saw the lights of McKenna's car backing away from the railway station.

"Micky, can you hear me?" Tobin responded with a groan. "Listen, I need you to find a way to undo my belt so I can slip my hands back over my head. Come on, man, we don't have more than a few minutes." Tobin fought the pain in his leg and used his teeth and tongue to unbuckle O'Shaughnessy's belt. With extraordinary effort, he bit down on the silver buckle and pulled the leather through the trouser belt loops. Colm felt the fishing line release and was now able to get his own hands into a position where he could use his teeth to gnaw through the nylon loop around his thumbs.

"I'll repeat the favor, Micky but first, I have to jamb my sock into that bloody drain hole to try and stop us sinking."

The boat was now floundering close to the middle of Lough Foyle, the small trolling motor losing its fight against the current from the river. It seemed inevitable that they would be flushed out to sea when Colm and Micky finally noticed that Brendan Mulcahy was slumped, unmoving, in the prow.

"Better check him out, Micky, his head's completely under water." At this point, they had to be very careful, their mobility was restricted by their injuries and the boat had only two or three inches of freeboard left. Their situation was fast approaching catastrophe as the sock began to fail in its valiant attempt to become a drain plug.

"Jeezus, I think Brendan's dead, Colm. His eyes are open but when I let his head go back under water, there were no bubbles."

"Well, the bastard must weigh close to twenty stone. Tossing his body overboard might give you and me a chance to make it over to Moville. Check him again."

When Micky removed the gag, he discovered that Mulcahy had probably choked on the massive gold Rolex. He fished the watch out of the dead man's mouth and surreptitiously slipped it into his own pocket. It took O'Shaughnessy and Tobin the best part of five minutes to position their backs against the port side, using their good legs to ease Mulcahy's rotund corpse over the starboard gunwale. Trying to maintain the center of gravity was an extremely delicate task but with one last push, the leader of the Fenian Brotherhood plopped into the dark waters of Lough Foyle. O'Shaughnessy and Tobin rapidly scurried into the middle to prevent the boat from capsizing. The dead body reappeared as a bobbing black mass as the lightened boat spluttered away.

Both survivors noticed the beam of Moville lighthouse to starboard and steered the skiff towards the small harbor of the Donegal town.

"Colm, we will most likely walk with limps for the rest of our lives but at least we made it. I don't know about you but I have a list of people in my head and I'll be payin' them all a wee visit when the time is right."

"I am with you on that, Micky."

CHAPTER TWENTY-SEVEN

Do Not Mess with the Big Man

E arly the next morning, Malcolm McClain and Chez Orlowski pulled into the parking lot of the R.U.C. headquarters in Knock just as Paddy McBride was getting out of his Land Rover.

"What is Bill Larkin up to, Paddy? He sounded very mysterious on the phone," Malcolm said.

"Damned if I know but it sounded urgent. Keep your voices down, we've got company." A white Hillman Imp pulled up and parked beside the Land Rover. A young woman climbed out of the car, her face a mask of tension. She moved swiftly past them towards the front door.

McClain turned to his friend in shock and whispered, "My God, Chez, if I didn't know better, I'd swear that could be Siobhán's elder sister."

Inspector Larkin was waiting for them in reception as the three old friends entered together.

"Thank you for coming at such short notice. We are going to be meeting in my conference room and I need to apprise you of some strict rules. You will be introduced to the man who was responsible for the academy bombing." This revelation caused raised eyebrows and a sharp intake of breath. "He is under armed guard and will remain my prisoner until he is formally charged and brought to trial. I must ask you to give me your word that you will respect my custody and not, I repeat not, attempt to kill him on these premises."

"How about off these premises, Inspector?" hissed the Spider without a trace of humor. At that point, the young woman they had observed in the parking lot emerged from the bathroom. She had obviously been crying.

"Gentlemen, allow me to introduce Miss Mary O'Connell. Her daughter was one of those killed as a result of the bombing."

"Siobhán," Malcolm whispered softly as he turned to her. "Miss O'Connell, words cannot express how much everyone at our academy loved your daughter."

Mary nodded silent acknowledgement of his statement.

Rudy Gomez sat alone on the long side of a conference table that faced the group as they entered. Both his arms were handcuffed to his chair and towering over him were two R.U.C. sergeants, bulked up with flak jackets. Slung under each officer's right arm was a matte black Sterling SMG and they stared imperiously at the new arrivals.

"Well, well, last time we met, you were pretending to be a Spanish count. What is it today, Raphael? No matter what you tell me, I smell a Nazi lurking under the surface." Rudy was completely taken aback by the Spider's direct approach but had already decided to tell the truth, no matter what.

"Mr. Orlowski, my legal name is Rudy Gomez and I live in Argentina with my father, former Reichsleiter Martin Bormann."

McBride whistled softly. *This is going to be interesting. The Spider will probably try to kill him right here in the inspector's office. Should I try to stop him or not? Difficult choice!*

Once everyone had recovered from that revelation, they sat down and the inspector cleared his throat.

"First of all, I would like you to know that Mr. Gomez surrendered himself and has been quite forthcoming. I do believe that you will leave this room with a better understanding of recent events. However, before I regurgitate his testimony, I must ask Mr. Gomez about a new turn of events.

"Sir, can you shed any light on the recent kidnapping of Mr. McClain and Mr. Orlowski's teenage daughters?"

Gomez hung his head and pondered his new misery before speaking.

Oh my God, can it get any worse? I did not think they would act so quickly after I disappeared. Now Mary is going to hate me even more. He looked up and responded firmly.

"I am going to tell you absolutely everything I know. Martin Bormann is believed to have died in 1945. Obviously, he did not; he escaped to Argentina with half the world's money. I was barely a teenager when I reunited with my father. The man is a paranoid schizophrenic and believes the Spider sabotaged the Third Reich. We happened to notice the Spider Academy press coverage and went to great lengths to disguise our Argentinian connection when we made our first visit to Belfast to check it out. Once Mr. Orlowski had been positively identified as the Spider, and I'm afraid that task was entrusted to me, my father's first choice was to murder him by using a third party with no clue whom they were employed by.

"The Fenian Brotherhood botched up their assignment in catastrophic fashion, so my father's contingency plan is to use Nazi Special Forces to bait the Spider across the border where they will finish the job. A group of ten, highly trained men from Köln is temporarily based at Gortlee Castle in Donegal. I am certain they are the ones who abducted the girls. I doubt they have made it back to *Éire* yet or you would have received a ransom note."

"We locked down the border crossings within thirty minutes of the report. Ten men and two young girls will have problems leaving Northern Ireland. Of course, there are many unmarked roads that might account for delays," Larkin interjected.

Paddy McBride stood up and took charge of the room. His physical presence and unparalleled reputation commanded awe and respect.

"Inspector Larkin, I am going to need an office and a phone. For the sake of our girls' wellbeing, I request that you allow these kidnappers and the girls to make it safely back to Donegal. We get into a firefight en route, there is bound to be collateral damage.

"Malcolm and Chez, I want you both to listen very carefully to this man's story. To me, he does not portray the arrogance of a willing participant yet by all he has revealed; he has been an integral part of some extraordinary bad decisions—to say the least.

"Maybe he has finally grown a pair! By the time he has finished trying to save his soul, I hope to have established a high-level protocol between Whitehall and Dublin. I have a special unit of Black Widows Security based at the Hewlett Packard headquarters in Sligo. They are only 60 miles south of Letterkenny. Once I get clearance, they will chopper in to the Gortlee estate to perform reconnaissance. They might even get there before the Nazis. Anything to add, Chez?"

"These so-called Nazi Special Forces sound like a staffeln; young nitwits who were probably all infants during the war and have spent their entire lives playing soldier to emulate their fathers. I'm going with you to Donegal, Paddy."

"Me too," chimed in McClain.

"I wouldn't have it any other way, wee man. But first, stay and listen to Señor Gomez spill his heart out while I get things organized and Chez, please behave." Paddy stared directly at the Spider and what seemed like an eternity of tension-filled silence, was eventually ended by mutual nods.

"Remember this, you might be Janna and Teréska's dads but you made me godfather to both of them and I take that responsibility very bloody seriously."

It took almost three hours for Rudy to recount everything he remembered. The Spider stared coldly at him the entire time, which made him extremely nervous.

He frequently glanced towards Mary for support but she seemed overwhelmed by the gravitas.

"Okay, Gomez, I have heard enough. I would like to speak privately with Malcolm and Inspector Larkin," Chez said.

Larkin stood up and spoke to the room.

"Miss O'Connell, you may stay but I am instructing the sergeants to make sure you remain on this side of the table. We will return in ten minutes. Gentlemen, let's check on Colonel McBride's progress. Please, follow me."

Paddy was using Bill Larkin's office and had just hung up on a phone conversation when the three men walked in.

"Perfect timing. We have clearance to operate across the border. The Garda is going to supplement our team with three observers, all lads I trained myself so they will be quite useful.

"Our friends from Köln are travelling in a convoy about five miles apart. All three vehicles were allowed to pass through the border crossing outside Castlederg and the guards report that the young girls in the second and third cars did not look distressed in any way. The Garda reports that they re-formed their convoy in Castlefinn and are currently on the Carnowen Road headed for Letterkenny. They should be at Gortlee Castle in about ten minutes.

"A chopper will be here in twenty to take the

three of us to Donegal. Now, what did you learn from Gomez?"

"The man spilled his entire life's story. I almost feel sorry for him—almost. Right now, it all depends on getting Janna and Teréska back safely but I do see some potential opportunities." The Spider's last offhand comment created a great deal of intrigue.

"I believe he has finally found the courage to break away from Martin Bormann's evil influence. Whether he did it of his own free will, from the guilt of killing the children and staff of our academy, or from falling in love with Mary O'Connell, I don't really give a damn, but I do believe he is sincere. His information about the planned attack on the Munich Olympics is much appreciated, especially since I plan to be there with my team. Anything to add, Malcolm, Inspector?" Both men shrugged but said nothing so Chez concluded.

"Inspector, he is your prisoner but could you hold off on any formal charges 'til we get back? Keep him locked up here but let Miss Mary talk to him through the bars on a regular basis. It might encourage his spirit of cooperation so that when we return with our daughters, he might be open to a proposition I would like him to consider."

CHAPTER TWENTY-EIGHT

Just Like Old Times

As the white Alouette III helicopter touched down in the R.U.C. parking lot, the reception committee noticed it had 'Guardians of the Peace' emblazoned in a dark green Gaelic script on the underside of the fuselage. McClain whistled in amazement.

"Nice one, Paddy. How did you swing this little treat?"

"The Irish Air Corps is based at Baldonnel in County Dublin and its boss, Major General Sean O'Leary, trained at Sandhurst with our friend, Brigadier Bryan Zumwalt. This debacle has generated some tremendous heavyweight interest. As soon as I mentioned your daughters were in jeopardy, I think I could have got the whole of bloody NATO to respond."

Inspector Bill Larkin ran out of his building to catch them. "Mr. Orlowski, I'm glad I caught you. Your office manager, Bette Tarleton, called to say that she just received a phone call from the kidnappers. They are demanding that you immediately drive to Gortlee Castle in Donegal. You must come alone because if they detect even the slightest hint of a police presence, they guarantee that they will kill the girls."

Chez and Malcolm exchanged a look.

"One more thing. Gomez volunteered the name of the leader of the staffeln as Hans von Keller. He says you will both remember his father from Maribor. Does that make any sense?"

"Yes it does, Bill, yes it does. Thanks for all your help."

Over the noise of the rotors, Larkin yelled, "How are you chaps going to get the kidnappers back so I can formally arrest them?

The Spider shrugged—and climbed into the chopper without answering.

As they departed Northern Ireland and entered *Éire's* air space, Paddy motioned for them to put on headphones so he could communicate with them.

"We will be landing at the Old Quarry Business Park about a mile east of Gortlee Castle. The B.W.S. just arrived. They are aware that we have received a ransom note and must assume that the staffeln is already back at the castle. They will be setting up surveillance positions based on some floor plans they procured from the Irish Historical Society. It is a four-story granite structure; the lower floor used for service. Reception rooms are on the main floor, upper floors contain twenty bedrooms. The granite might cause some problems for our listening devices but we should be able to detect whether voices are male or female."

Malcolm McClain interrupted him. "I've been meaning to ask but felt stupid. Why did they kidnap Janna if the bait is to get Chez?"

"It is not stupid, Malky, in fact, it's a damn good question. Standard operational procedure is to keep your prisoner from panicking and Teréska and Janna will certainly be providing each other with moral support. However, the most logical reason they took both of them is to eliminate their chances of kidnapping the wrong girl. If they kill Chez, the hostages will be next, so our plan has to have impeccable timing.

"Let me ask you guys a question. Larkin mentioned that you will remember the leader's father from that stunt you pulled getting Malcolm out of Stalag XVIII-D in Maribor. Care to explain?"

Malcolm answered before Chez had a chance.

"Sturmbahnführer Abelard von Keller was the nasty bastard charged with hunting us down after Chez got me out. He murdered a good friend of ours in cold blood so Chez slit his throat with a razor."

"Well done, wee man and I think we must assume that his son volunteered for this assignment, so you will receive no mercy," Paddy offered.

"I don't intend asking for any," was the icy reply. "But I will get our girls back."

The voice of the Air Corps pilot crackled into their headphones.

"Colonel McBride, we will be touching down in less than a minute. If you take a moment, the town at eleven o'clock is Letterkenny and if you look to port, you might note a flock of about fifty sheep gathered in an open field. Track to the far end of that field and you will see a heavily treed area; that is the southern boundary of the Gortlee estate."

"I am seeing three black Land Rovers in the Old Quarry parking lot. Can you confirm them as friendly, Colonel?" McBride looked forward through binoculars.

"Affirmative, captain, they have the Black Widows Security logo on the doors."

The Alouette landed softly, no more than fifty feet from the assemblage of vehicles and the rotor went into idle so the three passengers could make a crouched run towards the reception committee.

"David Goldstein, meet Malcolm McClain and Chez Orlowski. What is our situation on the ground, David?"

"Greetings, Colonel and it's an honor to meet

your friends. We have fifteen B.W.S. specialists, three Garda observers, plus ten guests from the Institute. If you recall, a group of my former Israeli commandos is currently visiting our Galway facility for special training. Once they heard about the background of the kidnappers, they were adamant about joining my Sligo team for this particular operation. My men are currently on site and in full camo. Our advance scouts watched the staffeln return to the castle with their victims about ninety minutes ago......"

McClain jumped into the conversation with some urgency. "......How did the girls look?"

"They both appear to be none the worse but their hands are still tied and heads hooded; most likely they're also gagged. They're being held in the same room on the second floor, north side and we have the room covered by extremely sensitive audio surveillance. The two armed guards in the room with them are called Pietr and Friedrick; I can tell you the names of their girlfriends if you want! Each of those guards has been assigned to my best snipers should we feel the girls are in imminent danger."

McBride turned to Chez and grabbed his shoulder. The Ulsterman's hand was almost the size of the Pole's head and he crouched down to share his thoughts.

"My friend, just remember, it has been more than quarter of a century since we fought together; we are both getting old. Just play your part and let my men do theirs. I know there are only ten troopers in a staffeln and have no doubt that you are still more than a match for these young pups, but I have to get my goddaughters back home safely and it would be very nice if you could join them. Will you work with me on this, wee man?"

"Tell me what you need me to do, Paddy. But if they harm our girls, all bets are off."

McBride smiled grimly and shook his head. "I doubt those Nazi clowns have any clue about the favor I am doing them by asking you to back off." The humor was lost on Chez Orlowski, who had now completely assumed the unnerving persona of the Spider.

"Okay, Chez, listen up. Behind the Land Rovers is a blue Morris Oxford, ostensibly the car that you have just driven up from Belfast after getting the phone message from the kidnappers. You cannot leave this parking lot for another two hours or the timing will not be right. On that mark, drive alone to the front door of the castle and surrender yourself to von Keller. Demand the release of the two girls and see what happens."

"Well, I think we know what they plan on doing next; they kill me, kill the girls and scurry back to their nest."

"That might be their plan, but it is not ours. They will most certainly want to kill you before Teréska and Janna; otherwise, they lose their psychological hold over you and remember, you are the Spider, the legend that has haunted their entire lives by upending the Nazi war effort. Chez, I am banking that their plans for your demise will involve great ceremony and most likely be filmed for a personal screening to show Bormann back in Argentina."

"And?"

"Well, Chez, I have not been given a copy of the staffeln's script, so we will be adlibbing, to a certain extent."

Malcolm McClain grew frustrated listening to this. "How the hell can I help?"

"Malcolm, the first action we take will be to disable any perimeter guards they might have placed to ensure Chez arrives alone. At that point, we will control Gortlee Estate; nobody enters, nobody leaves. Our second action will be to rescue the girls. I am going to lead four of my best commandos into the room where they are currently held. We will take out the guards quickly and silently, and then transfer Teréska and Janna into your custody. Your job will be to calm them down after what must have been an extremely traumatic experience. The third action will be to rescue Chez. I'm afraid that's the part we have to play on the fly."

The Spider summed it up in a calm voice. "I have absolutely no problem with this plan. You secure our girls and leave me as the trophy sacrifice for ten Nazi thugs. It is an excellent plan. Let me know when the girls are safe and I will take it from there. I can hardly wait." The Pole then motioned for his two friends to come closer to him.

"My dear friends, I have a confession to make. Using my nom de guerre for the academy was a calculated risk on my behalf, as was feeding the baron de Cortada exactly what he wanted to hear during our lunch. In other words, I am the one responsible for bringing all this trouble to our doorstep. The deaths at our academy and the kidnapping of our children would never occurred if I had not baited the Nazis into revealing themselves. This is my chance to make amends, if things go horribly wrong, I am begging you to find it in your hearts to forgive me."

Paddy McBride had both concern and compassion written all over his face as he responded. "Chez, think of it this way, you are merely a line item on Bormann's list of people he hates. Someone had to flush him out and you used yourself as bait. Don't carry the guilt of the bombing and the kidnapping on your shoulders. This maniac is hell-bent on getting you; he has not succeeded yet. Malcolm and I will never allow that to happen—never.

"I am pleading with you; think about the grandchildren you have not yet met. I do not want you taking on a group of combat trained, heavily armed Special Forces. I just need you to distract them so BWS can overpower them by force. Bullets flying around will not help our cause. Anything you can do or say to focus their undivided attention on you will help my men get the drop on them. Good luck, wee man."

The Morris Oxford series VI turned off the main road and entered the grounds of the estate by passing a small gatehouse. Chez detected a flash of motion and noticed a man holding a radio dodge behind a tree. So he was not unduly surprised when the front door of the castle opened before his car crunched over the final yards of the long gravel driveway. Chez pulled to a halt in front of the main entrance into Gortlee Castle and took a deep breath. Two leather-jacketed men with submachine guns were beside his car before he could get out and demanded his name in heavily accented English. The Spider chose to reply in Berliner German.

"I am Czeslaw Orlowski, here to pick up my daughter and her friend. Please escort them outside and we'll be on our way." The armed thugs laughed at his audaciousness; they pulled him roughly from the car and frog marched him up the steps and into the magnificent foyer. One of the welcoming committee expertly searched Chez for hidden weapons, the other maintained ten feet of distance, his gun pointed unwaveringly at the center of the Polish hero's torso.

Chez sensed that other eyes were watching and on cue, a large door opened. A tall man with a somewhat familiar face strode towards him.

"Herr Spinne, what an honor. Please join me and my associates in the dining room."

Chez was manhandled into a stout, high-backed oak chair that had been placed in the center of the room; ropes were used to ensure his immobility. The Spider brought one of his old tricks into play by expanding his lungs and flexing all his muscles as the knots were being tied. When he relaxed, the ropes slackened enough for him to be able to gain a little movement. It was imperceptible to the others—but it was there.

Heavy drapes on the windows prevented any daylight entering and at the front of the room, a man operating a reel-to-reel movie camera stood on top of a heavy oak table. All electric lights had been turned off in favor of a dozen, smelly kerosene-burning torches. The effect created was eerie.

The Spider's eyes adjusted to the dim light and he found himself in the center of a ring of chairs, each occupied by a smirking member of the staffeln. Hans von Keller, wearing his dress uniform, sat directly in front of his prey. With his right hand, he raised a German cavalry officer's sword as he rose dramatically to his feet and commenced his role as the master of ceremonies.

"I call this court to order. It is hereby convened under the sacred guidelines of the Thule Gesellschaft for the purity of the Aryan race." He then pointed the sword directly at the Spider's throat.

"Czeslaw Orlowski, you have committed heinous crimes against the Third Reich. You are accused of murdering our beloved Führer and countless other brave sons of Germany, including my own father, Sturmbahnführer Abelard von Keller. How do you plead before this court?"

Paddy called this one exactly right, Chez thought to himself. *I hope the rest of his plan follows the script.*

"Guilty as charged but there's quite a bit more." Gasps of incredulity welled up from the staffeln. Encouraged by this, the Spider continued, "I also completely fucked up your V-2 rocket program, which, I am proud to say, probably cost you the war. I would like to add in my defense that both Hitler and your father were cruel, despicable monsters who deserved to die as recompense to free people everywhere." All seven young Germans in the theatrically staged room leaped to their feet, incensed by the unbridled temerity of their prisoner. He was twice their age, tied up and, worst of all, Polish. They were seething and pleaded with von Keller to let them rip him limb from limb. Against this very real risk, the Spider gambled that von Keller would want more camera footage before he swung the glinting edge of his blade against his neck.

The intense focus of every member of the staffeln was palpable, as the Spider continued his verbal assault.

"Now, as soon as you boys finish with this Wagnerian bullshit, I would like to see my daughter and goddaughter. Please hurry up or I will start to get really pissed." At this effrontery, several of the fuming staffeln again jumped to their feet again. Von Keller confronted them with his sword and demanded that they be seated. To give his men the salve of satisfaction, he transferred the weapon to his left hand and smashed his gloved fist into the Spiders mouth. Chez spat out a bloody tooth and smiled, "Is that all you've got, Hans? My wife has a better punch." Von Keller began to seethe and reared back to deliver another blow. The staffeln cheered enthusiastically but were shocked into stunned silence when, from a rear door to the room, a young girl's voice blurted out in Polish.

"I am so proud of you, Daddy!"

Within a heartbeat, all the electric lights simultaneously burst into life. A giant of a man wearing full camouflage barked out an order and dozens of similarly dressed soldiers materialized around the perimeter of the room. Their method of aiming their submachine guns left little doubt that they were no strangers to the weapon. With his 9 mm pistol creating an unwavering, ramrod stiff line from barrel to von Keller's forehead, McBride marched straight towards the master of ceremonies with tangible menace.

"Drop the sword, von Keller. Order your men to sit down very slowly in their chairs with hands clasped behind their heads. Any movement contrary to this simple request will be the last one of your life. Chez, please translate so there is no misunderstanding."

The torchlight and the Spider's tirade had masked the soundless entrance of the Special Forces from the kitchen. The harsh increase in candlepower devastated the Germanic theatrics and left no doubt that the newcomers outnumbered the seated staffeln by at least four to one. The unblinking barrels of multiple Sterling SMG's served to emphasize the hopelessness of the situation to the kidnappers.

"Tie their thumbs together and pile any weapons you find into the center of the room. David, take charge here, then escort these clowns to the Garda headquarters in Letterkenny; they are expected. The one at the front gate is still unconscious and the two who were guarding the girls are bound and gagged in the bedroom. I'll leave it to Inspector Larkin to petition for transfer of custody back to Northern Ireland.

"I almost forgot, the domestic staff are being held in a third floor bedroom by one of our Garda observers. Tell Sergeant Riley to convey our sincere apologies for the inconvenience to them. They are free to return to duty, at least until the Garda has a chance to have a little chat with their boss, Hermann Schmidt, when and if he ever returns.

"How are you doing, wee man, unbelievable performance!"

The Spider shook off the ropes as he stood up. In one fluid motion he side-kicked the arm off his chair and caught it with his left hand. Before Paddy could react, the Pole had swung the improvised oak club in an arc; stopping it an inch above von Keller's flinching head.

"Stupid motherfuckers cannot even tie a knot. Part of me was hoping that you would let me have at them. If von Keller's eyes showed me that he was about to get serious, I would have made him regret bringing that sword to the party. Having said that, the other part of me is very happy to see you, Paddy."

"Holy shit; that's about all I can say, Holy shit, wee man, I do believe you could have taken them." He turned back to his men and noted the shock the Spider had induced into everyone, friend and foe alike.

"Now, if you'll excuse us, we need to get Janna and Teréska back to Belfast. Their mothers are cooking dinner and I'm inviting myself," Paddy concluded.

Teréska ran across the room to her father, and threw her arms around his neck. Janna was right behind her. Though he was prepared to deny it, a tear or two rolled down the legend's cheek.

David Goldstein walked over to Chez in the front hall and shook his hand.

"Wow, that was quite a performance, sir. Paddy has told me many times about you so I should not have been surprised, but for the record, I was.

"My fellow countrymen have requested that I offer von Keller a choice before handing him and his friends over to the Garda." An intrigued Chez followed the young captain over to the still-stunned von Keller.

"Mr. von Keller, some of my men are members of the Institute and we would like you to consider returning with us to answer a few questions about your covert operations in Germany rather than being remanded in custody by the Garda." Hans von Keller assessed the smiling, curly haired captain's offer against the capital charges he was about to face both in Southern and Northern Ireland.

Oh, I like my chances of escaping from this young pup, he started to contemplate.

"I think I might be very interested. Tell me more about this Institute."

But the Spider had his own plans for von Keller and the staffeln. He patted von Keller on the cheek and gave him an exaggerated wink. "As a former dear friend of your father, I'll give you a few words of advice, Hans.

"The Institute that David refers to is better known as the Mossad; go with the Garda option on this."

PART FIVE

CHAPTER TWENTY-NINE

Belfast

"Well, Inspector, our boy Rudy might have chalked up some points in the sympathy column but he still has a long way to go," Paddy McBride said to Bill Larkin.

"Yes, Colonel, I heard the operation in Donegal went smoothly. My counterpart in the Garda has already called to offer assistance with the transfer paperwork. Kidnapping minors across an international border in an attempt to commit the murder of a citizen of the United Kingdom will be at the top of a list of charges. Of course, I will need you all as key witnesses."

Chez immediately voiced his concern.

"Inspector, if you don't mind, I am going to call you Bill. It seems like a lifetime since I shared the secrets of my past with you and Malcolm. At that time, it was still an exclusive club, Paddy and Bormann being the only other members of note; even Jadwiga has been spared most of the ugly details. Now, Letterkenny's jail is full of people who tried to squash the legend of the Spider and if there is a trial, the BBC and ITV will tell my story to the world. As a consequence, my family and I will be placed in considerable jeopardy. I would much prefer to let Rudy Gomez, Malcolm and Paddy be your only witnesses."

"I am terribly sorry, Chez. You are the entire reason the kidnapping took place. If you don't testify, any half-baked barrister with a wig will be able to get them off. That said, I suspect your arch-nemesis Martin Bormann and his Fourth Reich will be retaining an expensive Q.C. to handle the trial."

"It is a very treacherous stretch of road from Letterkenny to Belfast. Maybe……"

"….Not on my watch, Chez. And listen, I cannot hold Gomez much longer without charging him. He might not understand the British legal system but that Mary O'Connell is smart as a whip. She visits him twice a day; I've never seen two people so much in love. However, if she hires a solicitor and I'm forced to release him, Barry McKenna will hunt him down like a dog, so I don't think she is thinking rationally right now."

"Before we left to rescue our daughters, I told you

that I had a proposal for you to consider. I have not yet worked out the finer points but as soon as you can, charge Rudy Gomez with exactly the same long-winded offense you are going to lay on the staffeln. I would like him to be sitting in the Crumlin Road jail by the time you take custody of his friends from Köln. It has the makings of quite a reunion party."

"I will do no such thing unless you give me a damn good reason," Larkin spluttered indignantly.

The Spider stared the inspector down and gave him an uncompromising ultimatum. "Work with me, Bill, or I will not testify under any circumstances." McClain and McBride pretended to feign shock, but their long history with Chez caused them to put their trust in whatever he might be planning.

The wee man is up to something, they were both thinking and sure enough, the next words out of the Spider's mouth laid the groundwork,

"By the way, Bill, where is Miss O'Connell staying in Belfast?"

"She is at the Wellington Park Hotel. Are you going to tell me what you are up to?" responded the inspector.

"First of all, I need to talk with Malcolm and Paddy but I'll get back with you in the morning." Then the Spider reached across and grabbed Larkin's hand in a firm handshake. "Please let Mary and Rudy say their goodbyes here before you incarcerate him. Trust me on this one, Bill."

The Botanic Inn on the Malone Road shares a parking lot with the Wellington Park Hotel. It is a very popular watering hole for Queen's University students and is affectionately known on campus as 'The Bot.' Malcolm and Paddy chose a corner table in the lounge and ordered pints of Guinness while waiting for Chez to seek a private meeting with Mary O'Connell in the adjacent hotel.

If two of Northern Ireland's most famous sons were seeking anonymity, The Bot might first seem entirely the wrong place to choose. Before the war, McBride had been an outstanding front row forward on the national rugby team, in addition to holding the British Heavyweight boxing title for several years. McClain was, well, Malcolm McClain—'nough said. Word travelled like a bush fire and students began to drift into the lounge. Both men dutifully signed every piece of paper the excited college crowd thrust in front of them. Picking his moment, Paddy rose to his full height, looked down at the awe-struck students and spoke.

"Lads, Malcolm and I could use a big favor from you. We are going to have a private conversation and would like to make sure there is no eavesdropping by strangers. Can you help us out?" This trust was much appreciated by the students and immediately, tables and chairs were rearranged to secure that particular corner of the lounge. Rugby players did most of the furniture moving and then claimed the seats around the perimeter.

A bold young man presented himself to Paddy and Malcolm. "Mr. McBride, Mr. McClain, I am Joe Thompson, captain of the First Fifteen. My team is going to practice some bawdy drinking songs so no one will overhear a word spoken in this corner of the bar. If we get too loud, give us a nod and we'll calm it down to a dull roar."

"I think that will be perfect, but if you are going to practice drinking songs, I think you had better have something to drink. Tell the bartender to put the first round on my tab," Malcolm said.

Paddy added, "Nicely done, Malcolm. Hey Joe, the second round will be on me."

When Chez strolled into the bar almost an hour later, two burly Queen's rugby players blocked his approach until Paddy called out, "It's okay, lads, he's with us." A path was opened through the barricade to allow Chez access to the celebrity corner table.

"What the hell are you up to, Chez?" Malcolm questioned in a voice that had to compete against the singing. The three men leant in close to continue their conversation.

"Here it is in a nutshell. Something Bill Larkin said scares the hell out of me. Most of the loot the Nazis pilfered has never been recovered and as the self-proclaimed führer of the Fourth Reich, I suspect Martin Bormann might be one of the richest men in the world. As such, the chances of the staffeln walking out of the court with nothing more than a slap on the wrist are extremely high. Especially if his son is in the Crum on the same charges." McBride and McClain looked extremely puzzled but Chez continued unfazed.

"The staffeln has no clue what caused Rudy Gomez to disappear, or what happened to him in Londonderry, but I intend to fabricate a cast iron alibi for him. By charging them all with exactly the same offense, whomever Bormann hires will have a legal loophole that should encourage him to get Rudy's release out of the way first before concentrating on a defense for the staffeln. Once Rudy is out, I'll have another deal I want to discuss with him."

Paddy's frustration took over. "Chez, that is fuckin' nuts. Are you telling me that we risked our lives to let those bastards go free?"

"Only Rudy. I have no intention of letting the staffeln get off with kidnapping our daughters. I am just changing the rules of the game to work in my favor. Not a lot I can do if they are all together in the Crum."

Both Malcolm and Paddy had seen the look on Chez's face before; the most dangerous man either had ever met was now on a personal mission. Both resigned themselves to go with the flow.

"Paddy, I really don't give a shit about those punks but Rudy Gomez is going to help me nail his father and drive a stake into the heart of the Fourth Reich."

There were several seconds of awkward silence before Malcolm ventured to speak. "Okay, Chez, I'm afraid you might have lost it, my friend. Why in God's name would Gomez help you kill his father?"

"Because he now hates Bormann and all he stands for. More significantly, it's the only way he can escape Larkin throwing additional charges at him. Complicity in the academy bombing might result in a sentence of death; and an abrupt end to any wedding plans he and Mary O'Connell might be dreaming about."

Then Paddy thumped his fist on the table, causing their glasses to skid and the singing to stop for a few seconds. Paddy gave the rugby players a friendly wave and the singing resumed.

"....If I was Rudy, I'd play along with you to get out of jail, then lure you to Argentina, kill you and have a good laugh about it with my dad. Mary might be a great piece of arse but she's not the only woman in the world.

"That's what this bloody vendetta is all about. BORMANN WANTS TO KILL THE SPIDER!

Under your scenario, Bormann wins. What am I missing? Why the bloody hell would Gomez cooperate with you?" McBride's raised voice caused the rest of the Bot to quiet again so Chez had to whisper his response.

"I truly believe that Rudy is deeply in love with Mary O'Connell, and at the appropriate moment, she is going to tell him she might be carrying his child. That should make him take my deal—or I've completely misjudged my instincts."

CHAPTER THIRTY

A Meeting of the Minds

T he next morning found Chez back at the Royal
Ulster Constabulary Headquarters but this time,
he was armed with two boxes of glazed doughnuts.

"Good morning, Lucy. Please make sure only
deserving officers get their hands on these." The frumpy
receptionist changed her demeanor and started to smile.

"Mr. Orlowski, you are quite the charmer." However,
she followed this with a conspiratorial whisper. "I'm not
sure the doughnuts will work on Inspector Larkin.
He is in a dour mood today. He told me to send you
straight back to his office as soon as you arrived."

Chez went back to Larkin's office, sat down and laid
out his plan. He received an even angrier response from
Bill Larkin than he gotten from Paddy the night before.

"I have been on the Force for twenty years; I know

how to put perpetrators in jail. There will be no legal loopholes for these thugs to manipulate and I am deeply offended that you think I would endanger my pension for this charade. Von Keller and his group will be charged at the Crumlin Road Jail as soon as I can get my paperwork approved by the Garda in Letterkenny. I have already advised Judge Kirkpatrick that bail would be a very bad idea.

"You must rethink dropping the accessory to murder charges against Gomez because he is guilty as sin of killing four people at your academy. I will have a much tougher time tying him to the attempted kidnapping but I think I can do it. Why the bloody hell are you even suggesting that Gomez shouldn't swing for the academy bombing murders?"

"Because his father is a major war criminal, convicted in absentia at Nuremberg of complicity in the deaths of millions of people. Martin Bormann is evil personified and I am going to deliver his sorry arse to justice.

"Bill, I need Rudy Gomez to help me get into the lion's den."

The passion in Orlowski's plea had a profound effect on the R.U.C. inspector. For several seconds neither spoke, then Larkin broke the silence with a melancholy tale.

"My father was reported to have died under mysterious circumstances on D-Day. He was a full colonel in the Royal Ulster Rifles and captured just outside

Longueval on June 7, 1944. A couple of survivors testified that two men in black leather coats, silver skulls on their caps, culled Colonel John Larkin from the rest of the prisoners, pushed him into a car and sped off behind the German lines. His body was never found. I know that the Gestapo were technically under the command of Heinrich Himmler but the entire Third Reich was ruled by a pretty small group."

"Bill, current evidence points to Martin Bormann being the tip of the spear. This bastard orchestrated the Nazi Party's attempt at world domination and I know for a fact that Adolf Hitler was no more than a gifted orator controlled by Bormann. Remember, I was there in the bunker!

"May God rest your father's soul, but responsibility for whatever happened to Colonel John Larkin lands squarely at the feet of Reichsleiter Martin Bormann."

Larkin had no immediate response to this and paused to gather his thoughts.

"Chez, I think I may have a simple modification to your plan which creates a win-win situation for both of us. Interested?"

"I am all ears, Inspector."

Later that day, Larkin's phone rang. "Yes, Lucy?"

"Inspector, Miss O'Connell is here and would

like a word." Two minutes later, a polite knock on the closed door preceded the young woman with the flaming red hair. The inspector noted that she looked rested and for the first time since their unusual introduction, he detected no stress in her eyes.

"Mary, please have a seat. Did you say your goodbyes to Rudy? I'll be transporting him to Crumlin Road Jail within the hour and understand you have decided to return to Londonderry. Incidentally, may I remind you, please do not leave the country without informing me.

"As I believe you are aware, I have agreed not to charge Mr. Gomez with the deaths of your daughter and certain other people in return for his assistance. I want you to be crystal clear that what he is being asked to do is very dangerous and you may never see him again."

"I am prepared for that, Inspector. Rudy now understands his father's evil for what it really is and we both know we could never have a relationship while knowing that man is alive and trying to terrorize the world again. The risk is extreme but if he loves me half as much as I love him, it will be worth it. He and I are agreed on what needs to be done to save his soul."

Bill Larkin steepled his fingers and paused before replying.

"Mary, Chez Orlowski made a compelling

argument to steer me in this direction. I will proceed within strict ethical and legal guidelines but I have no control over the whims of Judge Kirkpatrick. Should it all work out, there will still be many hurdles to negotiate before you two can reunite. You do understand that, right?"

Mary O'Connell teared up and nodded.

"The alternative is a lifetime in jail, so this is the only chance we have. God will look after him."

Rudy Gomez was formally charged with the kidnapping of the two girls across an international border and the attempted murder of a British citizen. As he was signing the sworn statement that essentially established his alibi, he commented on how difficult it was to hold a pen whilst handcuffed. Inspector Larkin fished a small key from his pocket.

"Then you will most definitely have trouble dialing a phone. As we discussed, I need you to relay your circumstances to your father so he can organize your defense. I am going to take the cuffs off but I will be standing right here when you make the call." A black Bakelite phone was pushed towards Rudy. "Do you have the country and area codes to make an STD connection? And make it snappy, the cost of the call will appear on my expense report."

On the third attempt, Rudy made the connection and spoke rapidly in Spanish.

"Guillermo, it's me, Rudy. Is my father available?" Gomez held his hand over the phone and raised his eyebrows at Larkin. "He is comin....... Ah mi Padre, how are you feeling today?" He listened for several seconds and then started to converse in German rather than Spanish. "I have been arrested. The attempts by the Fenian Brotherhood to kill the Spider failed miserably and some innocent children were killed; all it served to do was piss off the entire country. The backup contingency plan went into effect and the staffeln tried to bait the Spider into leaving Northern Ireland by kidnapping his daughter; that failed too. We are all going to be charged with capital offenses and might never see the light of day again. You were right about one thing; the Spider is an incredibly devious bastard.

"British law allows me to make this one phone call and I am hoping you can at least get me a decent lawyer." Rudy paused and cast a glance at Larkin before continuing,

"No, I did not physically participate in either the murder attempt or the back-up kidnapping, but someone ratted me out. Vater, unless you can work some magic, I will be spending the rest of my life in a Belfast prison—or worse."

Rudy was silent as Bormann began to talk in an

agitated fashion. It was so loud that Larkin could hear him beyond the telephone. Then Gomez concluded with, "The officer in charge is named Inspector William Larkin with the Royal Ulster Constabulary. Listen Vater, I have to go, my time is up…." And he pressed the button to disconnect the call.

"So far, so good, Rudy, but I'm afraid it's now time to escort you to your new hotel."

His wrists were re-cuffed before Rudy Gomez left the Knock headquarters to cross the Lagan Valley en route to the Crumlin Road Jail. As he watched the dark blue van depart, Larkin turned to Lucy.

"Lucy, I hope you managed to record both sides of that phone conversation? Please locate somebody who speaks both German and Spanish. I understand Argentinian Spanish has its own little quirks so give the language department at Queen's University a call and see if they can help us out."

CHAPTER THIRTY-ONE

The Crum

S ir Charles Lanyon designed the Crumlin Road Jail in the early 1840's. Its classic Victorian penal architecture uses black stone to intimidate inmates from the moment local police discard them into the custody of the Her Majesty's prison guards. Rudy Gomez was escorted to a twelve-foot by seven-foot cell with a small barred, arched window punching through one wall just under the 10-foot ceiling.

"Gomez, put all your clothes into this plastic bag and dress in this orange kit. Kidnapping will get you ten to twenty and the bag will be returned to you if and when the judge grants you a release," a large, gruff guard ordered. "Otherwise, mate, you will be given a fresh kit every Thursday for as long as you are here. And don't look to me for a good behavior recommendation;

my daughter is about the same age as the girls you abducted and I intend to keep you off the streets for as long as I can, you miserable piece of shite."

Rudy complied docilely and the two guards laughed to each other. When they finally left him alone, the key and the old lock had a disagreement that caused a noisy clatter to echo around the old stone walls before the tumblers clicked over. The hollow noises of a jail become an indelible memory for the prisoners.

The next morning at sunrise, Rudy awoke to the staccato of guards rattling their wooden truncheons against each cell door.

"Okay ladies, let go of your cocks and grab your socks. D-wing prisoners prepare for exactly thirty minutes in the exercise yard. There will be absolutely NO talking; MOVE IT." The harsh conditions were calculated to instill fear and intimidation; Gomez could not see himself surviving here for more than a few days. Some of the prisoners used the yard to build their physical strength with pushups and similar calisthenics; others, including Rudy, slouched in a subservient silent circle.

The next day repeated the monotony, but the third day was very different. Joining the circle of silence were Hans, Friedrick, Pietr, Fritz and the six other members of the Köln staffeln. Rudy stared intently at Hans von Keller until the crestfallen leader felt his gaze and stared back. The staffeln nudged each other but maintained their silence. Rudy flashed them a smile and a wink. For the first time in a week, the young Germans felt that the Fourth Reich had not completely abandoned them.

But as time progressed, boredom, silence and depression overwhelmed the smiles and winks. The paranoia of uncertainty pervaded until ten days later. Just as the coveted morning exercise period was about to end, Senior Prison Officer Frank McCloskey walked into the yard. He stared hard at each prisoner as he tried to link their face with a name on his sheet of paper. Each time he confirmed a quarry, McCloskey tapped them on the chest with his truncheon to gain their attention. This action focused the eyes of the selected prisoner onto the tip of the wooden weapon, which then moved hypnotically towards the yard's perimeter wall.

"You; over there: NOW."

Eleven men were culled out. The rest were escorted back to their cells. McCloskey, a man who bore a scary resemblance to Benito Mussolini, double-checked his list before announcing,

"You prisoners will have your pre-trial hearing before the judge in thirty minutes. I will be transferring you into the custody of the Royal Ulster Constabulary.

They will escort you through the tunnel under the Crumlin Road and thenceforth, into a holding area beneath the courthouse. You may talk only after you've reached the courthouse and if you make it back by lunch, it's a delicious cheese sandwich today, so don't dally." McCloskey turned his back and four R.U.C. officers took over.

Once they reached the holding cells, Hans von Keller and his men went straight to Rudy and began chattering rapidly with him in German.

"What the hell happened to you? We thought you were dead. How come they managed to capture you before us?"

Rudy replied with the fabrication dreamed up by Inspector Bill Larkin.

"I went to Derry to organize some things with the Fenian Brotherhood and ran into a gang of street thugs. Things got nasty; they tied me up and threatened to kill me. Next thing I know, these men get into a firefight with the local police. Eventually, the police overran the house and I was taken to their local barracks for questioning. That's where I first heard about the botched bombing, so I knew the staffeln would try the kidnapping. I've overheard stories from the police—but what the hell really happened?" Rudy Gomez spoke passionately, at the same time feigning complete ignorance of the events that transpired in Letterkenny.

"Oh, the kidnapping itself went fine; we got the girls and returned to the castle. The Spider showed up on command and we were just about to film ourselves capping the bastard when we realized we had been completely duped." Rudy listened to von Keller's account with the open eyes and slack mouth of a teenager watching a horror movie. "All of a sudden, the lights go on and we find ourselves surrounded by over a hundred armed Israeli commandos. Not one shot was fired because we didn't stand a chance. They cuffed us and dropped us off at the local Garda station. Three days later, we were charged with kidnapping and attempted murder and transferred to this filthy hole."

"Well, that explains why I got jailed before you; I was already in Northern Ireland, in jail and carrying a West German passport showing Rosslare as my entry point. The R.U.C. must have thrown a net over anyone who speaks German. They drove me straight here from Derry and threw me in jail to see if they could link me to the kidnapping. It seems fairly obvious that they have managed to accomplish that..."

At that point in the conversation, the door opened and two policemen entered ahead of an elegant, bespectacled man in a bespoke pinstriped suit.

"Gentlemen, I am Sir Roger Merriweather, Q.C. I have been appointed by an organization based in Argentina to defend you against charges in front of Judge Kirkpatrick—assuming that meets with your approval?" Sir Roger waited for an affirmative response then turned to his escorts. "Officers, if you would be so kind, I would like to spend some time with my clients before we are summonsed before the judge."

The usher banged his gavel before announcing, "This court is now in session. All rise in the presence of the Honorable Horatio Kirkpatrick." As this was only a hearing and not a trial, the courtroom's spectator gallery had few occupants but those present included Inspector Larkin and Mary O'Connell who sat beside each other. Judge Kirkpatrick adjusted his spectacles and addressed the eleven men in orange jump suits.

"This hearing will finalize charges between Northern Ireland and the defendants arraigned before me. The court's main purpose today is to determine whether Mr. Rudy Gomez will be included with the other ten defendants when answering Charge One, the attempted murder of a British citizen, and Charge Two, the kidnapping of Teréska Orlowski and Janna McClain, and their subsequent abduction across an international border. Royal Ulster Constabulary Inspector William J. Larkin has submitted compelling evidence to this court that will be taken into consideration.

"If your legal representation is present would he please identify himself?" The man in the sophisticated pinstriped suit rose and cleared his throat. Sir Roger presented a stark contrast to the Crum kits but in truth, Merriweather made everyone in the court feel underdressed.

"If it pleases Your Honor, I am the Queen's Counsel, Sir Roger Merriweather, and I have been retained to represent all eleven defendants. My team and I flew to Belfast from London three days ago to prepare their defense and I would like Your Honor and the court to note my sincere appreciation for the excellent cooperation we have received from Inspector Larkin and his staff."

Hans von Keller whispered into Rudy Gomez's ear. "This guy is smoother than ice covered with baby oil. We might stand a chance of getting off Scot-free with this kind of muscle."

Judge Kirkpatrick cleared his throat. "Sir Roger, your reputation precedes you. Please brief the court on why I should separate the charges against Mr. Gomez from those against the other men. Currently, they are charged en masse."

"If Your Honor will permit, I offer the court my humble legal opinion that Mr. Gomez's case must be kept separate. This court is in possession of evidence that proves, beyond the shadow of a doubt, that Mr. Gomez is merely a victim of circumstance who must be released from incarceration at the court's earliest opportunity. Gomez's only crimes seems to be that he travels on a West German passport, speaks German as his native tongue and found himself in the custody of the R.U.C. within twenty miles of Gortlee Castle where the kidnapping took place.

"The other ten gentlemen are in a completely different situation. The facts of their unfortunate folly should be resolved with a simple apology. It was a case of mistaken identity, nobody was hurt and I am authorized by my clients to compensate the Orlowski and McClain families at the court's pleasure.

"May I first plead for Mr. Gomez's immediate release from custody, Your Honor?"

CHAPTER THIRTY-TWO

The Debt Must Be Paid

M ary O'Connell and Sir Roger Merriweather sat in the Barristers' Lounge at the courthouse and shared a pot of tea as they waited for Rudy Gomez to complete his paperwork. He eventually joined them, looking much different after showering, shaving and donning his civilian clothes. He went straight to Mary and pulled her into his arms. Sir Roger had not reached the pinnacle of his profession without possessing an uncanny ability to read human emotions. He knew he was now witnessing two young people who deeply cared for each other. He finally politely interrupted them.

"Ahem." Rudy turned to the elderly barrister but kept both arms around Mary.

"Sir Roger, I am not sure what happened in that

courtroom but I thank you with all my heart. What about Hans von Keller and the rest of the staffeln?"

"MI6 recently intercepted an interesting enquiry and asked for my assistance; it had been sent to the Bar from an organization based in Argentina. As you might imagine, my loyalties are completely at the behest of Her Majesty the Queen and Her government. I am privy to the background of Mr. Orlowski and the tremendous debt that the United Kingdom owes him, so in direct response to your question, the staffeln are toast. Despite heroic pleading on my behalf, Horatio ruled against me. They will spend the rest of their natural lives in the Crum, after which, they will most likely rot in Hell.

"You, on the other hand are being offered a lifeline; help the Spider bring Martin Bormann to justice and Her Majesty's government will provide you with a new identity behind which you and Mary will be able live out your lives in married bliss." Mary began to cry tears of happiness and Rudy hugged her tightly. The Q.C. smiled as he wondered if the two lovers would even hear his concluding words.

"I happen to be staying at Culloden and had a very interesting dinner last night with Horatio Kirkpatrick, Bill Larkin, Chez Orlowski and Malcolm McClain. In other words—I am very much in on the sting…."

"I cannot thank you enough, Sir Roger."

"Well my boy, your father, Martin Ludwig Bormann, would do well to abide by the complex legal precedent, 'do not fuck with Her Majesty.' You would think that the Nazis might have figured that out by now!"

Sir Roger Merriweather left the two lovebirds alone in the Barristers' Lounge. Mary grabbed Rudy's hands and pleading with her eyes, said, "Rudy, let's get out of here. We can take my car, cash the money and disappear. Trust me, once we get across the border, they will never find us."

"Mary, I love you more than life itself but I am going to honor my pledge. My father and his cohorts have killed millions upon millions of innocent people. I have an obligation to repay my debt to the Spider by helping him bring them to justice."

The beautiful Irishwoman bit her lower lip, and then dropped the bombshell.

"Rudy, my woman's intuition is telling me that I might be pregnant. It has only been a month since our wild fling at the Belfray Inn but I missed my period and I can sense my body adjusting to welcome our baby."

Rudy Gomez was speechless. He sank to his knees and showered Mary's stomach with a hundred kisses. His tears drenched her midriff. "Mary, this child already has the greatest mother in the world but his or her father still has a serious debt to pay.

"The cashier's cheque I gave you now takes on a new importance. Please wait as long as you can before you redeem the funds, the Schmidt Bank in Letterkenny is bound to inform my father when the cheque clears—a couple of months would be prudent. And don't worry, the funds are guaranteed so use your personal bank in Derry, banking privacy laws should protect you for a while. Then get the hell away from Derry, go into hiding and open a new bank account when you decide upon a place to live. Give our child the best of everything but tell him or her that their father is a good man at heart. I will do everything in my power to join you after righting this wrong."

"I understand, my darling. When you return to Ireland, visit the Kilkenny Design Centre. You'll find it beside the castle and my cousin Kathleen Maguire works there. Kathleen will tell you how to find me, I mean—how to find us!"

CHAPTER THIRTY THREE

A Little Help from Your Friends

Rudy Gomez spent the night at the Wellington Park with Mary. Next morning, when the Spider called their room to announce he was waiting in the lobby, she remained upstairs after kissing Rudy goodbye and sobbed uncontrollably.

He found the Pole pacing in front of the elevator lobby.

"Where are you taking me, Chez?" he asked immediately.

"We are going to Hollywood, my friend. It's just an intermediate stop to get credentials; tomorrow, we fly to London."

"Why California first?" asked the puzzled German.

"No," laughed the Spider. "MI6 has a covert operation called Laneside in Hollywood, County Down. It is about four miles east of Belfast and our best chance of keeping you safe while the likes of McKenna and Mulcahy are out there. I am on quite a few hit lists myself so I want us both to drop under the radar for a while.

"We'll stay the night at Laneside and then drive to RAF Aldergrove in the morning to fly military to Luton Airport in Bedfordshire."

"I'm sure you won't tell me, but how are you able to pull these types of strings?"

"You are absolutely correct, I won't tell you. Suffice to say, a lifetime ago certain people made me a promise and they have never let me down. You would be well advised to respect that principle, Rudy."

A vicious storm built a dark gray wall above the Isle of Man, forcing the Lockheed L-1329 JetStar to climb above the dirty clouds to escape a battering. Both pilots were part of a special Royal Air Force team assigned to the Secret Intelligence Services and the plane was well suited to flying under weather extremes. Its interior was configured with eight passenger seats, a small bathroom and enough headroom to be able to walk and stretch.

"This storm is pretty bad, chaps; it stretches all the way to the Swiss Alps. We'll be cruising at 21,000 feet to stay above it and I'll continuously monitor for any breaks in the cloud cover," said the pilot. "Odds are there won't be any so our descent will be in zero visibility until we get below fifteen hundred. The first time you see the ground will be seconds before touchdown. Just wanted to give you a heads-up and remind you to stay seated with the straps on."

The final minutes of the flight lived up to expectations. Heavy pellets of rain bombarded the cockpit as the plane carved its path downwards. On three occasions, they found pockets of negative pressure and dropped weightlessly for several hundred feet. Chez and Rudy both heaved their breakfasts into barf bags but noticed the two pilots took it all in their stride.

The undercarriage whined down as the JetStar broke through the cloud base on final approach. A calm voice from the right seat told Luton that the jet was on final approach to Runway Zero Eight and received instructions in return to take the third taxiway exit to Hanger Five. The pilot waggled the wings in defiance of the rain and touched down softly before applying reverse thrust.

"The ghost of Billy Fagan is alive and well," said the Spider quietly as they pulled off to taxi. The pilot in the left seat overheard the remark and called back,

"So it's true, sir? We were briefed that you actually met the legendary squadron leader. They taught us in flight school that he was one of the greatest pilots who ever sat in the left seat. Folklore has it that William Wallace Fagan was actually shot while flying but still made a perfect landing after he had already died?"

"I not only knew him, son, I loved him as a brother. I happened to be in the right seat on his last flight and confirm the folklore as fact. The wizard managed to land a Fiesler Storch in a cow pasture after losing his right arm to friendly fire, bullets that also rendered him completely blind. I called out visuals to him but I swear he had already passed away before we touched down. I also know Billy would have been very proud of the way you two flew through this storm."

The JetStar taxied through the deluge towards a non-descript building on the northeast side of the airport. Massive doors rolled open to allow the plane access and a large black Humber Hawk Series IV left the parking lot to follow the plane. After the doors closed to secure the building, the two passengers climbed down onto the concrete floor to meet a tall man wearing a tweed coat and matching hat.

"Mr. Orlowski, my boss, Sir John Rennie, sends his personal regards. Traditionally, I would be asking if you had had a pleasant flight but, what with this bloody weather, I'm rather glad to see you both made it!

"I am Commander Peter McDougal with Military Intelligence, Section 6; I will be accompanying you and Mr. Gomez to our London headquarters. You must forgive me, Mr. Gomez, you will be required to wear a blindfold for the last ten minutes of our thirty mile journey. What with your family background and all that, Sir John is not very excited about having Martin Bormann's son scoping out our location."

"That's perfectly acceptable to me, Commander. Perhaps when you get to know me a little better it won't be an issue."

"Perhaps," murmured the agent. He held open the car's large rear door for the passengers and called to the driver. "Full speed to HQ, James, but be careful on these slippery roads."

The isolation of Hanger Five revealed another benefit when, in less than 200 yards from the building, James turned right onto a country road, thereby exiting Luton Airport without Her Majesty's Customs and Immigration being any the wiser.

The big Humber picked up the M1 at Flamstead and twenty minutes later, glided over the Thames on the Westminster Bridge. They meandered into the London Borough of Lambeth, where the Secret Intelligence Services had tucked itself away on the thirteenth floor of Century House, a modern tower at 100 Westminster Bridge Road.

Not until they had entered the building and found their way to a conference room, did Commander McDougal remove Rudy's blindfold. "Welcome to the S.I.S. There is a pot of tea and some crumpets on the sideboard. Once you both have relaxed a little and recovered from your journey, I want you to meet my immediate superior to reiterate what you have in mind and how my department can be of help."

The origins of the British Secret Intelligence Services trace back to the fifteenth century when Thomas Cromwell recruited spies to inform Henry VIII about events of interest in Europe. Throughout history, most countries in the world have trained covert units within their military to collect information that might help them protect their borders or give them an edge in battle; Great Britain is no exception.

Prompted by the rising threat from German military expansion in the early twentieth century, the United Kingdom assigned responsibility for internal security to Military Intelligence, Section 5 and designated Section 6 as the department charged with gathering intelligence about Britain's potential enemies abroad—perhaps keeping an open eye on supposed friends as well.

Commander Peter McDougal and his department head, Colonel Harold Lewis, worked for MI6. Their internal section had responsibility for intelligence pertaining to the Nazi regime and as long as certain war criminals remained unaccounted for, MI6 kept the files open.

"Mr. Gomez, can you provide me with any proof that you are, in fact, the natural born son of Reichsleiter Martin Ludwig Bormann?" asked McDougal with his opening question.

Rudy's reply took almost three hours and left those present in no doubt.

"So the bastard did manage to escape; no wonder we never found his body under the Lehrter Bridge in Berlin! The other Nazis you mention as 'living the life' in South America confirms what we have suspected for decades from our research into the Odessa organization. Why should we believe that you are willing to betray your own flesh and blood along with these heroes of your youth?"

Rudy Gomez did not hesitate and responded with intense passion. "Commander McDougal, the men I have named, including Dr. Mengele, Klaus Barbie, Erich Priebke and most of all, my own father, are some of the most immoral and evil men in the world and responsible for the deaths of millions of innocent human beings. I have no illusions about surviving this mission but by bringing them to justice, I pray that my unborn child will be forgiven by God and allowed to live in peace."

CHAPTER THIRTY-FOUR

Selling the Chief

"I don't like it; I don't like it at all."

After almost a week of planning, Peter McDougal and Harold Lewis were in the midst of presenting their executive summary to Sir John Rennie, chief of British Secret Intelligence Services when the chief interrupted.

"The United Kingdom owes a tremendous debt of gratitude to the Spider. Her Majesty's father, King George VI, committed the full resources of our government to ensure a long and happy life for the Orlowski family. This preposterous scheme you have cooked up is fraught with danger and might very well result in the Spider's death. Should that happen, you can count on Sir Winston Churchill rising up from his grave and haunting us all."

"Believe it or not, 'C,' we felt the same way—until yesterday." Colonel Lewis addressed the chief as 'C,' not as a familiarity of rank but to acknowledge a tradition that traced back to the founding of the modern S.I.S. and an idiosyncrasy of the first chief, Sir Mansfield Cumming. Cumming signed all his correspondence with the letter 'C' written in green ink. Since Sir Mansfield, subsequent chiefs continue the tradition.

"The Spider made an extremely compelling argument, and to close this chapter once and for all would make Winnie extremely happy, I am damn sure of that."

"Maybe so, Harold, however I must state the obvious; Rudy Gomez was born a Nazi and has been steeped in their nonsensical Thule Gesellschaft drivel all of his life. His father sent him on a mission to deliver the Spider back to Argentina for execution and your primary plan does exactly that."

"Sir John, I'm afraid you are correct. We see very little chance that Chez Orlowski will survive this mission, with or without Gomez proving a Judas, so we must try our best to cover his back with covert Special Forces and our friends, the Mossad. It has been almost thirty years but this plan might bring closure to the whole Third Reich—Fourth Reich threat if things go our way."

"So why not just get the hacienda's address from Rudy and send the Mossad in? They did a spiffing good job in 1961 when they captured Adolph Eichmann, spiriting him out of Buenos Aires and back to Israel for trial before the Argentinians had any time to react.

"We all know the Spider has pulled off some pretty amazing stunts in the past, but he is fifty years old for God's sake. Surely you chaps can figure out a way to avoid him having to enter the lion's den?" Colonel Lewis sensed the chief's frustration but answered in a calm voice.

"Sir John, President Juan Peron and all subsequent Argentinian governments have been bought and paid for; in this regard, nothing has really changed politically since the end of the war. Argentina's GDP relies heavily upon the transferred plunder of the last war and the Eichmann incident caused exiled Nazis to threaten transferring their wealth to Paraguay if security was not beefed up. Rudy Gomez has only confirmed what we already suspected; Fortress Bormann is in Patagonia. If we go in there with force, I believe that Argentina will declare war on the United Kingdom. If you recall, MI6 recently received unsettling reports that Argentina has her eyes on repatriating the British Falkland Islands.

"Our alternative plan is to convince Bormann to leave his stronghold and travel to Germany. Once there, our agents could take over. The world still believes that Bormann died as he tried to escape Hitler's bunker but not having a body has encouraged all sorts of conspiracy theories; promulgating the idea that a Fourth Reich is being planned. If we can provide Bormann's body, we will present the world's media with tangible proof that he perished in 1945 as history recorded."

Sir John Rennie closed his eyes and remained silent for almost five minutes. Lewis and McDougal thought he had fallen asleep until his intense eyes snapped open. He offered his insightful recap to the two agents.

"Your alternative plan hinges upon Bormann's desire to live longer than his type 2 diabetes and sins give him the right," Sir John began. "You are suggesting that MI6 could disseminate information about a miracle device being developed by a German labora- tory. It is well known that Sir Walter Lister, perhaps the most eminent authority on the disease today, has published his belief that science will one day invent a surgically implanted device to control the advance of diabetes. Somehow, we'd have to convince Bormann that this German laboratory is in the short strokes of perfecting such a device."

Sir John stared hard at both his cohorts for confirmation and then continued.

"We will send Rudy Gomez back home with a mission to ensure that Bormann and his medical staff get word of the German research project. At that point, we can only hope that his father will be motivated to contact somebody at the lab for more information. The Spider's renowned ability to operate under extreme duress, coupled with his passion to ensnare the Reichsleiter, make him a perfect candidate for the role of chief technician at the German laboratory. He must convince Herr Bormann that this invention is the greatest thing since sliced bread and that he should leave the security of Patagonia to have one custom fitted in Germany. Hopefully, Gomez can convince his father to let him tag along. He delivers Bormann to the Spider and we are well on our way to having the tangible proof you desire. Gentlemen, what could possibly go wrong?"

Lewis and McDougal glanced furtively at each other. *Only about a million things could go wrong!*

Ignoring these negative vibes, Sir John announced his final decision.

"Subject to advising the new prime minister, Edward Heath, I approve the alternative plan. Under the circumstances, I much prefer that we persuade Bormann to return to Germany to play out the final act in our theatre.

"I definitely do not want Orlowski traveling to South America. However, in the role of point of contact in Germany, he could prove pivotal. In addition to the special qualities we have discussed, the Spider hates Nazis, speaks perfect German and can certainly handle himself if Bormann brings back-up muscle and matters get physical."

Commander McDougal enthusiastically endorsed C's approval and seemed reluctant to sully it with an obvious question. "Sir, there is little doubt that Chez Orlowski is a remarkable individual; I'd even dare to say unique, but his skills come from the streets; a product of hard life in labor camps. I'm not sure that he can assume the role of a technician with expertise in endocrinology?"

"With regard to the Spider's lack of any formal education, he has proved to be a very fast learner and we will juice him with the type of knowledge a senior technician might have without him having to answer deep probing questions. Notwithstanding, Peter, he is the best chance we have.

"Off the record, I'd still prefer to see the Mossad mop up the rest of these bastards."

CHAPTER THIRTY-FIVE

A Final Briefing

Outside the MI6 cocoon, nobody knew that Chez Orlowski and Rudy Gomez had spent any time in London and Commander McDougal was determined to keep it that way. As the Humber returned the three men to Hanger 5 in Luton he went over the travel details for the last time.

Turning to Chez, he began. "The JetStar will be dropping Rudy off in Southern Ireland. From Casement Aerodrome, he will take a taxi to Dublin Airport to catch a 7:20 p.m. flight to Buenos Aires on B.O.A.C. You will stay on the jet and continue to RAF Aldergrove where your car is waiting. Spend some time with your family and please give them my personal regards. After a couple of weeks, I will contact you about returning to London and then Frankfurt for special training." Chez nodded his understanding, and McDougal focused on Rudy.

"Rudy, this copy of *The Lancet* has been stamped 'Property of British Overseas Airways Corporation.' Your flight will take almost seventeen hours so you will read just about anything in the cabin, including a medical journal. It is dated two years ago and has been planted with an article by Doctor Fritz Huelbein. The good doctor claims that he might be on the verge of announcing a revolutionary means of controlling diabetes. Huelbein's device is being developed at the Steiner Laboratories in Frankfurt. Wait a week or so before bringing this article to your father's attention and then don't push it any more. We think it important that he comes to his own conclusion whether or not to try to contact Doctor Huelbein."

Questions flooded Rudy's mind. His chances of marrying Mary and rearing their family in anonymity depended upon a credible delivery of his side of the bargain.

"What happens if my father's vast resources uncover a similar copy of *The Lancet* magazine without the planted article? He is bound to have a covert operation in Frankfurt. What happens if they check out the Steiner Laboratories and there is no record of a Dr. Fritz Huelbein? But most important, why do we care about what happens in Frankfurt; I thought Chez was coming to Argentina with the device and that I was going to help him kidnap my father!"

"Good questions, Rudy. The July, 1968 *Lancet* has been completely reprinted to include our bogus article. Anybody contacting the publisher will receive the revised edition that, for the record, does not specifically claim anything. The publisher is very finicky about quack claims so we satisfied them by using some rather clever English dons at Oxford to tease the words of the article to their fullest extent.

"As to your subsequent question, the Steiner Laboratories are legitimate; they also happen to be a shill of MI6 that has been receiving funding from one of our philanthropic sources since 1947. Dr. Fritz Huelbein has been in charge of research since 1955. Their personnel records have been altered to include a trusted, high-level laboratory technician named Dr. Paul Schneider who has the physical characteristics of Mr. Orlowski. Chez, wearing a disguise, can be seen standing behind Dr. Huelbein at the lead-in to *The Lancet* article."

Then Peter McDougal cleared his throat nervously before adding, "In light of the obvious exposure to danger, Sir John is insisting that flying Chez to Argentina is out of the question. Every attempt must be made to persuade your father to meet Dr. Huelbein in Frankfurt rather than Patagonia. I would expect you and his personal physician to accompany him. Once you have delivered him, Chez will take over and you are relieved of your obligations. As promised, your criminal records will be expunged and I sincerely hope you will live a long anonymous life of bliss with your new family."

In contrast to their horrendous flight to Luton eight days earlier, the sun shone down from a bright blue sky on the entire route to Dublin. Casement Aerodrome is southwest of the Irish capital in Baldonnel. As a military airfield, it serves a useful purpose by allowing politically incorrect landings and takeoffs to take place under the blind eye of the Irish Government; the SIS and the CIA show their gratitude in ways to which the public is not privy.

As Rudy turned to step down onto the concrete apron, Chez shook his hand but not in friendship. It gave him a final chance to stare into the young man's soul.

"Rudy, at least five people have died in your attempt to kill me and you also bear considerable responsibility for the kidnapping of my daughter and goddaughter. Ordinarily, I would not put my trust in a man with such credentials, but there are bigger fish to fry. I expect to receive your telephone call in Frankfurt within the month. Let there be no doubt in your mind, I am expecting a double-cross but I'll live up to my word if you do the right thing for the first time in your life."

CHAPTER THIRTY-SIX

Northern Ireland

C hez managed to drive the twenty miles from RAF Aldergrove to Jordanstown despite waves of weariness that threatened to sweep over him but the expectation of seeing Jadwiga and his family generated a source of energy that kept him awake and in the final minutes of his journey, he was back to being his old self.

The McClain/Orlowski compound was located on the short portion of Glenkeen Avenue bounded by Church Avenue and Lenamore Drive. At both these intersections, black Land Rovers blocked the last hundred yards to his house. Two tall muscular men in tee shirts walked towards his red Jaguar XJ6. At first, he was concerned but then Chez noted the logos, smiled and lowered his window as he secured his 9 mm pistol back under the dashboard.

"Let me guess, Paddy McBride has my house on lockdown and you lads work for Black Widows Security?"

"Mr. Orlowski, we are instructed to stop any vehicles from driving past your house. Even though we recognize you, you must show us some identification.

Both men spoke with lilting Aberdonian accents but the fact that they were well over six feet tall with chiseled physiques prompted Chez to have a little more fun.

"So Colonel McBride has the 'Ladies from Hell' guarding my house; a little overkill for a few amateur Nazis I would think......"

"....With all due respect, sir, how on earth could you possibly know we are from the Black Watch Regiment?"

"Because giant Scottish soldiers generally are. And the respect is all mine; the Black Watch has some of the fiercest motherfuckers I have ever met, hence the nickname, Ladies from Hell. To assume a six-foot, six-inch Scotsman wearing a kilt was a lady usually resulted in pure hell being unleashed upon whoever used the insult."

Both men laughed as they moved their vehicle then turned to salute.

"It is an honor to meet you, Spider, a genuine honor."

Dinner at home with an extended family that included the McClains and Paddy McBride required seating for sixteen. There was laughter and relief that Chez was safely home but after the children had excused themselves, a sober tone infused the conversation of the five adults who remained to nurse brandy snifters around the fireplace.

"I understand that you cannot tell us anything about what happened in London but I can read you like a book, Czeslaw Orlowski. Something extremely dangerous is about to happen." Jadwiga Orlowski had been married to the most dangerous man in the world for over twenty-five years. She knew that she could not control him and anticipated that her stomach would be in knots if he disappeared on another mission. The specter of bringing up their children on her own was omnipresent but she had worshipped him since the day they fell in love. Paddy flicked on the television to deflect the awkwardness.

"A badly decomposed body washed up on Portstewart Strand last week has been identified. Dental records confirm the corpse as Brendan Mulcahy, missing leader of the Fenian Brotherhood, an extreme Republican organization. The autopsy also revealed the probability that Mulcahy had been shot in the left knee, a form of reprisal popular with the IRA."

However, Paddy had his own interpretation of events. "I call bullshit on that red herring. Brendan Mulcahy was the bloody eejit responsible for blowing up the Spider Academy and killing amongst others,

Siobhan McKenna. I'll bet you a pound to a shilling that as soon as Mary O'Connell learned about Mulcahy's role from Rudy, she told Barry McKenna. That wasn't an IRA reprisal, that was one really pissed off Dad."

"I believe you might be right and I have a couple of comments of my own," mused Malcolm McClain, "We know Mulcahy had two sidekicks, Tobin and O'Shaughnessy. Until we see their bodies on a beach, we have to assume they are still out there and McKenna will be hunting for them like a hound dog."

"And the second comment," the Spider interjected quietly, "would be never to underestimate Mary O'Connell. I do hope she and Rudy are not planning a double-cross."

Contrary to what Barry McKenna believed to have been a conclusive execution, Micky Tobin and Colm O'Shaughnessy survived their ordeal on Lough Foyle but the injuries they sustained left them both severely crippled. Both men could hobble about by tucking a crutch under one arm, but nonetheless, each managed to carry a load of intense hatred in his heart. Barely four weeks after they had been left for dead, they began their own mission of reprisal.

Pumped up with morphine, the disabled terrorists

split their surveillance to cover both entrances to the Celtic Harp, a local Derry pub known to be popular with Padraig O'Hanlon, the leader of the South Derry Brigade and the man who had abducted them. A dirty, dark blue Ford Transit pulled into the rear parking lot at around 9:00 p.m. and Micky Tobin watched O'Hanlon and two of his henchmen enter the rear door of the pub. He shuffled around to the street side and found O'Shaughnessy sipping from a quarter bottle of Jameson as he leaned against an alley wall for support.

"They have parked in the back lot. Help me get the stuff from the car."

Just after midnight, Padraig O'Hanlon and his two friends staggered out of the pub with three giggling women in tow; all six knew the Transit would be seeing some action tonight. O'Hanlon got in the back and one of his henchmen, a brute large enough to convince Tobin and O'Shaughnessy that he was part of their kidnapping setup, sauntered around to open the driver's door. The engine turned over once, then triggered explosives concealed inside two duffle bags that had been strategically placed under the fuel tank.

WHHUMP! The heavy Ford left the ground and while still in the air, erupted into a giant ball of deadly flames before crashing back loudly onto the asphalt. Micky and Colm watched the mayhem from a block away. They finished the Jameson with one slug each and then squealed away in their rusted Austin 1100.

"That felt good. It might be the whiskey and morphine cocktail but Jesus, Colm, that felt really good."

"I will feel even better when we do away with McKenna, O'Connell and whatever that fuckin' German Spanish ponce is calling himself today."

"Fuck 'em all to hell, Micky!"

CHAPTER THIRTY-SEVEN

Into the Lion's Den

The B.O.A.C. Super VC 10 touched down late at Ezeiza International Airport in Buenos Aires. MI6 had funded Rudy Gomez only enough money for a one-way coach ticket and he was aching and tired from the cramped twenty-hour journey. As the plane taxied towards the terminal, the passenger adjacent to Gomez spoke out in an overly loud voice.

"Know what B.O.A.C. really stands for?" He immediately answered his rhetorical question with, "Better Off on a Camel." The soused passenger guffawed loudly at his own joke and several passengers laughed with or at him but all were eager to disembark and leave the fatiguing experience behind them.

At his first opportunity, Rudy found a pay phone and called Ambassador Ludwig Freude.

"Mister Ambassador, it's me, Rudy Gomez. I am home from Europe and need to get to the hacienda. I have been robbed and have no money so I must ask for your assistance."

"My goodness, Rudy, we were beginning to think the worst. Stay near the taxi stand outside arrivals. An embassy limousine will be there to collect you in about thirty minutes."

As he drove, the driver explained that Rudy would be staying at the Castelar Hotel and Ambassador Freude would meet him there for lunch. Rudy was very familiar with the famous hotel on Avenida de Mayo; his father always stayed there when in the capital and Rudy had often accompanied him as a teenager. So when the black embassy limousine swept onto the magnificent Avenida 9 de Julio, he knew they were less than a mile from their destination. He always marveled at this magnificent five-hundred-foot-wide avenue; its twelve lanes of traffic flanked by beautiful linear parks. The driver turned left on Avenida de Mayo and pulled to a halt in front of a 1929, eight-storey building. Gomez retrieved his small travel bag, thanked the driver and pushed through the wood and brass revolving door that presented the lobby. A smart young man at the conserjeria picked up his phone as soon as Rudy announced his name and within seconds, the manager approached with hand extended.

"Senor Rudy, it has been much too long. I do wish you were staying with us for more than one night. We have put you in your father's favorite suite and he has telephoned to instruct the hotel to extend you credit, so you can supplement your wardrobe on Florida Street before you leave. The ambassador will be meeting you in the bar for lunch in twenty minutes; let me personally escort you to your room so you can freshen up."

A mixture of over-exhaustion and fear kept Rudy in a fitful state of semi-consciousness all night. *Why am I the only offspring to remain with my father? What happened to my brothers and sisters? I have no idea where they are or if they are even alive. Why did it take me so long to detect the evil in him and the Third Reich?? I am actually petrified of seeing him tomorrow. The MI6 idea is so farfetched, he will see right through it and I will never leave Argentina alive.*

God, please help me.

By dinnertime the next day, the hacienda's black stretch limousine halted outside the Hacienda San

Ramon and Rudy Gomez emerged wearing a stylish beige linen suit accented by a dark blue cotton shirt. The private plane organized by Ludwig Freude had reduced the travel time by several hours and Rudy should have felt refreshed but his mind was still troubled by the reveries that plagued him throughout the night. He had never tried to deceive his father before; the man's characteristic probing questions would easily poke holes in his rehearsed story. He paused before approaching the front door and took a deep breath of mountain air. Rudy had a nagging premonition that his time on Earth was running out; he would never leave Patagonia to return to Mary and his child in Europe.

"Rudy, if I wasn't so glad to see you, I would be very angry that your mission failed so miserably. How on earth could you fuck up such a simple task and leave ten good men locked in jail?" Bormann confronted his son in the front hall.

"Thanks for sending that high-powered lawyer to get me out. The staffeln created their own mess but I was able to distance myself from them."

An odd look flashed across the old man's face as he sprang an immediate question at his son.

"Rudy, after you got out of jail, you disappeared for several days. What on earth were you up to?"

"I failed to kill the Spider because in Belfast's close knit society, I stuck out like a sore thumb. Northern

Ireland has two main rival factions and I managed to piss them both off. The Catholics beat me up and stole my money; the Protestants believe that I got off with murder and wanted to settle the score. The minute I got out of jail, I went into hiding, hitchhiked across the border into Southern Ireland and eventually made it to Dublin. I bought the cheapest plane ticket I could; landing yesterday with only a passport and fifty pounds sterling to my name."

The two men held eye contact in silence for several seconds. Fear began to constrict Rudy's throat.

I have absolutely no chance, he thought. *My father can smell deceit; he perfected it into an art form during the war.*

However, Bormann suddenly smiled at his son, "Good to have you home, Rudy. Let's adjourn to the dining room and you can tell me everything that happened. We'll open a nice bottle of our local Malbec and eat some Carne Angus."

Martin Bormann looked as though he had aged ten years whilst Rudy had been in Europe, but the young man was determined to bide his time before broaching the subject of his health. The old man was still totally consumed with his plot to disrupt the Munich Olympics and several days passed before the son plucked up the courage to ask the question, "How is your health, mi Padre? Has your friend, Dr. Heim, heard about the interesting developments in West Germany? A laboratory in Frankfurt is on the verge of making a major breakthrough in the treatment of diabetes."

"What the hell are you talking about? Heim would have told me if there was any chance of curing my curse. I pay him a colossal amount of money to keep me alive and he is the last person to want the spigot turned off by my death. He comes up with some crazy new cure almost every week but has never once mentioned a laboratory in Germany. The bastard has had me chewing flax seeds for the past month."

"Then maybe you should have Dr. Heim check out this article I read on the plane. I stuffed the magazine in my carry-on and almost forgot about it." Rudy tossed the rumpled B.O.A.C. *Lancet* onto the table and freshened his coffee. "It got way too technical for me and I admit I can't really comprehend if it has any merit, but what the hell, I thought it might be of help."

Bormann grunted and changed the subject without even picking the magazine up.

But three days later, Dr. Aribert Heim sought out Rudy Gomez. "Ah, Rudy, your father gave me your magazine article to read. I understand you came across it on your recent flight. May I ask when you started taking an interest in *The Lancet*?"

"When it became the only magazine I hadn't read on the plane," laughed the younger man. "I couldn't understand what the hell it was about, beyond my conclusion that some lab in Germany is claiming that they have developed a cure for type 2 diabetes. Isn't that the condition that's ravaging my father?"

"I read *The Lancet* whenever I can and find it hard to believe that I missed this article!"

"Well, I don't know why you didn't see it, but surely we have contacts in Frankfurt am Main who can check out the credibility of the researchers. What do they call themselves?"

"Steiner Laboratories, and the researcher interviewed in the article is Dr. Fritz Huelbein. For the record, I have never heard of him or his labs but that does not necessarily mean anything. Quite frankly, it sounds too good to be true, but I owe it to the Reichsleiter to check it out. He has progressive circulation problems and has started to lose his sight, if we can buy him an extra five years it will be a miracle."

Colonel Harold Lewis telephoned the Spider himself. The mission had been approved and funded. He had less than a month to become an expert in the treatment of Type 2 diabetes. MI6 needed him in London immediately and from there, he would spend time in

Frankfurt to become familiar with the workings of Steiner Laboratories.

Jadwiga was furious when her husband told her he was embarking on such a loosely conceived and dangerous mission. During that evening's dinner with the McClains, she let him know it in no uncertain terms and Margery was just as mad at Malcolm by default. Both marriages were already strained by recent events and the probability was high that tempers would reach boiling point.

"You are a couple of middle-aged men acting like fools. You have both contributed more than your share to this world; now you should be spending time with your families and leaving all this espionage bullshit up to professionals," Jadwiga lectured them, knowing in her heart it wouldn't make any difference.

Chez put his arms around her and spoke softly but loud enough for the McClains to hear his thoughts.

"Jadzie, I made an incredibly stupid mistake by endorsing our business as the Spider Academy. I always suspected that Martin Bormann had made good his escape from Berlin because I knew first hand that he was the mastermind behind the Third Reich. My ego got in the way and the nagging thought that he might be out there caused me to use my nom de guerre as bait. What I did not account for was Bormann's depth of hatred for me coupled with the immense financial resources he has acquired. I have kicked open a hornets' nest and both our families will suffer wave after wave of attacks until we get fatally stung. Please, please forgive me."

Jadzia Orlowski sobbed inconsolably and Margery tried to comfort her as best she could. In less than a minute, the crying suddenly stopped and the strength of both women congealed.

"Czeslaw, hand me a handkerchief please and then answer me this. When have the Nazis ever got the better of you? You and Malcolm need to call on every resource you have to stop this man before he hurts any more people.

"Margery and I will be safe here with Paddy's group securing the area but I've seen that look in your eyes many times. You are going to hunt him down whatever I say, so go with my blessing and come home in one piece, ukochanie."

CHAPTER THIRTY-EIGHT

Time to Bait the Hook

C hez Orlowski and Malcolm McClain drove a rental car to Larne and boarded the car ferry that would take them across the Irish Sea to Stranraer. The long drive from southwest Scotland to the south of England allowed the two friends much needed personal time together. The Spider Academy was being rebuilt and Malcolm had agreed to manage the facility while Chez was in Frankfurt. Business details were discussed but they both admitted sheepishly that the main purpose of the long road trip was to escape the wrath of their wives.

McClain pulled the last shift of driving and found a car-hire return location on the northern outskirts of London. The vehicle had served a useful purpose but driving through The City was much safer by taxi and besides, Chez would be staying for another week before catching a train to Frankfurt. Both men telephoned their wives from the road and knew from their conversations that the old proverb 'absence makes the heart grow fonder' proved true. Malcolm would return to Belfast in a couple of days to patch up any remaining domestic discord.

"We are staying at the St. Ermin's in St. James, please," was all Malcolm had to say to the taxi driver. London taxi drivers are renowned for 'the knowledge,' a rigorous training program that imbues an encyclopedic ability to find any address in The City.

The black Beardmore MK7 pulled into the hotel's horseshoe shaped drop-off driveway with the cockney cabby concluding his friendly, non-stop spiel with a prophetic, "Alright, Guvs, no doubt you will be 'aving dinner with MI6 in the Caxton Bar tonight. They all used to meet 'ere you know, Kim Philby, Guy Burgess, even Ian Fleming. MI6 'eadquarters used to be right behind the 'otel. Enjoy yourselves, Gents."

Chez and Malcolm were both shocked for a moment and then realized it was no more than friendly banter. They paid the fare and began to chuckle as they approached the front doors. Inside, a magnificent white stone staircase framed the lobby.

"Mr. Orlowski, welcome to the St. Ermin's. I have two messages for you." The attractive young lady in charge of reception had an eastern European accent and a dazzling smile. Chez recognized her accent as Ukrainian and responded with "Thank you," in her native language, just to watch the surprise on her face. He read the messages and waited for Malcolm to complete his registration.

"Malky, our taxi driver must be clairvoyant. My friends will meet us in the Caxton Bar at around seven but I also received a disturbing message from Paddy. Barry McKenna was shot and killed last night in Belfast. Come straight to my room and we'll try to find out the details."

The private line to Colonel McBride's office at Black Widows Security was answered by a terse young woman who demanded an immediate answer to her prepared security question, "What was the final score of the soccer game you played on the airfield in Semic?"

"Eight goals for the good guys, one goal for the others," replied Chez. The woman's demeanor changed dramatically. "Mr. Orlowski, I take it? Colonel McBride is at your house as we speak. He is expecting your call."

Paddy picked up the phone on the first ring. "Orlowski residence."

"Paddy, it's Chez. Malcolm is standing beside me. Is everything alright?"

McBride's deep Ulster accent was unmistakable. "Everything is fine but I have tripled security around your houses after Barry McKenna was killed last night. We captured one of the shooters but the other got away. No mean feat as both assassins are cripples and have to hobble around on crutches."

"So why do you think our families might be in danger?"

"We were dead on in our assessment the other day. Apparently, as soon as Mary O'Connell told McKenna that Brendan Mulcahy had been involved in the death of Siobhán, he drove up to Londonderry to execute him and his two henchmen. After popping their kneecaps, the three thugs were floated out into Lough Foyle in a leaky boat to disappear forever. However, as we saw on the news, only Mulcahy's body drifted to shore. The other two, Micky Tobin and Colm O'Shaughnessy somehow managed to survive long enough to reach medical care. Their miserable lives are now fixated on revenge and they popped McKenna first chance they got. O'Hanlon and some of his friends were killed earlier in the month; I have to think Tobin and O'Shaughnessy should be prime suspects.

"Bill Larkin has Tobin in custody but O'Shaughnessy escaped. The inspector graciously allowed me to have a few words with Mr. Tobin and he volunteered a list of names that the stupid eejits are blaming for their crippling handicaps."

"Apart from that being bloody ridiculous, how long is this list?"

"Four names, and Tobin admits to having killed

two; O'Hanlon and McKenna. The next name is Rudy Gomez followed by Mary O'Connell. As a precaution, I added you and Malcolm to the list by association."

"And Tobin volunteered this information?" Chez asked with undisguised incredulity.

"Let me just say this. Micky Tobin might believe himself to be a hard man, but you and I have seen ten times worse," Paddy added one more tidbit before he hung up the phone. "For the record, Mary O'Connell has managed to completely vanish. My gut tells me that this is of her own volition and not caused by O'Shaughnessy so I wish her well."   ·

Malcolm and Chez changed into dark business suits and took the lift down to the lobby. The Caxton Bar is neatly tucked under the southerly wing of the hotel and Chez ordered two half pints of Guinness as they waited for their guests.

"Malky, is it just me or was there something really weird about our taxi driver guessing we were going to meet a secret agent in this bar tonight?" Chez chuckled.

"Not very secret, I'll admit. But heads up, here come George Smiley and James Bond now." The two friends stood up to greet Peter McDougal and Harold Lewis and after the handshakes, Commander McDougal stated the obvious in sotto voce.

"It may surprise you to learn that the Caxton has been the bar of choice for MI6 since before the war. Consequently, I'll wager that our meeting will be duly reported to the secret agencies of half a dozen countries before we even order our drinks."

Malcolm tossed the commander a pleasant jibe laced with more than a hint of sarcasm. "It would have surprised us, Peter, if our taxi driver had not revealed your closely-guarded secret as he drove us here. The S.I.S might want to select a new watering hole."

"Hidden in plain sight, don't you know, old sport. George, the bartender, is in our employ but plays the field, so I am going to let him know we are meeting here with the famous Malcolm McClain to procure some tickets for the Arsenal game next Saturday; word will spread like wildfire. Well, well, there's our good friend Vladimir Drobny from the Czechoslovakian Embassy, sitting in the corner having a tipple. George will make a couple of quid tonight."

"In that case, I will buy the drinks to cement the story. What'll you have?"

Stares of recognition followed Malcolm to the bar, a common occurrence to which he was well accustomed. The bartender greeted him with a broad smile.

"Mr. McClain, what an honor. I thought that was you when you walked in. Staying at St. Ermin's, are we?" Malcolm smiled back and nodded but was unable to interrupt the patter. "If you don't mind, would you give me your autograph?" As if by magic, a sheet of paper and pen appeared in front of the former soccer star.

"Anything you would like me to write in particular?"

"How about: To my good friend George, sincerely, Malcolm McClain."

"Glad to do it, George, and I'll have two doubles of Glenfiddich for the gentlemen at our table. They are big Arsenal fans who work for the government and a friend of mine, Sammy Nelson, asked me to pass along a couple of nice tickets for Saturday's game. Apparently, they made Sammy's speeding ticket disappear a couple of months back," Malcolm whispered conspiratorially.

"I could do with a couple of friends like that myself, Malky."

Malcolm noted that his relationship with George had accelerated from 'Mr. McClain' to 'Malky' in less than sixty seconds but he ignored that and delivered the classic Belfast brush-off, "Ah well, there y'are now."

McDougal and Lewis drained their glasses with a nod towards the corner and Vladimir grinned back. The four men left the bar and headed for dinner in the West End.

Malcolm and Chez parted the next day. Before returning to Belfast, McClain took advantage of his time in the capital to visit some of his old footballing friends; Chez on the other hand, went straight to boot camp.

MI6 had spent an impressive amount of time strategizing ways of extricating Martin Bormann from his hacienda and Colonel Harold Lewis went to great lengths to stress the parameters of Chez's role.

"Over the next two or three weeks, we are asking you to become an expert on the pancreas. Your role at Steiner Laboratories will be as the long-time trusted assistant of Dr. Fritz Huelbein. As you are aware, we fund Steiner Labs in return for maintaining a front for our operations in Frankfurt. Fritz Huelbein has established a solid reputation as a research pathologist but we don't think he will be able to stand up to a grilling from Nazi medical experts. You, on the other hand, are an assistant and therefore not expected to be perfect. We will cram you on the medical aspects of our plan and I am confident you will be able to pull off enough of a tease to get the old man out of his lair. Any questions so far?"

"Yeah, what the hell is a pancreas?" responded the Spider with a grin.

CHAPTER THIRTY-NINE

London and Frankfurt

C hez spent the next week learning firsthand about the treatment of diabetes. Arrangements were made for him to live and work as a staff member of King's College Hospital under the tutelage of Sir Walter Lister. Sir Walter's great, great uncle, Sir Joseph Lister, had pioneered antiseptic surgery in the late nineteenth century; this development established King's College Hospital as one of the finest in Europe. Following the family tradition, the great, great nephew now led the hospital's diabetes and endocrinology department.

The previous week, Sir Walter had received a personal request from one of his Chatham House school chums asking that he give Chez Orlowski a crash course in the treatment of diabetes. The old friend, Edward Heath, also happened to be the prime minister of Her Majesty's government and with the importance of the Spider's mission being stressed as a matter of extreme national security, Sir Walter was not in any position to refuse.

Their first morning together was filled with tension. Sir Walter typified the upper crust of British society. The man had been on a privileged path since birth; Chatham House grammar school followed by Oxford University and admittance into the Royal College of Surgeons before his thirtieth birthday. Now in his mid-fifties, he was at the zenith of his career and recognized globally as a preeminent authority on the treatment of diabetes. Sir Walter also inherited the innate Englishman's distaste for unnecessary interaction with anyone outside his social caste.

This man I am asked to babysit is an uneducated Pole whose English, and most especially his grammar, leave a great deal to be desired. And Eddy wants me to teach him a working knowledge of diabetes in one week. Bloody hell, I'll wager the man never even finished high school. I told Eddy it was a futile task but he will still owe me a week at Cowes next August, no matter what.

As Sir Walter fumed silently, he was making the same mistake hundreds had made before him: he was underestimating the Spider.

Chez Orlowski had been gifted with a powerful clean intelligence, one uncluttered by social niceties and honed by a hard life of tough experiences. To his credit, it did not take Sir Walter long to pick up on the phenomenon, and he invited Chez to have lunch with him on the second day. By the end of the week, the two men had built up a viable rapport.

"Graduation day, Chez. You continue to amaze me but I am going to give you one last grilling before I let you go into the field.

"Dr. Schneider, would you please tell me what causes type 2 diabetes?"

"Research indicates that overweight people are the most susceptible to type 2 diabetes but age, race and genetics are also factors. In essence, glucose provides energy to our muscles, the liver makes and stores glucose then uses the bloodstream to get it to the muscles. Insulin is an important hormone that facilitates the glucose entering our cells."

Sir Walter nodded his satisfaction and followed up with another question. "And where, pray tell, does the body find this magic hormone?"

"It is made in a gland below the stomach called the pancreas...."

"....Not so fast, for very important reasons, you need to be more precise in locating the pancreas. After all, your dick is also below your stomach."

Chez chuckled at his mentor, and lowered his head in a mock Japanese bow.

"Yes, Sensei, the pancreas is located below and behind the stomach, in a bend formed by the duodenum.

In addition to producing insulin, the pancreas assists the small intestine to digest and absorb nutrients."

"Correct. Your invention will be attached to the patient's left side with a special tube surgically inserted into the pancreas. Why would you do that, Dr. Schneider?"

"Research at Steiner Laboratories indicates that we can electronically stimulate the beta cells in the islets of Langerhans to secrete natural insulin into the bloodstream. Our invention also monitors the patient's blood sugar level and can add artificial insulin if necessary."

At this reply, Sir Walter shook his head, but he was not criticizing Chez.

"Would that such an invention was here today, Chez. The fact is, I believe what you described is actually possible but doubt we will have the technology to produce such a miracle device in my lifetime.

"Just remember, your mission is to convince Herr Bormann that you and Dr. Huelbein have the goods. Your answers just convinced me that you do, but you will need to call upon a giant slice of the famous Spider's luck to pull this off."

"Thanks, Sir Walter, you have been most generous with your time and wisdom. Needless to say, the mission would have been impossible without you."

The famous surgeon stood. "It would mean a great deal to me and my wife if you would check out of the St. Ermin's and stay at our country house this weekend. I will get you to St. Pancras on Sunday morning in plenty of time to catch your train to Frankfurt. An old friend of mine, Eddy Heath, will also be a house guest; I think you two should meet."

At the Hacienda San Ramon outside San Carlos de Bariloche, Martin Bormann was intrigued by the possibility that a German invention could lengthen his life. He insisted that Dr. Aribert Heim call upon any resources he needed to verify *The Lancet* article.

"Berty, did you manage to find out anything about Steiner Labs and this doctor called Fritz Huelbein?"

"I am still working on it, Mein Herr. Dr. Huelbein and his laboratory have been in Frankfurt for some time. I spoke with several doctors who have sympathies with our cause; most have heard of Huelbein and a couple of them actually use the Steiner Laboratories for routine blood testing and other menial tasks. However, none of my contacts had any idea that the Lab was working on the artificial pancreas mentioned in *The Lancet* but they also admitted that the science was possible and would be a godsend to the world of endocrinology."

"Did you try calling Steiner Labs to talk with Huelbein himself?"

"Jawohl. He just left on a retreat to Switzerland and his staff refused to release his whereabouts. They did say that his main assistant, Dr. Paul Schneider, is in charge during his absence."

"Then get Schneider on the phone. Find out what he knows about this invention and if it is for real. You must explain my situation without revealing my identity."

It took several attempts from Heim before a phone connection was successfully made between the hacienda and Steiner Laboratories. There is a five-hour time difference between Argentina and Germany, so Rudy, Bormann and Dr. Heim were eating breakfast when the receptionist in Frankfurt finally picked up her phone.

"Steiner Laboratories, how might I direct your call?"

"This is Dr. Aribert Heim, I am calling from Argentina in the hope that I might speak with Dr. Paul Schneider?"

"One moment, Dr. Heim, I will put you through to his office." Berty Heim took the moment of silence to cover the mouthpiece of the phone as he smiled at the other two.

"I have a distinct weakness for women with a Frankfurt accent. I find it very—dare I say—sexy......
Ah, Dr. Schneider?"

"Ja, this is Paul Schneider. How may I help you, Dr. Heim?"

"I am calling from Argentina after reading an article you published in *The Lancet*. I am the personal physician to a very important Argentinian who has progressive type 2 diabetes. He has asked me to find out more about your experiments and if he might be eligible for the treatment."

The Spider was sitting in Fritz Huelbein's sparce office. Across the desk was the head of Steiner Labs, the man who was supposed to be in Switzerland. Berty Heim might indeed have found the receptionist extremely attractive but her name was Gill Bolton, a talented linguist from London branch who could have answered the phone in several different German dialects. As soon as the call was identified as coming from overseas, MI6 protocol went into effect.

"Dr. Heim, I must first tell you that the article you refer to was released, somewhat prematurely, about two years ago. A local reporter informed us that they had details of our experiments, so Dr. Huelbein took the initiative of preempting the local rags by publishing a project report in *The Lancet*. Back in 1968, we still had several important test results to verify...."

"....With respect, Dr. Schneider, can you now tell me categorically that you have invented an artificial pancreas?"

Chez paused at the interruption and smiled. He felt as if he was fishing and his hook had just sunk into the mouth of a giant bass. He winked at Fritz Huelbein before continuing in his native Berliner German.

"Artificial pancreas would not be the technical term I would use. It is a complex device that helps an existing pancreas normalize the production of insulin. My senior partner, Fritz Huelbein, is out of the country and we certainly will not be releasing any information until he returns and our lawyers confirm our international patents are in place."

Berty Heim started to lose his temper. "Does the damn thing work and will it cure diabetes?"

The Spider was as cold as ice in his response.

"Dr. Heim, as you are aware, diabetes mellitus takes many forms. I will not ask you to violate your patient's confidentiality but if I were to tell you the symptoms our device can normalize, you might be able to ascertain if it would be useful for your patient. Shall I continue?"

"I apologize, Dr. Schneider and yes, that would be most useful." Chez then read off a list of classic type 2 diabetes symptoms.

"High blood pressure, blurred vision, frequent urination, extreme hunger coupled with unexplained weight loss, fatigue and presence of ketones in the urine."

Berty Heim's mouth dropped. "My patient has all those symptoms. Are you telling me you have perfected a device that can cure him by normalizing his blood sugar?"

"Yes Herr Doctor, but we cannot release the device until the legal work on the patents has been completed."

Martin Bormann had been listening on an extension. His patience was at an end and he erupted into the phone.

"Goddammit, this is Juan Gomez, the fuckin' patient. I am slowly dying from diabetes and don't give a shit about your patents. Get hold of Huelbein and tell him this from me. I am prepared to purchase Steiner Laboratories for one hundred million deutschmarks. I will escrow the money in a Swiss bank account and release it when he satisfies two simple conditions. First, Huelbein will bring the device to Argentina and do whatever it takes to hook me up to it; second, my doctor, Dr. Heim, will verify the reversal of my symptoms.

"Are we clear on this, Schneider? It is pretty damn simple; he cures me, he gets rich."

The Rechsleiter's voice was so loud, it resonated through the phone in the Frankfurt office and Fritz Huelbein heard every word. He became very nervous and looked for support from Chez Orlowski but what he saw chilled him to the bone. The Spider's eyes had narrowed and a thin vicious smile played on his lips. At that moment, Huelbein knew that MI6 had chosen the right man to handle their side of the mission.

"Herr Gomez, I can understand the desperation your situation is causing. I am the only person privy to Dr. Huelbein's travel plans, however, I will try to contact him with your generous proposal. Do you have a phone number where I can call you back by the end of the week? By the way, your German is excellent."

"Schneider, I will call you back this time tomorrow. You will accept my terms or there will be no Steiner Laboratories by the end of the week." With that, Bormann slammed down the phone.

The Spider spoke to himself in a low monotone, *"I just spoke with Martin Fucking Bormann. Bring it on, you fat prick."*

CHAPTER FORTY

Emergency Regroup

Commander Peter McDougal was in trendy Sachsenhausen by half past eight in the evening. Fearing that Steiner Labs might already be under surveillance, McDougal asked Chez to meet him at Wagner's Restaurant in the fashionable Frankfurt suburb. Wagner's signature dish is weiner schnitzel served with a green, seven-herb sauce and the two men talked earnestly as they ploughed through the massive portions.

"Harold and Sir John are extremely concerned by today's phone call. Of course, having you or Fritz fly to Argentina remains out of the question, and the sale Bormann wants cannot be consummated. On the other hand, if he carries through on his threat to destroy Steiner Labs, he will not get the device either. Bormann is not acting rationally and as such, he's created quite the conundrum. What are your thoughts?"

The Spider's unfettered thought process had already formulated a plan. He laid it out as he and McDougal completed their meal with glasses of apfel wine.

"So Peter, I'll leave the finer details up to you, but Fritz has to disappear for a while and if you can arrange for some press coverage in tomorrow's German newspapers, it would certainly bolster credibility. In addition, half a dozen plain clothed Royal Marines at the Labs might make the staff feel a little safer. How long are you staying?"

"As long as it takes, Chez, as long as it takes."

The expected phone call from Argentina chirped its presence at exactly 4:00 p.m. and Ms. Bolton put it through to Huelbein's office. Peter and Fritz both crossed their fingers as Chez picked up the receiver.

"Herr Gomez, I presume?"

"Did you get hold of Dr. Huelbein to discuss my offer to buy Steiner Laboratories?"

"I am afraid matters have become extremely complicated. Fritz was spending a clandestine week with his mistress in Switzerland. I broke my vow of silence and tried to contact him last night. The hotel manager reports that they both went hiking yesterday and never returned to the hotel. Two miles west of the hotel, a serious avalanche has been reported and the Swiss alpine police are searching for them as we speak. All their belongings are still in their room so I'm driving there tomorrow to try and mitigate any scandal.

"The avalanche was large enough to merit mention in today's *Frankfurter Allgemeine Zeitung* but no hard facts about any victims were reported. So, Herr Gomez, I really do not want to discuss any business deals with you at this time, I have more urgent things on my mind. Good day, sir." The Spider slammed down the phone and turned to his companions with a broad grin on his face.

"Lunch on me if he doesn't call back within ten minutes."

Less than five minutes later, Gillian Bolton put though the second call.

"Dr. Schneider, this is Rudy Gomez; my father is listening to our conversation on an extension. He wishes me to apologize for yesterday's untimely outburst. Can you give me any further details about Dr. Huelbein's situation?"

"Not really, Herr Gomez. The hotel manager reports that two bodies have been found but not as yet, identified. With regard to your father, I have seen many diabetes patients over the course of my career and

I understand the desperation they feel as the disease advances. I will be in a better position to discuss helping your father after this mess gets sorted out."

Knowing the person on the phone yet pretending he did not, seemed weird but Chez was acutely aware that he and Rudy could steer the conversation for the benefit of the evil ears that listened on the extension.

"Please assure your father that my options will be a lot easier if I become the sole owner of Steiner Labs. Fritz and I created a corporation when we founded our company. We have a provision that transfers sole ownership to the other in the event either of us become incapacitated. Notwithstanding, there remains one insurmountable hurdle; German law will not allow me to take our device across international borders until international patents are secured."

"But couldn't you just slip one into your luggage and come to Argentina on holiday?"

"That would be breaking the law and no amount of money is worth me sitting in jail for the rest of my life. If you and your father would like to come to Frankfurt, I can personally install our latest beta version of the device. You won't need to hide it in your luggage because it will be implanted in your father's left side. We can sign the ownership transfer while you are here; I want to make sure Fritz's wife gets her fair share of the proceeds."

"Please hold for a minute, Dr. Schneider, I need

to discuss this in private with my father." Chez held his hand over the mouthpiece for all of two minutes as he waited for Rudy to respond. Then the distant voice crackled back through the earpiece.

"Dr. Schneider, you are correct that nothing can happen until the current ownership situation is clarified and we understand that the value of Steiner Laboratories will be significantly enhanced by the international patents. My father is willing to double his initial offer and will fly to Frankfurt for the implantation—but only after he takes ownership of the company. As such, we require you to fly to Argentina when your business affairs are in order and we know who in fact is in charge. He will sign the legal documents in Argentina, transfer the funds and then return to Germany with you. Your first-class travel and a substantial cash advance will be part of our arrangements.

"I will leave you a private number to call when you are in a position to respond. Thank you so much for your consideration."

"Thank you, Herr Gomez. Now, you must excuse me."

The phone line disconnected and Chez went over the general gist with McDougal in English.

"Bloody shite, they are calling our bluff; this is not working out well for the good guys, Chez," McDougal said angrily. "Any counter we make to avoid going to

Argentina will scream that we are trying to extradite Bormann to Germany. I think this is game over and we must send in the Mossad to kill the bastard. Let's discover that Fritz is alive and well and the bodies belong to someone else. He refuses to sell the company and that's that."

"Bormann is one of the richest men in the world. He will destroy Steiner Labs out of spite if he can't buy it. We have been dealt a hand and I am going to play it out. My gut tells me to trust Rudy so I am going to fly to Argentina and bring Bormann back; even though it may be in a body bag."

"Chez, the prime minister has expressly forbidden that you go to Argentina and he is bloody right. It is over; we gave it our best shot but we've lost this one. Once Bormann buys the company, he can check into a private nursing home anywhere in Europe and have Dr. Heim collect the device from Steiner. A Nazi surgeon he trusts can install what he thinks he has purchased. You must be aware that he does not need you after you sign over ownership. Your body will never be found."

"Peter, I am very grateful for everything the United Kingdom has done for me and my family but my true allegiance will always be to Poland and I can never forget how those Nazi bastards decimated my adopted country. When I escaped from Berlin in 1945, I met a young man named Hans Dorff. He led the true Berliners against the Nazi thugs. I doubt he is still alive but check on him if you can. I want to deliver Bormann, dead or alive, back to the Berliners he betrayed. Tell Malcolm to explain it to Jadwiga. She'll understand."

I seriously, seriously doubt that, was the nagging thought that haunted him for the rest of the day.

CHAPTER FORTY-ONE

Patagonia

During the next week, the Spider had one additional telephone conversation with Rudy Gomez. Again, careful not to reveal their relationship to prying ears, he sowed seeds that there had been no progress in finding the whereabouts of Dr. Huelbein or his mistress but now three unidentified bodies were currently held in the Swiss morgue. The ten-day period required by law for identification would expire in another two days, after which, he would be entitled to assume sole ownership of Steiner Labs and thereby the intellectual rights to the miracle supplemental pancreas that could extend Martin Bormann's life. The stage was set for Dr. Schneider to have a personal meeting with Bormann, sell the company and then return with the Reichsleiter to Germany for implantation of the device. The fact that there was no device did not worry the Spider; this matter would be brought to conclusion long before he had to enter an operating room.

Lufthansa #510, a direct flight from Frankfurt to Buenos Aires, pulled up to the gate in the early hours of the morning. Chez Orlowski was one of only two travellers flying first class which prioritized them to proceed into Terminal A well ahead of the rest of the passengers. He presented the well-worn West German passport that Commander McDougal had provided and smiled congenially at the immigration officer. The man spoke passable German and Chez surmised that most of the rest of his flight would be directed through this same booth.

"Welcome to Argentina, Dr. Schneider. May I ask the purpose of your visit?"

"I am catching the 9:30 a.m. flight to San Carlos de Bariloche where I will spend the next few days consulting on a medical matter before returning to Germany next week."

"Thank you, Doctor, have a pleasant stay in my country. Your luggage will clear customs at BRC as your ticket is technically a direct flight."

As he entered the Aerolinas transit lounge, the receptionist stopped him cold with a message. "Ah,

Dr. Paul Schneider, you have a guest waiting for you."
She gestured towards a sofa where Chez acknowledged the smiling face of Rudy Gomez. His senses immediately went on alert; MI6 had outfitted him with an almost undetectable, curly dark brown wig that matched his recently grown, Prussian moustache. In addition, he wore expensive photogrey glasses yet somehow, Rudy had recognized him instantly. With steady resolve, he remained in character and strolled towards the seating area.

"Guten morgen, Mein Herr, I am Dr. Paul Schneider." Then under his breath he whispered, "Rudy, I am very glad to see you but for Christ's sake, how do you know someone in this lounge is not watching us?"

But Rudy was well prepared and replied in conversational German, "Dr. Schneider, I am Rudy Gomez. My father asked that I meet you in Buenos Aires and requested I accompany you on the final leg of your journey to our home. We have a little time and I'm familiar with a delicious fresh pastry shop in the terminal. Would you care to join me?"

Very clever, thought Chez. *If anyone is watching, they will not expect us to leave the lounge as soon as I walked in. Moreover, I will certainly notice if anyone tries to follow us.*

The two men walked to the breakfast venue and it was not until they were able to find a remote table that Chez began to feel comfortable with the situation.

"Rudy, in the eyes of the world that exists on this side of the Atlantic, we have never met before this morning. If your father has any inkling of what we are up to, neither of us will see another sunrise. Where is his head right now? Is there any chance he'll fly with us to Frankfurt?"

"He talks like he will. The Steiner device is his only real chance of reversing the diabetes. He is still obsessed with disrupting the Munich Olympics; it is all he thinks about and he's determined to live long enough to gloat over his handiwork. By the way, you're not still going to coach the British team, are you?"

"As a matter of fact, no. This is my final mission and if I survive, I want to concentrate on rebuilding the Spider Academy. Hell, maybe I'll be lucky enough to have grandchildren some day and be around to teach them how to vault! By the way, how did you manage to recognize me in the lounge?"

"I didn't. I gave the receptionist your name and told her to send you over when you came in. Don't worry, Chez, I still cannot believe it's you. The disguise is very effective."

"That's a relief, but for now, let's concentrate on what we need to do. Time to head for Patagonia?"

They kicked up a cloud of the local red dust as the plane taxied towards the Bariloche terminal. Chez had a window seat and commented the moment his sharp eyes took in the scene on the apron.

"This airport is full of military vehicles. What's that all about, Rudy?"

"The 12th Mountain Infantry Regiment is based here. Nothing out of the ordinary. I heard a specialist security group from Europe is conducting joint Alpine exercises with them over the next week or so. The 12th are crack troops and my father sends them quite a bit of money. It allows him to treats them like his own personal security force."

"Wonderful," replied the Spider sardonically. "Thanks for letting me know in advance."

Martin Bormann and Dr. Aribert Heim were both seated in the study at the hacienda when Rudy ushered in his guest.

"Gentlemen, may I present Dr. Paul Schneider from Frankfurt." Both Nazis remained seated but gestured for the younger men to join them. It was just after noon and a servant brought out a large platter of cold cuts and cheeses for a light lunch. After polite small talk about Chez's flight, Bormann cut right to the chase.

"Can I assume that you now have complete authority to act on behalf of Steiner Laboratories and that you brought the necessary legal papers for me to review before I purchase your company?"

"Yes, Herr Gomez, but please remember, certain considerations must be satisfied by both parties before any deal can be consummated." Bormann's eyebrows furrowed like a thundercloud. He remained silent for a few seconds before uttering a measured reply.

"Of course, Herr Doctor, but with respect I must in turn remind you that I have already given you one million deutschmarks as a non-refundable retainer, not to mention an expensive plane ticket. You on the other hand, have yet to prove your device works—or even exists!"

The Spider could not help thinking, *I have never been scared of any man but this one makes my skin crawl. I am face to face with the very Devil himself!*

"Herr Gomez, you and Dr. Heim are quite welcome to ask me any questions you want. I did bring our latest test results with me and I think you will find them very encouraging. As you know, I am not a medical doctor; I am a scientist but I do have a reference who has agreed to speak with you by phone or in person if you are willing to visit King's College Hospital in London. Sir Walter Lister is perhaps the most eminent authority on diabetes in the world and he is very familiar with the Steiner Labs and the device I helped invent. Call him right now if you want."

The Nazis looked at each other and Bormann

nodded his head as if to answer an unasked question. Heim turned to Chez in response.

"Sir Walter is indeed a legend in his field and I think you might just have answered all our questions with that single referral. Give me his direct line and I will make the courtesy call during business hours in London. In the interests of complete disclosure, the reason that we will not be visiting him personally is that we are both, shall we say, personae non grata in England. In case you have not already figured this out, Senor Gomez, the gentleman seated before you, is better known as Reichsleiter Martin Bormann."

The Spider feigned suitable shock as he thought to himself, *And disclosing that information to me is tantamount to my death sentence. I am most certainly not going to sign any papers here. If they are going to try to kill me, I must trick them into doing it in Frankfurt.*

Chez Orlowski might have described the next couple of days at the hacienda as pleasant—if he did not have a recurring urge to break the Reichsleiter's neck whenever he was within three feet of the monster. Dr. Aribert Heim continued to ask exploratory questions about the device and Chez, well-rehearsed at King's College Hospital, had no problems handling them all with aplomb. It reinforced his conclusion that Sir

Walter Lister had been contacted and the credibility of the Steiner Laboratory's device thereby confirmed. As such, the pleasant hospitality that Chez was being afforded made perfect sense. He was ostensibly the head of Steiner Labs and they were at least supporting the pretense that they would need him to continue running the place after their purchase.

A somewhat awkward moment occurred during dinner that night when Chez caught Bormann staring at him. He smiled and took the initiative.

"Do you have a question, Herr Reichsleiter?"

"I can tell from your accent that you are from Berlin and I assume that you are of an age that served the Fatherland during the war; I am just wondering if our paths might have crossed. There is something about you that is vaguely familiar."

"I would certainly have remembered meeting you, sir, but I was excused service due to a debilitating lung problem. My father was a doctor and I worked as an assistant in his medical practice, which is where I developed my desire to help people." The smooth answer was accepted begrudgingly with a grunt from Bormann and the matter was dropped.

Rudy Gomez confirmed all of the Spider's conclusions when they managed to get a few minutes alone together.

"Chez, be ready to travel home tomorrow morning. My father is committed to making the trip to Frankfurt for the surgery. He told me to tell you that his lawyers have approved your documents and the agreed two hundred million deutschmarks will be transferred from Zurich into an escrow account at the Deutche Bank headquarters in Frankfurt as soon as you transfer the company to him. However you were right, he will be insisting that you sign the papers before we leave."

"Rudy, I smell a rat and doubt that any funds will be escrowed in Frankfurt. It is critical for me not to divest ownership of Steiner Labs until I get to Europe. I have to think of an excuse to delay the signing until after our plane lands safely in Germany; once he owns the company, I not only lose my only bargaining chip, I lose my life.

"When he revealed his true identity to me, it was a calculated move on his behalf to make me aware of his immense power but I am certain he has no intention of letting me reveal the whereabouts of a war criminal to the world. As long as he believes that the device exists, my odds of staying alive remain a helluva lot better in Frankfurt than here. If I manage to pull it off, who is going with us and how are we getting to Frankfurt?"

"Looks like just you, me, Berty Heim and my father. The military is sending a Bell 212 Twin Huey to the hacienda at ten o'clock tomorrow morning. As you noticed, the 12th Mountain Infantry is playing war games with some foreign special forces and the

Bariloche Airport is on lock down until Thursday for mock exercises in counter terrorism. As such, our private plane has been grounded. As a form of apology, the Huey will transport us 200 miles south to Neuquén. Once there, the Presidente Perón International Airport has many regular Aerolineas flights to Buenos Aires, so we will have no trouble connecting with our Lufthansa flight to Frankfurt. My father will reveal all of this to you tonight at dinner."

"Just for sport, ask what the seating arrangements will be on the flight to Frankfurt. I am betting only three tickets have been purchased!"

The next morning, the four men drank coffee on the outside patio of the hacienda and waited for the military helicopter to arrive.

"Dr. Schneider, I am a little disappointed that you did not bring the signed papers to breakfast. You have had them since yesterday and my lawyers need everything in place before we leave for Frankfurt. Is there a problem?" Bormann demanded curtly.

"Not at all, however, I noticed a small discrepancy with the address. Perhaps it would be better if my lawyers in Frankfurt corrected this one sentence. Both parties have approved everything else so the revision should not be an issue. We will then be able to sign clean originals in Germany to perfect the deal." The mood became tense and Bormann began to fume as he struggled for a response. During the awkward silence, Chez caught sight of a man walking towards the stables. His warning antennae went on full alert, but he wasn't exactly sure why. Another man came out of the stables and talked to the first.

Oh shit, those are the men who were with Rudy, or should I say, Rafael de Maldà, baron de Cortada, when I first met him in Belfast. I doubt they will recognize me but this could rapidly turn into a disaster.

"Gentlemen, I am going to have to relieve myself before being bounced around in a helicopter. Rudy, could you please direct me to a bathroom?"

Rudy got up politely and escorted Chez into the dining room.

"Through the hall; first door on your…"

"…Rudy," hissed the Spider, "There are two men over by the stables who look a lot like your travel compadres when I met you in Belfast. Inspector Bill Larkin would like to have their heads on a platter for murdering a bartender—but my immediate problem is that they can upset our applecart in a heartbeat if they identify me."

Rudy hurried over to the window and strained his eyes towards the stables.

"Shit, you are right. Their names are Lucas Romero and Franco Ramos. We relegated them to another of our properties in Tierra del Fuego as punishment for abject stupidity. I thought they would have frozen to death by now and have no idea why the hell my father has allowed them back here."

"I repeat; if they recognize me as the Spider, your father will never believe that you are not a co-conspirator. Maybe he recalled them to check me out. If that's the case, we are both dead men."

The instant that Rudy and Chez returned to the patio, the Spider noticed the change in Bormann's demeanor and instinctively knew that his cover was blown. Before he could react, he felt the cutting edge of a facón blade against his neck and from behind, a rough hand ripped off his wig.

"Nice try, Herr Spinne, I must admit, the lure of living without diabetes almost colored my judgment but I have a habit of always planning for contingencies and undertook my own covert investigation into Steiner Laboratories. Yesterday, my men visited the missing Fritz Huelbein at his home in Frankfurt, so I am very aware that there is no device. He didn't exactly know who you are, but admitted that you are working for the British government. I used Rudy as bait until I got my confirmation from Frankfurt and then, knowing I could no longer trust my own son, I flew Ramos and Romero up from Tierra del Fuego to make the identification. What a gift!"

The Spider could see two armed gauchos on each side through his peripheral vision, sensing at least another two were behind him. He had a strong suspicion that they might be Ramos and Romero.

"My diabetes will eventually kill me anyway but I shall just have to die happy in the satisfaction that I have caused you pain beyond your wildest imagination. I have decided to invite some of my closest friends to watch your final minutes. Your painful exit from this world will occur exactly one hour after I execute the sorry bastard whom I thought was my son."

The Spider suddenly dropped to his knees; his left hand grabbing Franco Ramos's wrist as his right elbow crushed into the gaucho's unprotected groin. The Argentinian screamed in pain as his right wrist snapped. Chez grabbed the knife before it hit the ground and sliced Ramos's throat in one continuous fluid move. The four gauchos beside him were too close to use their guns without endangering Bormann and Heim, but the Spider with a knife is lethal in any circumstances. Two of the thugs were dispatched easily and swiftly; mounting fear was evident in Bormann's eyes as the odds began to swing in the Spider's favor.

But Chez never saw the blow from Lucas Romero that caught him under the left ear. His world dissolved into blackness.

CHAPTER FORTY-TWO

The Best Laid Plans of Mice and Men

I n the San Carlos de Bariloche airport, the war games had concluded for the day and Colonel Miguel Rodriguez of the 12th Mountain Infantry Regiment was catching up on paperwork as he sat alone in the main passenger lounge. An adjutant approached him.

"May I get you some coffee, mi colonel?"

"Perfecto, Juan and please locate the British commandant and ask him to join me."

Ten minutes later, a massive man in alpine camouflage sat down beside him.

"That was an exceptional dawn exercise, Miguel. Your men have improved enormously over the past week. I am happy to report that it has become increasingly difficult for the Black Widows to infiltrate your airport perimeter."

"Much appreciated, Paddy, but that is not why I asked to speak with you. Something unusual is going on at a giant hacienda just north of here. I've always suspected that it might be owned by Nazi war criminals because they keep everything very secretive. Once or twice a year, they send my regiment a large donation in return for any protection we might provide; sometimes they might be having a large party that last two or three weeks, other times they just might need an armed escort for a day. I have never actually met the owner but he seems to have powerful friends in Buenos Aires.

"Anyway, because our exercises shut down the airport we received orders to fly three people from the Gomez hacienda to Neuquén this morning. About twenty minutes ago, that plan was suddenly cancelled. In its place, I am ordered to lock down the hacienda for up to a week while a group of VIPs assembles to attend a special meeting. What do you make of it?"

"I'm afraid it's not good, Miguel. When I told you we scheduled these airport security exercises at the last minute to catch you unprepared, that was only partially true. There cannot be many haciendas of the size you mention this close to Bariloche and I believe it might be the same hacienda where a friend of mine is staying. I scheduled this trip to Argentina primarily because I need to be close by in case he got into any trouble. From what you just told me, I think my friend might be in deep shit." The British soldier silently weighed his options and then presented his requirements to Colonel Rodriguez.

"I have immediate need for a couple of Hueys to get me and my men to the hacienda; we'll try a hot extraction if it's not too late. I'll have to rely upon you to dream up an explanation for Buenos Aires. Maybe you say we went rogue and stole them but, rest assured, I will protect your career as best I can." Colonel Paddy McBride had known his Argentinian counterpart for over a decade and had already decided that the younger man would be perfect to head up Black Widows Security in South America.

"Paddy, hold on just a minute. I think we both know who these VIPs are. I am under strict orders to turn a blind eye and never mention it, but fuck that, maybe now is the time to take a stand. The Nazis are a tremendous embarrassment to my country, therefore, I would like to suggest an alternative plan."

"I am listening, but make it quick, Miguel. Apparently we don't have much time."

"As requested, I will lead a squad from the 12th to secure the hacienda. I suspect it will take Senor Gomez, or as local rumor has it, Reichsleiter Martin Bormann, a couple of days to get his fellow war criminals together, so your friend, the Spider, will most likely be kept in one piece until the glorious get-together takes place. Remember, Bormann is expecting me to protect his property so I will use that as an excuse to check for any places your friend might be incarcerated. At the earliest opportunity, I will make it my business to extract the Spider and bring him back here. I think there is an excellent chance he might still be alive."

As McBride listened to this plan, his two index fingers tapped together in front of his pursed lips. This continued for almost a minute after Colonel Rodriguez had finished talking. Finally, the giant Ulsterman tossed out his own thoughts.

"I'm afraid it doesn't fly, Miguel. Martin Bormann controls the purse strings of your government and he will come after you with everything he has. I appreciate your bravery but I will not be able to protect you from the aftermath. However, I do like the first part of your plan, so go to the hacienda as expected and let me know if the Spider is still alive. In the meantime, I will attempt to reinforce my Black Widows with additional Special Forces and simultaneously arrange for the Royal Navy to open a back door for us to escape through if we are successful.

"My men will wait here at the airport until you tell me the party is about to begin. Then we will supplement the 12th to eradicate the cancer your country has endured.

"Heads will be cracked but I am betting if we get rid of Bormann and his cronies, your government might grow some balls."

"Paddy, I cannot guarantee the safety of the Spider if it comes down to a full blown fire fight. Bormann has a small army of heavily-armed thugs at his hacianda…"

"…Trust me, Miguel, dead or alive, the Spider would not want it any other way."

CHAPTER FORTY-THREE

The Hacienda San Ramon

As consciousness slowly returned, the throbbing in the Spider's body only increased. Pain was everywhere; his hands, arms, legs but mostly the left side of his head. Through the fog, a familiar voice called his name.

"Chez, thank God, I was beginning to think you were dead." Chez managed to open his eyes and turn his head towards the words. In the dim light, he saw another man suspended from a horizontal pipe in a manner similar to himself. "Rudy, is that you?"

"I am afraid so. My father had suspicions about my behavior since the Belfast trip and Ramos and Romero were brought back to the hacienda to not only to identify you—but to rat on me. Apparently, they paid more attention than I thought to my first encounter with Mary O'Connell and took unnecessary pleasure in branding me as a philanderer who was delinquent in paying attention to our mission to kill you. I really don't know what I did to piss them off; I have known them both since I came to Argentina and thought they were my friends.

"They both recognized you instantly from our lunch in Belfast, despite the disguise. There is something in the way you move that cannot be concealed. So my flagrant ignorance branded me as your accomplice." Chez noticed that Rudy had dark bruises around both eyes.

"Your father do that to your face?"

"Hell no, my father manipulates from behind the scenes. He has about forty outlaw gauchos on the payroll, men who will do anything he asks without questioning. Smacking me around in front of him gave a couple of the sadistic bastards nothing but pure pleasure. We are both to be kept alive until Klaus Barbie and the rest of the Fourth Reich leadership get here. I will be killed as a traitor but your execution is the main event and I'm sorry to say, it will be dragged out and extremely painful."

"They can do as they like," the Spider shrugged. "I have taught myself many ways to mask pain. They will not get any satisfaction out of me."

The Spider was now lucid enough to take in his surroundings. The room had the dank smell of a basement. It was about eight feet in height with a dirt floor and three narrow awning windows at the top of the one exterior wall. Strong lariat ropes secured both him and Rudy; their wrists looped over a horizontal black iron pipe supported by hangers screwed into the floor joists above. Rudy's height allowed the tips of his toes to touch the floor but Chez's shorter stature caused his entire weight to be suspending from the pipe.

"Do we have any guards to worry about?"

"Lucas Romero for the most part; spelled by various other thugs when he needs to eat and sleep. It is pretty much twenty-four hour surveillance but they do leave to take food and bathroom breaks. For the record, we don't get either of those luxuries; I am hungry and smell like a sewer. Wait, I hear him coming back."

"Then I am going to pretend to be unconscious."

For the next hour, the Spider hung motionless from the black pipe. He felt the rope slowly biting into the skin of his wrists as his mind raced to analyze the dilemma. Suddenly, the sound of helicopter rotors vibrated the air and Romero rose and left the room to check out the excitement. As soon as he left, Rudy whispered urgently to Chez.

"That must be the army detachment. My father

has ordered the 12th Mountain Infantry Regiment to provide security for the handful of his cronies he has invited to witness our executions. These old Nazis have been extremely paranoid since the Mossad snatched Adolf Eichmann off a bus in San Fernando. The Fourth Reich has threatened the Argentine government with massive reprisals if that ever happens again."

"Rudy, you were conscious. How did they get the rope between our wrists over this damn pipe?"

"They didn't, a couple of thugs stood me on a barrel while my wrists were tied. Then they kicked the barrel away. The pipe is an old heating pipe made of fairly thick metal."

Rudy watched in amazement as the aging gymnast suddenly jack-knifed his heels up and into the six-inch space between the pipe and the floor joists. With his weight off his wrists, the Spider grabbed the pipe with one hand and tried to work a knot with the other. But his weight had pulled the knots tight and none of the bands surrendered. So he resorted to rubbing the rope between his wrists against the sharp edge of the nearest hanger. He took both hands off the pipe to facilitate this and his stomach muscles began to scream but he kept at it until the rope parted.

"Someone's coming," hissed Rudy Gomez urgently. The Spider grabbed the pipe again and swung his legs back to vertical just as the door opened. Lucas Romero noticed nothing amiss, grunted and sat down in his chair to read an American motorcycle magazine he had found.

Chez eventually let out a low groan. Romero glanced towards him briefly but then went back to coveting a red Harley Davidson in the magazine he held. It was indeed a beautiful bike but more probable he was enjoying its unlikely rider, a young lady who was completely naked except for a pair of goggles. Chez waited a few seconds and then mumbled some more drivel.

"Back in the world of the living, are we? What the hell are you moaning about?" Chez repeated the nonsense, this time, a little louder.

"If you don't shut the fuck up, I will knock you senseless so I can enjoy my magazine in peace." Again, Chez mumbled his indecipherable gibberish at the gaucho. Lucas Romero stood up and threw his magazine onto the seat.

"You stupid bastard, you've asked for it." He strolled towards Chez and balled up his fist.

His prisoner then spoke calmly in their common language, English, "Can you see my toes, Lucas?"

Puzzled, Lucas Romero looked down. The Spider let go of the pipe and drove his pointed elbow onto the top of Romero's skull as he fell. The gaucho collapsed to his knees but was unable to protect himself from the sinewy arm that locked around his neck.

"Just out of interest, Rudy, which one of your gauchos killed the bartender in Belfast?"

"It was Franco not Lucas."

"No matter, both of them gave us the death sentence. Bill Larkin can close the book on this one." And with that, the Spider snapped Romero's neck.

Chez located the gaucho's facón knife and sliced through the knots that held his wrists and ankles. He pushed a barrel under Rudy's feet and did the same to release him. The two men spent the next few minutes rubbing their joints to restore blood circulation but the Spider did not miss the opportunity to relieve Romero's lifeless body of an old revolver, which he tucked into his belt along with the facón.

"Chez, outside this room are forty of my father's personal thugs supplemented by a platoon of elite mountain troops. Tomorrow morning, the Fourth Reich will start arriving and I'll bet each one will want to come into this room to gloat before the execution. We have to escape tonight. I have spent most of my life on this hacienda and know every inch of it, so we do have a small advantage."

"Believe it or not, Rudy, I've been in worse situations. What served me well was to do the very opposite of what your opponent is expecting. Show me how you would get from this room to the most likely route you would take to escape this hacienda to safety."

Rudy led the way out of the basement prison and Chez followed him along a corridor to a set of stairs.

He whispered urgently, "At the top of these stairs

is our main kitchen. At this time of day there are going to be at least a couple of servants preparing dinner. The back door from the kitchen leads into a service yard. Once outside, we will be exposed for about one hundred meters until we reach the tree line of the Valle Encantado. Those trees will conceal us as we climb down to the river and break into our boathouse. A small river flows down the valley for about three miles until it joins the much larger Rio Limay. From the confluence, we must then head upstream but should reach the east end of Nahuel Huapi Lake after about ten minutes. With any luck, we can get to within two miles of the Chilean border just by staying on the lake."

"Sounds like a plan that might work. What type of boats do you have in the boathouse?"

"There are a couple of row boats but we'll have to take the motor boat. We can drift silently with the current until we reach the El Rio Limay but we will definitely need the Evinrudes to get us upstream to the big lake."

"One last question, Rudy. By chance is there any place here in your house where we can hide?"

The Spider's question puzzled Gomez and he paused for several seconds before deciding to answer. "As a matter of fact there is. When I was fifteen years old, I found a portion of the attic above my bedroom that could only be reached from the ceiling of my closet. As a teenager, I would retreat there for hours and read. Nobody ever found me and I always felt secure, but surely you are not suggesting we risk staying in the house? One of the other gauchos will be replacing Romero in just over an hour and we have to be long gone by then."

"I am definitely going with you to the boathouse, Rudy. I just want to weigh all my options. How would we get from here to your room if we cannot make it past the kitchen?"

"Don't even try it, Chez. You would have to go up the main staircase at the front of the house. My room is to the left of the one you have been staying in."

The escapees climbed the stairs and walked boldly into the kitchen. As a result of their confinement, the two fugitives had an unpleasant pungent smell clinging to them. It caused both the kitchen staff to turn towards them as they entered. Rudy and Chez leapt forward and clamped their hands over the startled women's mouths before they had a chance to scream for help.

"Pinch her nose shut, Rudy, and hold on until I tell you. It will only take about a minute." The struggling gradually diminished as the two victims slowly succumbed to a lack of oxygen. "Okay, lower them gently to the floor and let's head for that river valley.

These two will be our best witnesses when they wake up. And leave the kitchen door open behind us."

With Rudy leading the way, they had made it to within a few yards of the tree line when a shout rang out from the direction of the stables.

"Keep going, Rudy; fast as you can. You have less than ten minutes to get that boat started. No real need to be quiet anymore; gun the engine and head for Chile."

"You are not coming with me?"

"You have fulfilled your part of the deal, Rudy and deserve to get back to Ireland to enjoy your new family. But I am guest of honor at your father's party; it would be rude for me not to show up.

"I've got Romero's gun and will buy you as much time as I can."

"Good luck, my friend."

"And to you, amigo."

CHAPTER FORTY-FOUR

The Party at San Ramon

C olonel Miguel Rodriguez sat in a Huey parked on the forecourt of the hacienda and dialed an encrypted frequency into the radio to connect him with Colonel Paddy McBride at the Bariloche airport.

"Paddy, we have an unexpected wrinkle in our plans. I seriously underestimated your friend, the Spider." Rodriguez heard a chuckle on his headphones.

"Ah well, there y'are now. You're not the first, not by a long shot. What has the wee man been up to now?"

"He has escaped. Bormann had him and his son, Rudy Gomez, trussed up in the basement to await public execution in front of an assembly of Fourth Reich VIPs but we just found the guard's body with no trace of any prisoners bar some frayed ropes."

"One guard—for the Spider! Now there's a total mismatch. Any idea where they went?"

"Actually, they seem be headed towards you. They knocked out two servants in the kitchen and were last seen headed towards El Valle Encantado with four of Bormann's pet gauchos in hot pursuit. About ten minutes ago, my men heard gunshots and I just got a report that all four of the gauchos are dead. I sent a squad to follow their trail and it led to a boathouse where we verified they commandeered the hacienda's motor boat. If they can make it to Rio Limay, they will only be about three miles as the crow flies from Nahuel Huapi Lake. Should they reach that large body of water, they'll be well on their way to Chile!

"Bormann is throwing a tantrum because his guests are starting to arrive. He just sent three or four pick-up trucks crammed with armed gauchos to try to intercept your friends, so I could use a little help from the Black Widows. We are going to monitor the trucks from our choppers and try to prevent a deadly altercation."

"I have a nagging concern, Miguel; it is not SOP for the Spider to leave any kind of trail. In fact, the little shit has been known to become almost invisible whenever he has a mind to. Tell me quickly about the Nazi royalty that is headed for the hacienda."

"Well, Bormann is in a tizzy; no public execution of his arch enemy and all that. Listen, I've got to gather my men. We have been cleared to use our Hueys to chase the boat. I'll keep you informed about the Nazis, but most of them are already here. Gotta go, Paddy."

Twenty minutes later, Miguel Rodriguez was back on the encrypted line with Paddy McBride, his voice teeming with urgency.

"Paddy, take down these coordinates and get your arse here immediately; we have a really bad situation. We are at the road bridge where Route 40 crosses the Valle Encantado. I have a couple of men down but we have managed to secure the area. You should be able to get here in less than ten minutes."

Colonel McBride and the Black Widows had anticipated something irregular might happen and they were airborne within seconds. The pilots were ordered to head directly over Nahuel Huapi Lake and pick up Route 40 on the east shore before the coordinates were even plugged in. Once over the road, the formation of four Huey helicopters swung north at speed and raced to rendezvous with Colonel Rodriguez.

On final approach, three of the helicopters peeled off and hovered to give cover to McBride's squad, which went straight in.

Paddy opened the side door of the Huey and surveyed the scene on the ground over the sights of his 9mm submachine gun. A small boat had smashed into the side of a bridge that supported four pick-up trucks. On the south bank of the river, a squad from the 12th Mountain Infantry surrounded two dozen gauchos who were kneeling with their hands clasped behind their heads.

As soon as Paddy landed, Colonel Manuel Rodriguez ran at a crouch under the spinning rotors. "Follow me, Paddy and I'll bring you up to speed.

"Okay, those clowns over there work at the hacienda. They raced by truck to this bridge and ambushed your friends as they came down the river. As you can see, the boat crashed over there."

"What is the casualty situation, Miguel?"

"There are ten wounded or dead gauchos and two of my men have superficial wounds. In addition, I do have one severely injured person who is receiving emergency medical treatment; you will have to make an identification but I doubt he will survive. He was an occupant of the boat and we managed to fish him out of the river. I'm afraid he has multiple bullet wounds and has lost a lot of blood. We could not find the other occupant."

Paddy raced ahead of his Argentinian counterpart and pulled the medic roughly aside. He would remember the elation he felt when he identified the victim with guilt for the rest of his life.

"Rudy, it's me, Paddy McBride. Try to relax and breathe, you'll be okay. Where the hell is Chez?"

Rudy Gomez contorted his face with effort but his failing voice became almost inaudible as he gasped, "Chez left me after we got to the boathouse. Said he had a party to go to. Check the attic above my bedroom and ...and tell Mary I love h................."

McBride checked for a pulse but found none. He gently picked up Rudy Gomez's corpse and walked slowly back to his helicopter.

"Dammit, Miguel, my men will look after those gauchos. You have to head back immediately; your men at the hacienda are in great danger. The Spider is about to take on the Fourth Reich and does not realize that the 12th is on his side. He will massacre everything and everyone between him and Bormann if we can't find him first.

"Rudy said something about the attic above his bedroom. Let me travel with you; the Spider will not respond to anyone but me and I need you to help me find Rudy's bedroom. I hope we're not too late."

Martin Bormann was preparing to host a lavish lunch for the six war criminals who had dropped everything to respond to his exuberant command. They in turn, had travelled varying distances to attend the execution of their hated nemesis, the Spider.

Bormann advised each of them of the current situation as they arrived but his embarrassment still ran deep as he looked into their faces.

Standartenführer Walter Rauff, Dr. Aribert Heim,
Gestapo Captain Erich Priebke, Hauptsturmführer
Klaus Barbie, Dr. Josef Mengele and SS-Gruppenführer
Ludolf von Alvensleben had all filled their glasses with
the most expensive brandy they could find in the liquor
cabinet as immediate compensation. They now awaited
a more adequate explanation for the enormous inconvenience each had suffered.

"My friends, as you know, the rat has escaped
with my son. We know they are on the river somewhere between this hacienda and the lake so I have
dispatched my gauchos in trucks along with the military in Huey helicopters. They are checking various
intermediate locations to intercept them. The Fourth
Reich owns this country and these fugitives will find
it virtually impossible to escape its borders. If you will
indulge me for the next couple of hours, I anticipate
their capture shortly. We will drink and dine together
in the expectation that their execution will make your
exhausting journeys worthwhile."

The helicopter carrying Colonels McBride and Rodriguez raced back to the hacienda and landed in the
service yard close to the kitchen. Rodriguez radioed to
the rest of his detachment.

"Land in the forecourt and secure the perimeter

of the house, we need a few minutes to check out the upper floors. Await the eventual arrival of the Black Widows but hold off entering until my signal."

Rodriguez found his way from the kitchen to the main staircase and went upstairs with Paddy McBride. They heard noises emanating from the dining room but the rest of the house was quiet. McBride covered the upstairs corridor with his Heckler & Koch MP5 as Manuel Rodriguez opened each bedroom door. They sought any clues that might indicate a room belonging to the late Rudy Gomez. The third bedroom had a faint smell of cologne so he checked the closet. The clothes hanging within were in keeping with the style of a young wealthy Argentinian man, so with time running out, he tapped McBride on the shoulder.

"I think this might be it, Paddy. What do you want me to do?"

"Guard the hallway, I'll take it from here." Paddy's wingspan had no problem in knocking on the ceiling of the bedroom.

"Chez, it's Paddy," he whispered as loud as he dared. "The Black Widows have hooked up with the 12th and, if you are up there, I would appreciate your help in taking down some Nazis."

A voice close behind him gave him a start. "What the hell took you so long, you old reprobate? Any news of Rudy?"

"I am afraid that a gang of gauchos ambushed

him on the river. He died about ten minutes ago in my arms. He managed to tell me that you might be hiding above his bedroom and I figured it would take my dulcet voice to convince you to join us."

"Sometimes you can be a complete dick, Paddy. I am truly sorry about Rudy but right now, I am totally focused on killing every Nazi in the dining room. I was just about to go down there with this AK47 I borrowed when you come barging in on the party...."

"...Calm down, wee man, there's plenty of fun to go round. Meet Colonel Manuel Rodriguez of the 12th Mountain Infantry. You and I will stay here under cover until the rest of the helos land, then we're are going sneak downstairs and present you to the Fourth Reich as their guest of honor. I have flown in some special forces from Europe but it could still get very hairy."

Well, well, well, thought the Spider. *I'll wager a pound to a shilling that Paddy is bringing David Goldstein and the Mossad to the party. I am tempted to say this is not fair, but I won't—it is rather sweet poetic justice.*

As four additional Hueys joined those on the ground, Colonel Rodriguez and six of his men walked into the dining room.

"Colonel Rodriguez, what the hell is going on

out there?" demanded Martin Bormann, irate at the interruption.

"Some reinforcements, Senor Gomez. My men located both your son and the Spider. Unfortunately, your son was killed by your own men but I will bring the Spider before you momentarily." Bormann spread his arms wide and beamed a wide smile as he turned to his comrades in triumph.

"Gentlemen, as I promised, your journeys were not wasted. Fill your glasses and toast to this momentous occasion. Prost!"

"PROST!"

Rodriguez and his men took the opportunity to position themselves strategically around the dining room as the celebrations began. The doors opened again and the Spider entered in front of a phalanx of fierce looking men wearing alpine camouflage. He had his hands behind him and the Nazis assumed he must be manacled. Bormann was ecstatic and rose to his feet at the far end of the table.

"Well, well, well. If it isn't Herr Spinne; my life is complete. After I finish this brandy, I am going to blow your brains out and then pour myself another…"

But the Spider stepped forward and placed both his palms on the dining table. Bormann recoiled in shock; the arch enemies were only ten feet apart. The Polish hero locked eyes with the Reichsleiter and killed the buzz in the room with an ice-cold retort in his perfect Berliner German.

"Not one scintilla of remorse for Rudy? He was ten times the man you are, but you are right about one thing, Bormann, your life is complete. Any of you filthy bastards even flinch and you die where you sit. If you are in any doubt, ponder this: Colonel Manuel Rodriguez of the Argentinean 12th Mountain Infantry Regiment is extremely eager to liberate his country from your Nazi scourge."

The Spider paused to scrutinize the shocked faces around the table.

"I am extremely pleased that you have invited me to be your guest of honor so I took the liberty of inviting a couple of my friends to share in the festivities. I'm sure you all recognize the big man behind me as Colonel Paddy McBride but perhaps your biggest thrill will come from meeting the gentleman to his right, Captain David Goldstein of the Mossad."

The Reischleiter opened his mouth to respond but no sound came out. The Spider's eyes were boring into his soul and he knew the length of his time on earth could be counted in seconds.

"Martin Ludwig Bormann, you were the mastermind behind the Third Reich and responsible for the deaths of millions. But the misery and sadism you imposed upon Europe served to strengthen the resolve of those brave men and women who resisted you and your ilk. This day, I am honored and proud to represent all the lives you have destroyed.

"You miss Adolf Hitler? Prepare to meet him in Hell, motherfucker."

The Spider's right hand disappeared behind his back for a split second. When it reappeared it was holding the handle of Lucas Romero's facón knife. The Reichsleiter might have conjured a glimmer of hope had it been any other weapon, but the Spider with his weapon of choice inspired nothing but panic that flooded his brain. The Pole slowly grasped the tip of the knife between the index finger and thumb of his left hand and reared back. The facón whirled down the length of the table and was buried up to its hilt in the Reichleiter's heart.

McBride whistled softly in appreciation. "Strike three, and you are out. Next batter." The rest of the Nazis cringed; trying to make themselves as small as possible when Paddy stared them down. "Time to go home, wee man."

"Ah well, there y'are now," the Spider responded.

The End

EPILOGUE

1999, Twilight Begins

Of all their many great days on earth, this day would rank near the top on both men's lists. Here in Belfast, the Irish Football Association was showcasing a friendly international game between Northern Ireland and Wales as an excuse to pay tribute to the two special men. Both were feeling the ravages of time but the roar of appreciation from the twenty thousand-capacity crowd gave witness to the respect they had earned from living lives as athletes, war heroes and philanthropists.

A public address announcer attempted to set the tone. "And now, ladies and gentlemen, the moment you have all been w…" But the crowd suddenly recognized a giant of a man walking towards the center spot and drowned out all sound from the speakers.

Everyone loved the colonel and he waited patiently for the clamor of his fellow citizens to subside before he picked up the microphone.

"Thank youse all for coming to Windsor Park today and showing your gratitude for the life and careers of my two best friends, Sir Malcolm McClain and Sir Czeslaw Orlowski. If you could collectively add together everything you think you know about them, I promise it wouldn't amount to a tenth of what I know.

"The Lord Mayor has a couple of wee medals to hand out before getting the game underway, so please give a big warm Belfast welcome to Malky and the Spider."

Two hours later, the game ended in a three to one win for the home team, and a happy crowd slowly dispersed to begin celebrating in various bars along the Lisburn Road. The three friends returned home with Jadwiga and Margery to celebrate over dinner with their extended families.

"That was a great meal, ladies. Let the kids do the dishes and the five of us will sit around the fireplace in the library and tell tall tales."

"Phone call for Uncle Paddy in the kitchen," yelled Melanie Blando, one of the Orlowski granddaughters.

The big man excused himself, leaving the McClains and Orlowskis to organize themselves and pour drinks. They had hardly sat down when Paddy rejoined them, wearing a quizzical smile on his face.

"Well, that was a very interesting phone call. Do you all remember Mary O'Connell, the stunning redhead who fell madly in love with Rudy Gomez all those years ago? Last I saw her, Inspector Bill Larkin asked her not to leave Northern Ireland without telling him, but then she completely vanished into thin air. When Rudy died, I promised him that I would pass on his last words to her but damn it, I could never find her, and believe me, I've tried pretty damn hard.

"Larkin has long since retired but I maintain a relationship with his replacement, Nicholas Wiggins and we feared the worst, even suspecting that the deranged cripple who escaped the McKenna assassination might have popped her off. What was that eejit's name. ...Colm O'Shaughnessy, I think. Anyway, I kept the file open because of my promise to Rudy and last week, a cross reference appeared on the BWS main server. An incident mentioned that a thirty-year old man named Rudy O'Connell was arrested for beating up an elderly cripple—in Kilkenny of all places. The young man's defense was that the cripple attacked his mother with a knife."

"And I bet that young man has flaming red hair

and the cripple is called O'Shaughnessy," Malcolm interjected.

"And you would win the prize, Malky. Anyhow, I sent a couple of Black Widows down to County Kilkenny to get an address or a phone number and I got both. Inspector Wiggins was the person I just talked to on your kitchen phone. He wanted to know if I would like to represent him in transporting O'Shaughnessy back to Belfast. He has an open warrant for him in the death of Barry McKenna."

"Do you want us to go with you, Paddy...."Chez began.

"NO!!!" shouted Margery and Jadwiga at the same time and Paddy laughed.

"Thanks for the offer, Chez, but I have my men waiting for me down there and I'm going to drive down tomorrow in the morning. This way, I can take Mary out for dinner, say what I have to say and pass on condolences from all of us.

"You have to admit, that wraps up a couple of loose ends rather neatly. Now, I'm thirsty for a little of that Black Bush the four of you are tippling."

Malcolm poured an inch of the liquid gold into a glass and pushed it across the coffee table to his friend. "Not so fast, big man. While we are in the mood, there are a couple of other loose ends that need to be addressed."

"Like for example?"

"Like for example, we were never told exactly what happened to those Nazis you captured in Argentina?" Margery McClain asked with her 'butter wouldn't melt in my mouth' smile that she knew Paddy McBride could not resist.

"Okay, Margery, we'll do a tell all. But I'm going to insist the five of us keep what you learn tonight to yourselves, agreed?" Five glasses were clinked together to seal the oath.

"After we gate crashed the Nazi's lunch party in Patagonia, Chez and Martin Bormann had a delightful dinner conversation. Unfortunately, the Reischlieter got severe heartburn and fell into a body bag." Jadwiga just shook her head and stifled a giggle.

"We transported his body by helicopter through the Cardenal Antonio Samoré Pass and into Chile. Once across the border, Black Widows Security from Santiago met us with a truck. After sixty miles of bouncing on mountain roads, we made it to the docks at Puerto Montt where a Royal Navy frigate was waiting for us. The captain had us underway before the Chileans had a chance to figure out what we were up to."

It all came flooding back to Chez and he jumped in with some of his personal memories.

"It took us four rough days at sea to get around Tierra del Fuego and into the south Atlantic. When we reached the port of Stanley on the east coast of the Falkland Islands, MI6 arranged for a military transport plane to deliver Paddy and me, along with our cargo, to Frankfurt. The very first thing I did when I got off the plane was call Jadwiga, right Paddy?"

"That's the way I remember it, Chez." McBride supported his version with a big grin. "Commander McDougal met us at Rhein-Main Air Base in Frankfurt. Peter had an old friend of ours with him, Hans Dorff. Hans had proved invaluable to us on our last trip to Berlin during the war and, quite honestly, we never expected to see him again. But Chez and I had asked MI6 to try to find him and turns out he had risen to a management position of some authority in an East Berlin hospital. Anyway, our work was complete and we flew home to Belfast from Frankfurt while McDougal and Dorff escorted the body bag to Templehof Central Airport in the American sector of West Berlin.

"The official story of what happened to Martin Bormann during the last days of the war has always been somewhat of a mystery. Most of the evidence that he died trying to escape the Führerbunker in Berlin came from diehard Nazis, all of who were committed to confusing their interrogators. Everything seemed to point to Bormann killing himself under the Lehrter railway bridge. For a quarter of a century, that bridge and the surrounding area was put under a magnifying glass but not a trace of the dead Reischleiter was ever found. Then, a miracle; in

December, 1972, just a few months after we got home to Belfast, his body was found just where the Nazi witnesses said it would be. Dental records matched and a long autopsy conclusively proved that he had been buried there all the time."

"You have to be bloody joking," laughed McClain. "Bormann's body had hardly the time to decompose since you popped him in Argentina!"

"Who are we to argue with a report signed by Hans Dorff himself, the man whose hospital completed the autopsy?" smiled Chez sardonically. "About ten years ago, I met Hans for dinner at the Adlon Hotel in Berlin to celebrate the wall coming down. He shared with me that there was an extraordinary amount of red dust found in Bormann's lungs but that detail was expunged from the autopsy."

"Why go to all that trouble?" interjected Margery to which Chez answered dramatically.

"There is no soil type in Berlin that produces red dust—but it is all over the damn place in Patagonia! The bottom line here is that Sir Winston Churchill, God rest his soul, was intent on bringing closure to the war. The five of us in this room know what really happened to Adolph Hitler and Martin Bormann. Suffice to say, both bastards are rotting in Hell and it serves no useful purpose to rewrite the historical accounts of their demise."

"This gets more exciting by the minute; two more

questions. What happened to Rudy Gomez's body and you still haven't told us about the other Nazis, the ones you left with the Mossad."

Paddy, as always, pandered to Margery's persistence. "Chez and I buried Rudy at the hacienda and a friend of mine, Manny Rodriguez, arranged to have a nice granite headstone erected at an appropriate time. I must remember to tell Mary and her son about that; they might want to visit some day.

"With regard to Barbie, Mengele and the rest, we were so intent on escaping with Bormann, we really didn't stop to say goodbye to our other Nazi friends at the party. Which was a real shame, because about a week later, they managed to bribe some Argentinian troops to ambush David Goldstein and the Mossad as they were smuggling them out of Argentina. David and his lads fought their way to safety but, as best I know, Walter Rauff, Aribert Heim, Erich Priebke, Klaus Barbie, Dr. Josef Mengele and Ludolf von Alvensleben all managed to avoid justice and survive into old age. It was all I could do to persuade Chez not to go back!"

"I got the top two; the ones that counted. Na zdrowie!" Jadwiga, Margery, Malcolm and Paddy raised their glasses to join Chez but Malcolm McClain stood up and offered another toast,

"To the Spider."

"The Spider," concurred the friends conspiratorially.

"And with that, I have one last question. Where the hell is our grandson? I thought he was going to swing by and say goodnight before he went out to celebrate with his cousins," McClain grumbled.

As if on cue, raucous cheers emanated from the front foyer, causing Chez to comment, "Well, I do believe that young Remington has arrived to grace us with his presence."

Today's ceremony before the game at Winsor Park had certainly set the tone for a memorable day but the icing on the cake came from watching a teenage winger from Carrington United score two of the Northern Ireland goals on his international debut.

Teréska Orlowski had married Janna McClain's older brother and their union produced an athletic protégé. The boy had been exposed from birth to two rather special coaches. Remy McClain had not let them down today and he had a giant smile on his face as he walked into the library to hug his two grandmothers, his Godfather Paddy and of course, his Poppa and Poppy.

"Not so fast, Remster, you took way too many touches before scoring that second goal," complained the eighty six-year-old McClain.

"Apart from that, you could have had a third if

you hadn't let that Welshman foul you!" snorted his seventy nine-year-old cohort.

"I get no breaks from these two, Nanna, no breaks at all."

Thank you

AUTHOR'S NOTES

A s the great Sir Winston Churchill is quoted as saying, *"In wartime, truth is so precious that she should always be attended by a bodyguard of lies."*

Whether this fictional work managed to evade the bodyguard by exposing some truths, we shall most likely never know. A few brave and driven souls devoted their lives to make sure no rock hid a war criminal from justice, but most young people in the 1940s and 50s welcomed the peace as closure to an extremely violent chapter of history. Loose ends were neatly wrapped up, all the bad guys were pronounced dead, champagne corks were popped and babies were started—one of them, me. Nagging whispers that the evil mastermind had escaped to try it again fell on reluctant ears.

I hope the World War II buffs that reach this

page will forgive me weaving fantasy and rumors into historical and geographical truths. For those readers interested, I offer the following resources for your entertainment:

> ***Grey Wolf: The Escape of Adolf Hitler,*** Simon Dunstan and Gerrard Williams, Sterling Publishing, 2011.

> ***The Hunt for Martin Bormann, Charles Whiting***, Pen & Sword Digital, 2011.

> ***Martin Bormann, Nazi in Exile, Paul Manning***, Lyle Stuart, Inc., 1981.

> ***Escape from the Bunker***, Harry Cooper, Sharkhunters International, 2010.

And a couple of videos, which record the official history:

> ***The Bunker*** starring Sir Anthony Hopkins, Time-Life Productions

> **Downfall**, starring Bruno Gantz, Momentum Pictures

READ A SAMPLE OF

BALLS

OF LEATHER AND STEEL

THE FIRST BOOK IN THE SPIDER TRILOGY

CHAPTER NINETEEN

1943 – Revenge is Sweet

L eft alone with Malcolm in the Brodnik living room, Chez calmly summarized their predicament.

"The Germans will be here shortly, my friend. You must hide in the passage and wait for Savo and his men. They'll get you to Semic and freedom by tomorrow."

"Sounds like you're not coming with me," Malcolm said, frowning.

"If we both leave now, the Nazis will be suspicious of an empty house and might search and find the passage. There might not be enough time for Savo to get back here and rescue us. I'll keep them occupied here for a while before I..."

He broke off abruptly, swinging to squint into the blaze of headlights that suddenly flooded the interior of the house.

"... join you in the tunnel," Chez finished calmly.

"Shit! Time to scramble!" Malcolm said.

He followed the back of the Spider as it bounded upstairs to get a better view from the front bedroom.

"You sure you want to play the hero?" McClain said uneasily. But then, he had never looked into the eyes of a close combat adversary. Flying Officer McClain had been used to killing his enemy from 20,000 feet.

The odds were not insurmountable as far as Chez was concerned. Outside, on the flat forecourt only two Krupp troop transporters had drawn up, joined by the two motorcyclists; a patrol of fourteen soldiers in all.

"Hardly a full magazine load," Chez judged coldly. He had been up against worse odds, and *'The Spider'* had always managed to survive.

Then suddenly, the odds against them lengthened as another pair of headlights materialized behind the Krupps. One of the bikes revved up and turned back towards the new arrival, its headlight clearly illuminating a staff car with an SS major in the front passenger seat.

"Well, well, well," Chez mused softly. "It looks like our favorite Sturmbahnfuhrer has decided to follow this lead himself. That makes it personal for all of us... and in turn, leaves me rather looking forward to the next few minutes."

The soldier who had remained to observe the house was reporting to SS Major von Keller who remained seated, ramrod straight, in his Mercedes.

"Herr Major, two elderly people and two younger men headed up the valley in a small bread truck about twenty minutes ago. I judge that at least two other men remain inside the house."

Von Keller then stepped from the staff car with careful deliberation.

"Corporal, take the other motorcyclist and one troop carrier. Catch that damn bread truck! If it remains headed up the valley, they must be climbing over the top of the mountain to Rogia and then back down into the Drava Valley and Maribor. They have a twenty-minute start but there's only one road. In the meantime, I'll radio for troops from Maribor to block that road at the river. They have no escape. SCHNELL!"

While the pursuers sped off up the valley, von Keller turned sharply to address the remainder of his patrol.

"Until I can determine whether our prime suspects have remained here or taken flight in the bread truck, we will stay to interrogate the two inside. I rather suspect that McClain will be trying to escape in the truck—but he will find himself back here for a little chat regardless."

"In your dreams, Sturmbahnfuhrer," Chez grinned.

"The chances of them finding—let alone catching—Savo in those mountains are somewhere between slim and zero."

Then it was time to focus on the immaculate bastard in the polished black boots and jodhpurs. The major raised a megaphone and addressed the house. Simultaneously five Wehrmacht soldiers trained their headlights and machine pistols on the windows, a sixth staffing the MG-42 light machine gun mounted on the troop carrier.

"I know there are at least two of you in the house. You have five minutes to surrender and step outside."

The surrounding facets of the old marble quarry gave von Keller's already amplified voice an added quality of menace. Malcolm reflected back to the movies he had watched at the Arcadian on Albert Street, goggle-eyed as a kid in Belfast. No money needed from those who had none; two empty jam jars had been enough to get a front row seat. A smile flickered across his face. "Seems this is another fine mess you've got me into, Ollie," he said quietly.

Chez looked blank: going to the cinema had never been part of his childhood prison camp experience but he thought, "Damn, this Irish guy has ice in his veins.—I kinda like that!"

Regardless, their survival time was shortening by the second.

Malcolm blinked, as without warning, his

companion suddenly ripped a sheet from the Brodniks' bed then pulled up the casement and proceeded
to hang the linen outside. McClain was about to blink
even harder when the Spider's shout in German took
on a most uncharacteristic whine.

"I have Flying Officer McClain here. He is very
badly wounded and the occupants of the house were
sent to get medical help. We surrender! Allow me
a minute to get him downstairs ... but please don't
shoot."

Malcolm spoke no German but the meaning was
easy to follow. "What the hell ...?" McClain began to
blurt before Chez whirled urgently.

"Shut up an' follow me to the Wine Vat in the
barn."

Without waiting, the Spider turned and led the
way downstairs, navigating each flight in one effort-
less jump. On reaching the ground floor, he darted
left into the kitchen where a rear door went directly
into the barn. By the time Malcolm caught up with
him, the young Pole was already holding open the
Wine Vat's secret access to the passage. He gestured
for Malcolm to enter. With the Irishman inside the
void, Chez started to close the secret door from the
outside.

"You go ahead, Malcolm. There is one small detail
I need to take care of before I catch up."

Sturmbahnfuhrer Abelard Hans von Keller was exceedingly pleased with himself. Although he had not expected it to be this easy, he had the two bastards he wanted and could leave it to others to apprehend the Partizani bit-players in the bread truck.

There was no hurry, which afforded him time to savor his coming rehabilitation in the eyes of his superiors. With the knowledge that McClain was virtually back in the bag with no harm done to his career, von Keller pleasured on being able to exact retribution on that still-mysterious traitor to his Fuhrer's beloved Third Reich; the man with the Berliner accent who had almost pulled off the successful kidnapping of his prize.

Walking briskly back to his staff car, he could already feel the adrenaline coursing through his body. He vividly imagined himself placing his gleaming jackboot between the bastard's shoulder blades before shooting him in front of McClain.

Sliding into his car seat, von Keller reached into the glove compartment, retrieving a short, black ebony cigarette holder into which he carefully pushed a Balkan Black Sobranie. He had never permitted himself to become an inveterate smoker—the Fuhrer would have disapproved—but there were occasions when one could justify a brief, discreet deviation from the SS model of perfection. He thumbed the flint of his silver, monogrammed lighter and pulled the rich, satisfying smoke deep into his lungs. He smiled a cold smile and murmured out loud, "As you stagger through that door, you treasonous cretin, appreciate your last few moments on this earth ..."

The major felt a slight pinprick, the irritation of a mosquito biting his neck. It was a curious sensation in itself. As he swatted it, a dark spray splattered the inside of the windshield in front of him. Puzzled, Hans von Keller slowly raised his warm, wet left hand until he could see the sticky glint of what could only be his own blood. While he was still frowning in confusion, a strong hand clamped across his sagging jaw and he heard a soft Berlin accent from the back seat.

"I am not a treasonous cretin, Herr Major, because I do not consider myself a German. I am Czeslaw Orlowski, a proud Pole and one of those resistance fighters you hold in such contempt. You might know me better as 'The Spider'?"

As von Keller's carotid artery continued to pump out warm blood, his body involuntarily began to shut down. With a supreme effort, he compelled his brain to focus on analyzing the facts: *Unmistakably, he had just heard this same voice from the upstairs window: He had detected neither movement from the house nor the slightest sound since returning to his car: He had not even felt the blade slice his throat.*

He still felt little pain; it made no sense and, for the analytical mind of Sturmbahnfuhrer Abelard Hans von Keller, that came as a terrible revelation.

"Spider, Spinne ...? But you're a myth. You don't exist outside the pipe dreams of your filthy Partisa ..."

Nevertheless, before he slipped down to the eternal flames of Hell, von Keller heard the voice softly utter the last earthly words he would ever hear.

"With fond remembrance of Goran ... and Biba!"

Chez slid silently out of the car and dissolved into the shadows. But his luck finally ran out as he returned to the barn and was climbing to negotiate his way through the roof trusses towards the wine vat. Suddenly, a powerful flashlight snapped a fix on him. He had little option but to freeze.

"Come down right now, whichever one you are, or you'll be shot," demanded Corporal Manfred Gimmstadt, one of three grey-uniformed Wehrmacht troopers in the barn.

Then, a most unexpected event occurred.

"I believe you may be looking for me as well?" Flying Officer Malcolm McClain called almost conversationally from behind them.

Without understanding his English, the three soldiers whirled in shock. Gimmstadt re-directed his torch towards the new challenge. When, the confused corporal directed the beam of his flashlight back into the rafters, he found them empty.

"Verdammt!" he snarled, quickly returning his torch to illuminate McClain. This caused a second furious soldier to train his Schmeisser on the seemingly nonchalant British flyer. The third slung his machine pistol across his chest and motioned for McClain to step forward, hands above his head, to be searched.

Commendable standard practice, only Gimmstadt did not realize he was dealing with a man from Belfast. McClain's demeanor transformed into a whirl of action as he took one step forward to grab both lapels of the German's uniform. In a crisp motion, he pulled the soldier towards him, simultaneously smashing his forehead into the bridge of the trooper's nose. A brutally unsophisticated but extremely effective tactic known colloquially as giving 'a stitch' by those fighting for survival around the Springfield Road.

Allowing his victim's semi-conscious body to slump to the floor, Malcolm swung on the second soldier and in a continuous, flowing movement, stabbed the ball of his right foot straight into the man's crotch. With this leg still airborne and the unfortunate soldier already doubling in agony, Malcolm completed the scissor kick with a roundhouse left foot to the soldier's right temple.

When kicking a leather ball, a professional football

player's boot can travel at over 75 miles per hour, and McClain had perhaps the most lethal left foot in the game. The second guard was brain-dead before his body hit the floor. Two down in as many seconds, McClain was already pivoting to dispatch the last captor when he stopped in his tracks.

Before his eyes, the beam of light that had started the debacle began to rise steadily towards the rafters. Then the torch dropped with a clatter to the accompaniment of a strangled gasp. McClain could just make out Gimmstadt's frantically flailing jackboots as the corporal swung higher and higher. Malcolm recovered the lamp to illuminate the elevated soldier dangling helplessly, his neck pinioned in the vice-like grip of the Spider's thighs. Hanging effortlessly from the rafters, Chez rotated his hips savagely, first to the left and then right. There came a snap and Corporal Manfred Gimmstadt's corpse joined his inert comrades on the floor of the barn.

"Well done, Chez," Malcolm announced almost matter-of-factly as the Spider landed like a cat in front of him. The young Pole's respect for his foreign charge had tripled in the last few seconds.

"Now for the rest of those bastards!" McClain said but Chez restrained him with a hand.

"Enough, Malcolm. Remember, my prime mission is to get you safely out of here. Though, I'm starting to think that you are looking after me!"

Just as they were ready to close the secret passage door, they heard urgent shouting from the courtyard.

"Hold on here for now, Malcolm," Chez grinned as he caught the gist of the guttural conversation. "If they've found what I suspect they've found, then we might not need to negotiate that long damp passage."

Apparently, the three Wehrmacht soldiers remaining outside in the yard with von Keller's increasingly nervous SS driver, had become restless while awaiting Chez's promised surrender. Even more unsettlingly, Corporal Gimmstadt's party who had entered the barn to prevent any back door escape had not reappeared. Nor had they heard the reassuring sound of shots from within. Direction was needed ... *but where the hell was Major von Keller when the arrogant bastard was needed?*

They soon found out. The panicked shouting Malcolm and Chez had heard provided evidence enough. To compound their disarray, the soldiers then ran back to the barn to locate their missing men and tripped over three bodies, only one of which retained any signs of life.

The decimated squad's sergeant, a grizzled veteran of the Russian front, stared at the seemingly vacant farmhouse and made a battlefield decision.

"Load the bodies into the Krupp, leave the staff car for now and we'll return to Maribor for orders!"

Only while they were carrying the dead major to

the troop carrier did one of them see the salutation, pinned to Sturmbahnfuhrer von Keller's chest by the Thiers Issard cutthroat razor Chez had commandeered from the Brodniks' bathroom.

The square of paper showed the infamously feared caricature of a spider. Beneath the oval with eight legs was a terse message in German.

READ A SAMPLE OF

A
GORDIAN
WEB

BOOK TWO IN THE SPIDER TRILOGY

PROLOGUE

From worse to worst

E uphoria should have abounded that spring, but there was none. In their hope-filled dreams, the sun shone, birds sang and the air was crisp and clean, but these dreams shattered against hard reality. At the very least, those Poles who survived the six-year Nazi scourge would rejoice in the freedom of self-government, but the situation deteriorated from worse to worst.

The brief interlude created by Germany's retreat from Poland and Russia's establishment as 'the new landlord,' allowed Polish Resistance, known as the Armia Krajowa (AK), to melt into obscurity. This nettlesome decision was predestined by Premier Joseph Stalin's massive Soviet forces taking a ringside seat during the Warsaw Uprising to watch the AK and German garrison decimate each other. Stalin, the self-proclaimed 'Man of Steel,' ordered his invading armies to adopt the role of passive observers, boasting he preferred to occupy a Poland unencumbered by annoying freedom fighters. The sixty-three days of genocide on the streets of Warsaw went a long way to accomplishing that mission. President Władysław Raczkiewicz and the Polish government-in-exile finally ordered all surviving Armia Krajowa freedom fighters to disband on January 20, 1945, in preference to certain death in a Gulag labor camp.

Stalin knew exactly what he was doing, as members of the Armia Krajowa were far from subservient during the years of oppressive Nazi occupation. In fact, they aggressively resisted giving up their country to Adolph Hitler. Gestapo tactics never quelled the AK in Poland or for that matter, the Partizani in Yugoslavia and those two brave groups worked to drain the resources of the Third Reich, eventually driving the Germans to distraction.

Throughout these intensely difficult times, hearts were uplifted by the exploits of a fearless Polish folk hero known as the Spider, or Pająk. The legend sprouted from the deeds of a young AK patriot called Czeslaw Orlowski, who claimed graphic responsibility for the mayhem he foisted upon the enemy. His infamous calling card depicted an oval surrounded by eight legs— a pająk. The fable mushroomed over time by the AK crediting every successful sabotage to the Spider and leaving his calling card at the scene.

The People's Commissariat for State Security, the dreaded NKGB, was painfully aware of the unifying effect this 'legend of the Spider' was having upon the proud Polish nation. If the spirit of this populace was to be crushed, they knew they had to eliminate the Spider very quickly and very publicly.

But first, they had to find him.

However, even the copious files of the NKGB had failed to note that their quarry had spent the past eighteen months on a series of secret missions for British Special Forces.

One of the most brazen took place right under the nose of Dr. Joseph Goebbels and his Nazi Ministry of Propaganda causing massive embarrassment to the Third Reich and a corresponding surge of patriotism in London. The Spider engineered the daring escape of one of Britain's favorite sons, international soccer icon Malcolm McClain from the high-security POW camp in Maribor and as a by-product, a strong bond of friendship developed between Orlowski and McClain.

But a subsequent mission trumped even that success when the Spider led a marauding band of Polish and Yugoslav guerillas on a seemingly suicidal mission to destroy the final testing of Germany's V-2 rocket program; a weapon of such technical sophistication it would assure dominance in the theatre of war. The scientist needed just a few final tweaks before presenting their Fuhrer with certain victory and an eternal place in history as the Emperor of Europe. However, the ants ate the elephant and the decline of the Third Reich was ensured.

The British wartime Prime Minister, grateful for the heroic exploits that had quantifiably saved millions from death or servitude, was persuaded that political asylum for the Spider would be both a justified and popular conclusion to these adventures. So the Brits also sought the elusive Pole, but for entirely different reasons than the Russians.

The NKGB, given its number one priority by Premier Stalin to find the Spider, used their disciplined, methodical practices to identify traditionally Polish-occupied regions in eastern Germany that might have high potential as his hiding place. Neither side was yet aware that after urging his Krakow division of the AK to retreat into obscurity, Czeslaw Orlowski married his sweetheart and settled down as a nondescript farmer in Żagań, a small bucolic town in Lower Silesia.

By unfortunate coincidence, Russian armies massed

rapidly in this area as Stalin planned to repatriate all lands east of the River Oder back into Poland, thereby laying claim by the Soviets to strategic access to the Baltic.

The noose was tightening and the Spider could feel it inching closer. Several weeks before, he had pleaded his predicament by letter to Malcolm McClain, his dear friend in England, and even managed to persuade a Red Cross delegation to attempt delivery.

Who knows if it made it past the keen eyes of Russian censors? It's this damn uncertainty without hope I could do without, Chez worried.

Malcolm, my dear friend.

I hope you are in good health and still playing for Blackpool. Jadwiga and I are happily married and live with her mother and four sisters on a small farm. I cannot reveal where because I'm afraid our days on this earth are numbered.

The many hours we spent together during the escape from Maribor were dangerous at the time but all I remember is the joy we shared when talking about our girls and the many

children we would have after the war.
I have dreamt about our future kids
growing up and playing together but
the Russian armies are hunting for me
with intensity you cannot imagine; the
soldier who kills me will be rewarded
well and I sense the end is very close.

If this letter reaches you, know you
are in my thoughts. When we last
parted on the runway in Semic, do you
remember promising that if I ever got
in trouble you would send a couple
of lads from Belfast to bail me out?
Well, a couple might not be enough,
I am a stalked animal with a price on
my head so we will probably never see
each other again.

I hope you have found bliss with your
beautiful Margery. Enjoy your love,
your family and your freedom. They
are the most precious things in this
life. Your prayers would mean a great
deal at this time; I am in desperate
need of a miracle.

Your friend forever.
Czeslaw.

PART ONE

CHAPTER ONE

1945 – Hidden in Plain Sight

He was puzzled, but couldn't quite put his finger on why. Long before the cock crowed he lay wide awake and restless, trying to reconcile an uneasy feeling coursing through him. It was a familiar sixth sense; one that had never let him down and saved his life on many occasions. What was it trying to warn him about? The peril could not be inside or outside the immediate farmhouse because his geese provided cacophonous security. No, this pressure in his temples had not yet manifested itself into anything recognizable so his tortured mind strained to filter the cause of his alarm. Perhaps it was an out-of-place sound somewhere in the distance. And then it all crystalized,— there were no sounds. The wild animals of the valley must have retreated behind the security of silence in the face of some intrusion into their world. The danger would surely head his way and he needed to be ready.

Although it was late February and bitterly cold in this part of Silesia, the young farmer had beads of sweat covering his forehead as he raised himself off the pillow. He decided to get up and walk around to clear his head, so he glanced over at his wife, Jadwiga, to make sure she was still asleep. Her large brown eyes popped open the moment she felt his gaze upon her. Now there could be absolutely no doubt that something was wrong,—but what?

"I feel it too, ukochanie, this will be the day they finally find us. Hug me close," Jadwiga whispered.

There was a thin film of ice all over the metal water jug in the bathroom. Czeslaw filled the white pottery basin and sluiced the cold water over his head and torso before drying himself rigorously with a rough towel. It brought a pink sheen to his skin, which he quickly captured with a fresh flannel shirt, tucking it into his work pants as he returned to the bedroom. Jadwiga was now anxiously peering into the farmyard through a small gap in the curtains.

"Czeslaw, I can see one of our geese, she is sleeping but moved her head. At least for now, our yard is secure but you need to leave the farm immediately. I can buy you time by sending them on a false trail...."

"......I appreciate your love and your bravery—more than I can say—but that simply won't work, Jadzie. The Russian troops will hand you over to the NKGB and I could not live with the thought of what those bastards might do to you.

"Get your mother and sisters up, pack essentials and hide out at the railway station. I'm going to contact a couple of old friends who might be able to shed a little light. I'll meet you there as soon as I can—but if I'm not there by noon, catch the next train to Poznan and stay with your cousin, Franek. The Germans abandoned Poznan to the Soviets last month so there's still great confusion there, but your Russian will serve you well. I'll rendezvous as soon as I feel it's safe. Don't worry." He kissed her tenderly and left the room, pausing only to grab his dark blue woolen jacket.

The frozen ground crackled underfoot as he pushed his old Wul-Gum motorcycle from the shed to the edge of the farm before pounding all his weight onto the kick-starter. As he passed through the farm's five-bar gate he was planning to turn right towards the town, hoping to arouse Szymon Grabowski. Żagań's elderly postmaster was a proud man who still kept tabs on what was left of the Polish resistance in this area. The thought brought a grim smile to Czeslaw's cold lips.

"That old goat will be able to tell me if something is brewing."

Szymon lived above the Post Office and the young man could be there in less than five minutes. Then, for some unknown reason he stopped and stared into the night sky. His mouth pursed in determination and relying on instinct, he suddenly swerved left and accelerated towards Przemcow.

Since settling down on the farm, Czeslaw always rose at dawn to begin his chores; swilling pigs, planting or harvesting crops, lugging great pails of water to the house; backbreaking tasks small farmers perform in all corners of the world. When finished, he would sometimes unwind by cruising the thirty kilometers to Przemcow and assist Zenon Majewski at his small grocery store. Zenon had once helped Czeslaw out by lending the young stranger some of his murdered son's clothes to make him more presentable for a pending date with his future wife, Jadwiga. Czeslaw had never forgotten this act of kindness and the frequent visits with the old man allowed him to replace some of the load a missing son might have carried. In truth, Czeslaw also enjoyed Zenon as the father figure in his life and it never hurt if the old man filled the young farmer in on any unusual troop activity in the area.

On this occasion, there was no cruising. The Wul-Gum roared through the crisp night air at purposeful speed and the closer Czeslaw got to Przemcow, the stronger his intuition warned him about danger ahead. By the time he was within sight of the village, he had to pull over and take deep breaths to regain control of his heartbeat. As he carefully concealed the motor-cycle within a thick copse of mature trees, his persona morphed into his alter ego, the Spider.

By now, birds were welcoming the new day and frosted dew tossed off sparkles from the light growing in the pink sky to the east. A tall, healthy pine tree allowed him to climb unobserved onto a high branch where he waited patiently for the sun. As daylight arrived, the perch gradually afforded him a clear view of Plac Wolnosci, the small square containing the Majewski Grocery Store. Nothing appeared amiss,— but the hair on the back of his neck seldom lied.

ABOUT THE AUTHOR

G uy Butler was born in Blackpool where his father, Malcolm Butler, did in fact play for the famous Blackpool Football Club. When his Dad retired, the family moved back to Belfast, Northern Ireland, where its roots go back to the 17th century. Guy spent his youth playing soccer all day and bass guitar in a band called 'Johnny and the Teenbeats' all night. The other group in town was Van Morrison and Them, who went on to much bigger and greater things.

Despite the resultant horrific grades, he managed to get accepted into Queens University's College of Architecture, where he played soccer for the Northern Ireland national colleges' team against Wales, Scotland and England.

Guy currently owns a boutique architectural firm

that specializes in golf resort design all over the world. While *Balls of Leather and Steel* was mainly written at 35,000 feet en route to China, Nigeria and the Far East, Guy chiseled time away from his busy architecture office and home life to craft *A Gordian Web*.

The Butler family lives in Orlando, Florida. Learn more about Guy Butler and his architecture and design firm by visiting www.guybutlerarchitect.com.

Connect with the Author Online
TheSpiderTrilogy.com
Facebook.com/thespidertrilogy

Made in the USA
Columbia, SC
16 February 2021

33057698R00269